Angel's Downfall

An MC Romance Trilogy The Harder They Fall

Kristen L. Proc

D1519595

This book is dedicated to my mom. She's always been my rock and my biggest supporter. Thank you for cheering me on and always believing in me.

Contents

It's not always where you come from, it's the direction in which you're going.

Chapter 1

Alexa

I walked into the bar slightly dragging my heels. I wasn't huge on socializing; It was hard pretending to be the social butterfly everyone expected me to be. I had done my makeup, a rarity for me, blew dried my hair and put on a short red and pink paisley wrap dress that swished when I walked with flutter short sleeves and it screamed summertime. My tan-heeled booties made me a little taller than my 5'3" body and I even had to admit to myself that I felt sexy. Not that I'd flirt with the likes of this crew I was about to hang out with or anyone else in this dingy bar to be honest. I was working down the street when my best friend that I've had since fourth grade texted me to come and meet up at the local bar. Before I could even text her back, my phone pinged with a long drawn out, 'pleeeeeeaaasseee'. Sarah was an overly friendly, sunkissed blonde with a heart of gold. We went to college together and stayed really close when she interned at my mom's then law firm.

The parking lot was crowded with motorcycles and cars; I had parked my Dodge Challenger on the street just in case I needed a fast get away and wasn't blocked in by the people standing around smoking and making out. Tommy's Bar was a local joint; pool tables and typical bar food; booths and tables scattered about. I can't even remember the last time I was in a bar. I don't drink really. I don't like the feeling of losing control or making a fool out of myself; so I choose to stay sober but I've been known to nurse a beer or two to not raise eyebrows from people around me. It's easier to just blend in when you don't stand out for something; even something as silly as being sober.

I didn't mind being the wallflower. My mom is the District Attorney and as soon as people learn my name; Alexa Ramirez, they know instantly who I am. My mom taught me to be vigilant with my social activities; being kind and thoughtful and not causing her any types of bad publicity.

The stale cigarette smell hit my nostrils along with the beer and sweat that lingered in places like this. It was clean enough and there was definitely a mix of young and older crowds here. College kids and underage kids hoping to score a few beers before they got kicked out; run of the mill working class people, myself falling into that group. And then of course the local motorcycle club thugs. They kept to themselves mostly. Hovering over tables, playing pool or talking in hushed tones up at the bar. Most people knew to just stay away from them. They were like bees; if you don't mess with them; they most likely won't mess with you. Los Demonios Locos were the local M.C. and were a mix of younger and older guys; some looking like they just got out of jail, tatted up from neck down and some looked like the hot guy next door. Maybe that's their m.o? Safe amongst the crowds, blend in to fit in? Word was that the DL's were gun traffickers; smart and scary. My mother had the job of dealing with some of the trials and investigations of the D.L.'s; so I've heard her speak of them from time to time.

I'm tired from a long hard day at work; so I promised myself I'd go to the bar; spend some time with my friends and head home to crawl under my blankets that I could hear screaming my name. I have a small group of friends that I love to be with, Sarah of course and her boyfriend, Josh. They've been together since senior year in high school. We all went to private school together. All of our parents are rich or politically tied in one way or another. Randy, the famous plastic surgeon's son, and a few jocks turned medical students that show up in town from time to time. We bond mostly because we come from money... we don't necessarily all work... and for most of this group, they only date within the same social status.

I work with a few local charities, set up by my mother

of course, but I'm passionate to work with kids that have been displaced. Living within 50 miles of the Mexico border; there have been waves of immigrants and most lately, children. Children being sent to America alone, without a single item besides the clothes on their backs. And I really love being that person that helps them when they are so lost; organizing clothing and shelter for them. I smile for them so they know I will help keep them safe.

As I walk into the bar; a few heads swivel my way but I keep my eyes up as I look for some familiar faces. Sarah sees me first and yells my name. Of course she looks like she's half in the bag; so I slap a smile on and wave as I make my feet move to the back side of the bar.

"Alexa! Oh my gosh you look so cute! I'm so glad you finally came out with us!" she slurred a bit and stumbled in my direction. But Sarah was a professional drinker. She can hang with the best of them and never loses her dignity by acting like a drunken fool.

"Thanks, I ran home for a quick shower and to get changed. I didn't leave the shelter til almost 9:30!" There was some weird bedding confusion and I had to shuffle around some cribs for a few babies that got processed today. It was definitely a rough one." I walked to the back of the bar where there were some dart games and high top tables.

"Hey guys! Have you been here a while or something? It's only 11:30 and you've got a table full of empties!" I put my purse down and gave hugs to everyone standing around. Sarah's boyfriend Josh had a sloppy smile on his face, he was sweet and doting to Sarah; a millionaire's son but you would never know that about him. Josh was a professor at a local community college and really passionate about history. He and I got along really well and he never poked fun at me for my quietness or my lack of drinking. He even volunteers at the shelter from time to time to read stories to the children.

"Hey beautiful, lemme get you a drink." I slid Randy's arm off from around my shoulders and gave him a quick pat on the back. I don't know why Randy hangs out with the likes of us; he's stuck up and bratty and lives off his parent's money without a single regret. I'm surprised he even steps foot in this bar, it's not somewhere you'd ever see an actor or famous internet star or someone just as wealthy and stuck up as he is.

I bowed my head and grabbed a few bucks out of my purse; giving Sarah a knowing wink. "That's ok Randy. Thanks but I'm not even sure what I'm in the mood for." I turned towards the bar and heard his annoying remark, "'ha.. I'll get her in the mood for something." Gosh he was annoying. I know he's had a thing for me, but I think mostly it's because he knows how wealthy my mom is and that I don't date; like ever. I had a few boyfriends in high school and then in college, but I'm just not into it. I haven't met someone that is worth my effort; right now those children need all my support and I'm perfectly happy that way.

The bar is packed. Shoulder to shoulder, everyone is into their conversations or trying to get the bartender's attention. But there's a little opening between two leather vests. Great, Los Demonios. I see the one guy peer at me over his shoulder and he was actually polite enough to scoot over a bit so that I can belly up to the bar. Ok, how bad could this be? He seems nice. I'll just make it quick. "Hey, thanks for letting me squeeze in." I didn't look directly at him. He definitely was intimidating. He had longish hair, a few days scruff on his face and a bunch of patches on his leather vest. "Mmmhmm". That's all he said back. Ok, simple enough. I was trying to make eye contact with the bartender to make this a quick visit; but he was swamped. Pouring shots and flinging beer around like it was Mardi Gras or something. But then I felt eyes on me from the other side. The other vest was looking at me. Before I could turn my head to say 'excuse me' hoping this guy would be just as polite; I could smell his cologne... woodsy and musk and male. I could see his hand wrapped around his beer and the tattoos peaking out around his sleeve. I lifted my head giving a cursory glance and he was doing the same.

"I'm sorry, I'll be out of here in a sec, I just need a drink".

I flashed him a small smile but when my eyes met his, the air whooshed out of my lungs and I felt my knees get weak if only for a second. He was handsome. Dark hair that looked carelessly messy and tanned olive skin. His eyes were a milk chocolate brown with long lashes. Strong cheekbones and square jaw with a goatee. His goatee was dark with a few strands of grey in it hinting at his age but it's his lips that I instantly found. Lush lips, tanned and kissable. Oh my god, was I staring? Or was he staring at me. Shit. "I"m, I'm, sorry.. jeez.. umm.. this bar is really packed."

"That's ok, I got you. Hey Joe!" He gave the bartender a simple wave and Joe came right over. "Whatcha drinking?" He looked at me and I still felt zapped. I know I'm shy but this guy damn near shut me up. His eyes were kind as they searched my face and his lips slightly tilted up at the corner. I can see the bartender impatiently pacing as he waited for my reply.

"Uh, I'll just have a beer. Uh, Corona." Jesus I sounded like I just graduated high school or something. What was wrong with me.

"Not a big drinker, huh?" He turned his body a bit towards me, giving me his attention but now I got to scope out the whole package.

"No, ha.. not really." I smiled up at him again. Trying my damndest to keep my eyes from wandering to his lips or down his body. From the fast glance that I took, I could tell he was tall. He had thick thighs that parted around the bar stool and the long sleeve tee shirt that was under his vest was tight enough to make out solid, thick biceps and strong shoulders. Jesus, was I swooning over this guy? Get a hold of yourself Alex!

I was quickly snapped back into reality when I felt Randy brush up against my back. "Alex, you good? I was waiting for you." He put his hand on top of my shoulder, fingers slightly brushing my neck. It was a dick move and possessive. Maybe he was concerned with who I was standing next to or maybe he just wanted to show them that I was spoken for.

"Yea, I'm good Randy... just grabbing a beer. I'll be back

there in a sec" I shrugged his hand off my back and gave him a tight smile; hoping not to sound like a complete bitch to him for checking in on me. He gave a couple quick glances and nod to the two guys now flanking me and tucked tail back to our friends. I turned back in time to see my beer being delivered.

"Thanks!" I was about to hand Joe the bartender my money when the god wearing the vest next to me put his hand on top of mine and gave a head nod to Joe. Joe walked away and went back to his patrons. I was surprised and looked up to say thank you but the words got stuck in my throat. His hand overtop of mine felt electric; warm, and firm.

"My treat Alex." he smiled down at me; not a creepy smile like he was just trying to hit on me; but a genuine smile that I felt instantly in between my legs and creeped up to butterflies in my stomach.

Angel

"My treat Alex." I smiled at her and placed my hand on top of hers. She looked like a tanned goddess in that sweet little dress. Soft brown curls down her back and big lush lips that tipped up at the corners. She stood close to me; I felt her body heat and she smelled like coconut and lemons. I didn't buy her the beer just to hit on her; actually; I didn't know why I was giving her my attention at all. But that smile she gave me; the way she looked nervous to be standing next to the likes of me and my brother. I felt my cock harden as her hand stayed put under mine and she tried to find the words to say thank you.

"Thank you. You didn't have to do that." she slid her hand out from under mine and brushed a few strands of hair away from her face.
"So, you know my name; what's yours?" I couldn't tell if she was just being polite in asking or if she really was interested. But she didn't make a move to pull away from the bar and regroup with her friends.

"Angel." I put out my hand to shake hers. I really just wanted to touch her again; feel her warmth and see if I could make her smile again. That smile sprung my cock to life as I tried to not stare at her lips or the way she licked them and she thought of what to say next.

"It's nice to meet you Angel. That's a beautiful name. Well, I should get back to my friends." She looked down at her feet then back towards the girl she was talking to after I saw her enter the bar. I was always looking over my shoulder, especially in these small town bars. Never know who's gonna show up to ruin your night. That's when I saw her. She breezed through the door looking a little nervous; scanning over the crowd probably looking for someone. But I couldn't take my eyes off of her. She looked like sunshine amongst a sea of clouds. She was a tiny thing with strong looking legs; toned and looking lickable with those little boots on. She has a small waist and beautiful tits, perfect handfuls well hidden behind her dress. But her face was that of a goddess. Glowing tan skin, pink plump lips and honey brown eyes. Her hair was long and soft looking, waves down her back that looked carefree and yearned to be pulled. She shook my hand softly hesitating for just a brief second and turned her body to leave. Her absence was immediately felt and I watched her walk away like I was a lost puppy.

"Damn Angel, did you fall in love or something?" My brother Roman punched me in the shoulder to snap me out of my fog. I took the smile off my face quickly and shot him a look that told him to shut the fuck up. "Fuck she's hot. I bet her little douche bag boyfriend thinks so too." he quipped.

"Shut the fuck up bro. No way she's with that ass clown." I flagged down Joe for another round of beers and added a shot of Jameson. My dick was still hard from thinking of her and a shot was a good replacement for a cold shower. I glanced back from time to time to check on her; still chatting with her friends and nursing the beer that I bought her. "We gotta head out in 15, get ready for that shipment." Roman said casually and chugged the rest of his beer and waved to Joe for another.

I dreaded nights like these. Don't get me wrong, I love the brotherhood that I was brought into, the club and protection we provided each other with. But the things we did in the middle of the night; when I longed to be somewhere else, anywhere else; made my chest ache and I can feel it poisoning me. Hardening my soul and screwing with my mind. The motorcycle club thrived on illegal trade. Guns, ammo and other favors for other local M.C.s. Girls and drinking, even dabbling in gambling and fighting competitions; we were all business when it came to the hard stuff and we were supposed to live like kings off the fruits of our labors. In the beginning, the girls and drinking were amazing. I fucked my way through the slew of girls that would hang out at clubhouse. Silencing my thoughts for a few hours with a blow job or a lapdance. I never wanted to be a criminal; but there wasn't much else for me to live for.

Chapter 2

Alexa

I tossed and turned until I couldn't take it anymore and peeked an eye at the alarm clock next to my bed. Damn. 6:43am. It's Sunday morning and I wish I could sleep in a bit but I would be lying if I said I wasn't an early bird. I thrive in the mornings; love my morning coffee and work out. A good sweat to get the anxiety out of the way for the day. I rolled over to my side and closed my eyes for a moment and there he was. I can see him clear as day in my mind. Warm skin, dark hair and kind eyes. Lips that looked like they were sweet and kissable. I felt the wetness pool between my legs and I clenched my thighs. What was I doing last night flirting with a motorcycle thug? Sarah gave me a little bit of shit about it when I got back to the table. Laughing and said I needed to be more careful who I squeezed my tight ass between. I laughed it off but it was Randy that gave me the death stare. The guy just hated feeling unimportant but also, he hated that I wouldn't give him the time of day. I let my hand wander down my chest; my skin was warm from sleep and felt my body buzz when I thought of Angel. He touched me and I damn near had an out of body experience. I can't even remember when I'd reacted to someone like that. Instant want and need. I wanted him to dip his head near my neck and whisper sweet words to me so that I could take his male scent in and live there for a few moments. Ugh, whatever Alexa... I highly doubt he'd want anything to do with my boring ass. The guy probably has a different girl every night.

I got up and made myself a steaming cup of coffee and flipped on the news. The local news showed that my mom was holding a press conference about the influx of Mexican families crossing the border. There was a lot of debate on how everything should be handled, protests erupted near the border and some violence always seeped into downtown. There was a lot of opinion about whether the U.S should get involved with immigrants and how we should be handling these poor souls that were fleeing their country. But these children. It's so sad. They don't speak a word of English and have no idea how to find their parents even if they were given back to Mexico. That's why I loved and hated my job. It made me so sad for them and scared for their futures. We opened up the children's shelter in the downtown area a year ago; and it's been at full capacity since.

The work week went on the same way; shuffling children around to different locations; relying on local businesses to donate clothing and provide meals. I met up with my mom on Wednesday's for lunch in the city. This Wednesday we went to this cute outside BBQ place that was delicious. We tried not to talk about work; but work was all we knew. My mom, Sonya, had a tough upbringing. Coming from a family of lawyers, her life was in the books and she thrived on helping others. A real humanitarian. I was so proud of her when she became the D.A.. Of course things got tense at home; we moved to a gated community and had security for when she was out. Her security guards were two beefy men, Rob and Ben and her personal assistant was never too far away either. I grew up with my mom always working but we lived with my grandmother who helped raise me. Tough woman she was. Smart, a little bit sassy but she loved me so much. She passed away during my first year at college. I was devastated. Abuelita taught me so much about love and dedication; compassion and how to be present in life. I always believed she shaped me into the woman I am today.

Angel

Roman and I headed out on the bikes early in the morning. We wanted to get out of town for a few days; drive through the desert and visit some brothers from the adjoining MC. We worked all Saturday night into the early hours of Sunday morning. We had a shipment of guns that came in from New York that needed to be smuggled into Mexico. We used tunnels to move the larger shipments; our club prospects got the shitty job of moving them through the musty, dark tunnels. I didn't feel bad for them. I did my fair share as a prospect along with a million other remedial tasks.

The sun and the desert air felt great on my skin. I was in a good mood for once. There was nothing like the machine under my body and my brother and I spending time on the road together. It was always him and I. I practically raised him. He's three years my younger. Our mom passed away when we were young; I was just six and Roman, three. I don't remember that much of her, but I remember the way she sang me to sleep or when she danced in the light of the bonfires we'd make; probably high as a kite. My dad never told us how exactly she died, but from what I can assume was an overdose. My dad was a deadbeat. I barely remember him working, but he was always gone. We were all in and out of rented rooms and shacks, relying on handouts from neighbors and school charities to get by . I dropped out of school after tenth grade and started working at a bike shop running errands for this guy named Mack who owned it. I made sure my brother finished high school. He was a good kid, but just like me; he didn't get a fair shake. Roman got caught up in a gang and was constantly in trouble or hiding out at some girls' house. I was always putting my ass on the line for him. When I turned 18, my dad got arrested for murder. I still remember the police tearing down the door at the hotel we were holed up in and tackling dad to the ground. Thankfully I was awarded custody of Roman and took care of him ever since.

I made my way through my twenties working my way up to mechanic at the motorcycle garage. Mack was into some shady business on the side; but I tried to keep my nose clean and worked on fixing up motorcycles. I was good with my hands and a quick learner. I made enough money to keep some food in the fridge and paid rent on time. Roman and I rented small places here and there; moving to the next when the neighborhood got too rough to tolerate. By that time, Roman worked all night as a bouncer and slept all day. I know we weren't going anywhere fast. But when the police showed up at the garage and threw me in a pair of handcuffs; I didn't realize how much my life had sucked.

Alexa

Sarah convinced me to meet up again at Tommy's Bar downtown. It's been one hell of a week so I definitely wanted to blow off some steam and maybe I'd be lying to myself if I wasn't hoping to see Angel again. What's that saying? Good girls love bad guys. Yea, I get that may be true, but when I looked into his eyes... it wasn't all bad. There was softness there, maybe some pain... and definitely a lot of lust. I wore a black skater skirt with a tee shirt tied at the waist and a jean jacket over top. Sneakers to keep it casual and my hair long with loose curls. No reason to try and beat the humidity that summer brought on.

The usual suspects were there when Sarah and I walked in. Sarah was helping out at the childrens' shelter so I drove her over knowing that her boyfriend Josh would take her home. Josh and Randy were playing a game of pool and some other of Randy's friends were hanging over some touristy girls that smiled and giggled every two seconds. "Gosh, Randy again? Why's he been hanging around so much lately?" I whispered to Sarah.

"Ugh girl, he's got it bad for you. Josh said he hasn't shut up about you all week. I guess seeing you hang over that biker dude last week got him all riled up. Just ignore him. He's an ass and he'll lose interest when he realizes you don't put out." Sarah smirked. She knew I was not into casual sex or even interested in a relationship. Maybe I was a tad stubborn and really focused on work.

"Ha, jee thanks. Make me sound like a nun, why don't you." I elbowed her with a smile. "Anyway, I never gave him a clue that

I was interested in him. I wish he would just back off. He slightly creeps me out anyway." Randy was your typical fuck boy. Picky to a fault; always on the hunt for someone to keep around that was just as pretty as he was. And rich.

"Hey ladies! Hey Alex. Damn you look good tonight." Randy slung his arm around my shoulders and kissed the side of my head. Yuck. Jesus, get off of me. I ignored his comment and politely ducked under his arm and busied myself with grabbing a pool cue. I teamed up with Sarah and waited for her to rack the balls. I gave a quick scan to my surroundings and that's when I saw him. He was in a booth this time across the bar with a few more of his 'brothers' from the Los Demonios Locos. He was staring right at me. He looked serious, I can see his jaw ticking from here and he fisted the beer in his hand and his lips were pressed into a hard line. I felt flustered all over again. Butterflies and sudden dizziness in my head. I gave a small smile and then glanced back down at the pool game I was supposed to be starting. Fuck, just one look at him and I'm a mess again.

I tried my damndest to get my head into the game and conversation when Josh and Sarah were talking about throwing a Fourth of July party. They volunteered my house since it had the biggest pool and plenty of parking. Nevermind the fact that the house was always fully stocked of food and drinks; even when my mother was away, she encouraged me to have friends over and have fun. Anyway, I had two weeks to think about the party and the details but already Sarah was putting a mental list together of who we'd ask over and if we can get a DJ. If it weren't for my outgoing friends, maybe I would be a nun. I was a homebody for sure but my anxiety and shyness never allowed me to throw ragers or party like a 20 something year old at my house. My mom lived 80 percent in a swanky apartment in the city by her office and courthouse; leaving me home to do whatever I wanted.

"Oh shit. Did you see your leather bound man is here!" Sarah sputtered out as she stood in front of me with her back towards Angel and I peeked over her shoulder. "Yes, I've noticed."

my eyes shot out around Sarah's shoulder and he was looking at me. You can tell he was at least trying to stay interested in his friend's conversation but his eyes were on me. He gave me a small secret smile with his lips turning up slightly at the corner and it warmed his features. It gave me goosebumps, everywhere. I must have been smiling like a silly fool because Sarah snapped her fingers in front of my face.

"Hello, earth to Alex. Jeez you've got it bad for this guy. Why don't you just walk up to him, grab him by his leather vest and make out with his hot ass!" She laughed at her own brazenness as if her nor I would ever do anything like that. But damn, if that thought didn't cross my mind. For the next hour I played pool, chatted with Josh and some of his buddies that showed up. Before you knew it we were a large crowd taking over the back side of the bar and two pool tables. I was trying hard to keep tabs on my motorcycle god but the crowd was too thick to see him anymore.

I heard the sound of boots behind me and I smelled leather and that same woodsy male scent as it washed over me like a warm breeze. He was behind me. I looked up fast enough to see Sarah in front of the pool table with a girly smile on her face and I knew Angel was behind me. "Can we get in on the next game?" His voice was deep but soft at the same time; with a hint of a spanish, mexican accent. I felt chills go up my spine and before I got a chance to turn around, Josh replied, "yea sure man, let me just kick this guys ass and the tables' yours."

I turned around slowly and he was close, so close to me. I was short in my sneakers and when I looked up towards his face I only reached up to his chest. I tilted my chin to meet his eyes and a breathy, "hi", was all I could manage.

"Hi again. You and your friend want to play me and my brother?" Before I could even answer, Sarah gave a very eager "Yes!" and scooted around the table so she could introduce herself.

"Hi, I'm Sarah.. and well, I guess you know Alexa. My boyfriend, Josh is the tall adorable one over there and some of the guys are guys he works with." She stuck her hand out to shake hands with Angel and his brother and I was slightly jealous that she was touching him and I didn't get to again. Angel never did take his eyes off of me and walked around the pool table to rack the balls and grab pool sticks. He kept a little smirk on his face as well as I did; like this little unspoken secret we kept between each other. His other 'brothers' moved into our crowded space to play a game with Josh and his buddies.

"This is my brother, Roman." Angel moved around the table quietly. I watched his smooth strokes of the pool cue and the smack of the balls. I didn't know how stupidly sexual this game could be. But I couldn't stop the buzzing in my head of just the thought of his lips on my lips or his hands on my body. I was mesmerized by the way his arms held the pool cue as he took his shot. His firm shoulder muscles and biceps. He pulled up his long sleeves up to his forearms where his tattoos showed a bit more. I shook myself out of the thought when it was my turn and tried not to bend over too far over the pool table; attempting to keep my modesty intact. The game continued pretty quietly; small talk from Sarah and Roman. And the guys playing next to us kept it civil and I can tell our friends were pretty intimidated to be playing with the M.C.. Josh bought a round of beers for everyone when the games were nearly over and Randy wasted no time to rush over to me and Sarah after we lost our game. Angel eye fucked the hell out of Randy. Clenching and unclenching his jaw. He was definitely leery of him.

Sarah and I thanked the guys for the game and hung up our pool sticks. Angel surprised me when he grabbed my elbow. He stuffed his hands back into his pockets and shoulders slightly raised. Maybe he was a little nervous to talk to me one on one. It was so hard and soft with him. Hard exterior with his intimidating stance, tattoos, leather and patches on full display but his eyes and voice were so soft, gentle yet almost demanding of my attention.

"Do you wanna sit with me? Roman just ordered a pizza and should be here in a sec." He stood so close to me. But this time when he spoke, he dipped his head toward my neck and I could feel his warm breath on my skin.

"Yea, I'd like that, thanks." He led me to the booth with his hand on the small of my back. The contact alone was enough to make something stir inside of me. Sarah saw where I was headed and came and sat down across from us in the booth with Josh and some of the other guys they were with. It was an odd combination. Motorcycle guys, us.. me. But we all hit it off; talking about local news and some politics. A couple of the guys were our age and went to public school in town. I slid in next to Angel. He had his arm resting on top of bench so it was easy for me to cozy up next to him without it seeming like I wanted to crawl into his lap. The conversations seemed to grow distant as we honed in on each other. The world faded away and all of a sudden, it was him and me.

"So, why haven't I seen you around here until last week?"Angel spoke softly, his chocolate brown eyes warm with slight smile lines hugging his eyelids.

"Oh, I've been on rotation for volunteering at the Migrant Childrens' shelter down the road. Sarah works there with me too; this is our second week at this location. And Josh is doing night classes at the college building two blocks over. So this was a good meeting point." I couldn't help being slightly nervous; I was rambling for sure. This man that I've been fantasizing about for the past week is now closer than I thought could be possible. I tried to keep eye contact with him, but my shyness was getting the best of me and I was fiddling with the silverware that was on the table. "Sarah is an occupational therapist and I'm a social worker. But I'm working on my child psychology degree." When I looked up, he was hanging on my every word... looking at my lips and I blushed when he licked his lips in response to my attention to his.

"Okay, okay, I have to ask," Roman butted into the conversation. He seems much like his brother, warm on the inside; big tough guy on the outside. He was a bit shorter than Angel, stockier, maybe a few years younger and had hair down to his shoulders that today was tied in a low ponytail. "What's with the asshole giving us eyes from across the room? He does realize he's way out of his element, right?" Roman was referring to Randy. Once again, Randy was making a pest of himself. He looked like he was power drinking and kept his face furrowed in our direction; specifically mine. I tried not to even look his way. I didn't want to give him any ammunition to come over and start anything with these guys. Not just because these guys may or may not be criminals or thugs; but I don't want to see Randy get beaten to death over some unrequited love situation. I didn't like the guy but I wasn't about to be a jerk about his feelings.

"Oh, Jesus, that's Randy.. just ignore him. We do." Sarah chuckled into her beer.

"Yea, he's just pissy that Alex here wants nothing to do with him. The guy could be a cool dude but he gets in a huff when he doesn't get what he wants." Josh added in; always trying to be the most diplomatic. He was never one to be an asshole for shits and giggles. "His daddy is a big shot doctor in the city and Randy skates through life from his good looks and his dad's money".

Ugh this conversation is not going well. The last thing I want to do is talk about money or how some guy has the hots for me while I'm bubbling with nerves sitting next to Angel. Angel looked like he was mad. Jaw clenched tight, face stern and hard and his eyes were boring a hole in Randy's head. I feel like I needed to change this conversation quickly so I put my hand on Angel's knee; gliding his attention back to him and I.

His eyes came back to mine and I felt him relax. Pizza arrived and we all had a slice. All this pent up sexual frustration needed a diversion; I felt like I was ready to burst. It was well after 1am and some of the bar's patrons started dispersing. Angel and I made light conversation. He asked me about my volunteer work and I told him how I grew up in the outskirts of town and that I loved the desert. As we talked I felt his hand on the side of my thigh. Slowly, leisurely, his thumb trailed up and down the outside of my leg in lazy circles. My heart was beating so hard and I could feel my insides turning to goo with just his touch. When he realized I wasn't going to push his hand away; he slid his hand over my knee, gently palming my leg. His touch was soft while his hand felt slightly calloused, the pads of his fingertips rough and manly. As we were finishing our beers, my second of the night; his fingertips started to play with the inside of my thigh. Sliding a touch higher each time. He made me breathless.

I'm sure my face was a little red and I couldn't tell if I was panting or if that all was in my head. But when I peeked up at Sarah, I knew she knew something was happening under the table. She gave me a quick wink and started to tell Josh that she was getting tired. Within a few minutes she started to gather her belongings and said goodbye to all the guys. Josh finished his beer and stood up. He shook hands with everyone and when he shook Angel's; Josh gave him a slight nod that seemed like secret guy language. Angel nodded back to him and then glanced around the room. There were only a few stragglers left.

Angel

"I guess it's getting late." I looked at Alexa's parted lips and didn't want this moment to end. Feeling her skin under my fingertips was amazing. Her thighs slightly parted while I explored with my fingers. I traced lazy circles in the middle of her thigh, her soft skin prickled with goosebumps and her breath hitched if I inched higher. Her cheeks were a perfect shade of pink and she licked her lips as I spoke to her. If there wasn't an audience, I'd have taken her right there. My dick was hard and I was practically begging to taste her mouth.

"Do you want to come home with me?" Alexa asked as her cheeks turned a bright shade of red. "I mean, I'd like to keep talking with you. Um, we could just hang out. Oh shit, I'm not very good with this. I um.." she brushed the hair back from her face; her body fidgeting in the seat.

I let out a little laugh. She was adorable when she was

nervous. I tipped my head down and gave her a wicked smile. "So you want to take me home? Is that what you're asking?"

"Oh my god. I um, just would like to get to know you better. I um, was having a really nice time with you." she put her head in her hands and a nervous giggle escaped from her throat. "Jesus, I suck at this. I don't want you to get the wrong impression of me. I just... I don't know. Forget it, I'm sorry." she looked a little defeated when she finally looked back up at me. I knew she wasn't the type of girl to bring dudes back to her house. She was smart, and sweet and definitely too good for me. But I wasn't ready to let her out of asking me to come home.

"Yea. Alexa, I'd love to come hang out with you. No pressure. I'm not a total dick." I gave her a smirk and put my hand under her chin and tipped it up to look at me. "I'll be a complete Angel."

She batted her eyelashes at me and said with a nervous laugh, "okay, let's go then."

Alexa slid out of the booth and headed to the pool tables where her jacket was hung up. I gave my brothers a nod and Roman slapped me on the back. He knew better than to make a crude comment. This was a good girl. I wasn't just gonna take her back to the clubhouse to get my dick wet. Alexa was putting her jacket back on when I saw Randy slide in front of her. Everything went black. My body was moving before I could even put a thought together. He was in her face and he grabbed her wrist. Somehow Roman got to her before I did. My brother always had my back and would take on anyone without a second thought.

Alexa

I cannot believe I just blurted out asking him to come home with me. What the hell was I thinking? Omg, can my face get any redder at this moment? I just asked a guy to come home with me that I've met twice and duh! Of course he's probably thinking he's gonna get laid. Shit, what did I get myself into. My intentions were just to not to end the night. I really liked talking to him and well, him fondling my bare thigh didn't hurt my decision either. My head was fuzzy from all his touching and to be honest with myself; I just wanted to see where this could go. Maybe I was getting tired of acting like a nun!

"Yea. Alexa, I'd love to come hang out with you. No pressure. I'm not a total dick." he gave me this little wicked smile and I couldn't help but laugh and shake my head. He took my chin in his thumb and forefinger and tipped my chin up to meet his eyes again. "I'll be a complete Angel."

I nodded my head with a sigh and batted my eyelashes in response to his still sexy smirk. "okay, let's go then." and I got up and went to grab my jacket off the wall in the back. I was putting my jacket back on and heading back out towards the front door when Randy jumped in front of me. I didn't think he was even here any longer so I threw up my hands on his chest when he surprised me; getting into my personal space. He grabbed me by my wrists. Hard.

"What the hell Randy, let go of me." I shot out. He let go quickly but inched closer to my face.

"What the fuck are you doing Alex? Are you seriously fucking going home with him? That piece of shit?" and he gestured back to Angel. He was mad; and drunk. He slurred his words slightly at the ends and his eyes looked dead and hollow.

"Randy, that's none of your business. What's gotten into you?" I backed away until my legs hit the table behind me but he reached out and grabbed my wrist again. This time he pulled my body towards him. One second I was being gripped hard on the wrist; the next I felt a firm arm come around my waist from behind and pulled me away from Randy.

That's when I saw Angel's tall frame step in between us. He grabbed Randy up by the collar of his shirt and brought him to his face. That's when I realized it was Roman that pulled me back. "It's ok... let's wait for Angel outside." Roman whispered in my ear. I had no choice but to comply. And honestly, I felt more safe with Roman and Angel than Randy whom I've known since grade school. I looked over my shoulder as Roman guided me to-

22

wards the door. Angel's body was tense and rigid. Randy looked like a ragdoll in his hands. Before the door swung closed behind us, I heard Angel's stern voice say, "You don't touch her. Alexa is not yours to touch. I will break every fucking bone in your hands if I see otherwise." And with that, the door closed and the night's cool breeze allowed me to take a relieving breath.

"It's fine. Angel won't do anything stupid. Unlike that ass bag in there." Roman lit up a cigarette and offered me a playful smile. Angel came out a moment later putting his hands on either side of my waist and searched my face.

"You ok? He didn't hurt you, did he?" Angel looked so serious, searching my face to see if I was afraid of him or afraid of the situation I just walked out of. Before I could answer he put the palm of his hand ever so gently on the side of my face and took a deep steadying breath.

"Im ok. I'm sorry about all that. We tried to warn you about Randy. I'm just shocked he grabbed me like that." I felt ashamed that I put Angel in that position. "I don't know what he was thinking."

"Well if he wants a problem with the DL's then the dumbest thing he can do is put his hands on their property." Roman pipped in and Angel shot him a warning look. "Well, we don't treat women like that. One of us was bound to put him in his place." Roman laughed off his comment, sucking on his cigarette and moving toward the rows of motorcycles in front of the bar.

"Can I still follow you home?" Angel stepped back allowing me a second to decide. But I still wanted him; still wanted to see this through.

"Yes. I'm parked on the street, the black car over there." I pointed towards my black Dodge Challenger.

"Huh," he said with an amused laugh. "That's your ride?" Angel headed down the steps of the bar towards my car as I unlocked the doors. He admired the machine and opened the door for me.

A little smirk crossed my lips as I sat down. "Yes, Angel." He waited til I buckled my seat belt and shut my door for me. I rolled down the window allowing the cool breeze to fill my car. "My place is about 15 minutes outside of town."

"Okay, I'll be right behind you." I waited as he turned and walked back to his bike. He strapped on his helmet and started up the bike; the rumble that came out of it vibrated through my body.

Chapter 3

Alexa

I gripped the steering wheel as I pulled out of the bar parking lot. My hands were sweaty and my heart thumped so hard in my chest. I clenched and unclenched my thighs just thinking about Angel at my house; in my space. I was excited with a healthy dose of nervous as hell. I'm not sure what was coming over me; my sudden eagerness to flirt with danger or the actual want to spend my time with a guy and maybe have him run his fingers over more than just my bare thigh excited the hell out of me. I watched his headlight in the rear view mirror and the butterflies and goosebumps washed over my body over and over again. "Alex, this will be fine. You'll be fine. Angel is more than fine. Don't chicken out. Just breathe." I kept giving myself this pep talk as we headed out of town.

Soon the traffic faded away and we entered the desert where the homes became more sparse and larger developments sat tucked into the peaks and valleys of the desert. Within a few minutes, we pulled up to the large gated community where I lived and I rolled down the window to punch in my code. Angel's bike idled loudly behind me and for a split second I remembered that security will for sure think it's odd that a motorcycle is sitting in front of my house. My head swam for a second thinking about the possibility of security banging on my door to see if everything was ok. The gate opened for us and he slowly pulled forward and we wound around the mansion-like homes until we got to my driveway. I hit the garage door opener where I park and opened the adjacent one so that he can pull into the garage as well. Problem solved. No one will see his bike.

My mother's house was beautiful. Two stories, white stucco estate with black trimmed windows. Uplighting in the landscaping made the house look warm and dreamy. Beautiful cacti and desert flowers encompassed the entryway and lined the driveway. The main house sat nestled into a valley with a huge circular driveway and amazing backyard. The house consisted of a generous gourmet kitchen overlooking a pool complete with a waterfall you can jump from and a large patio with a firepit and jacuzzi hidden behind strategically placed landscaping. There were six bedrooms, library, office and a two story family room that housed a huge stone fireplace for chilly nights. Caddy cornered off the main house was a four car garage with a complete guest house above it. I lived in the guest house. I loved the privacy of the space and I didn't have to worry about the maid, or my mom's assistants barging in while I was walking around in my pajamas. I had my own entrance on the side of the garage or up the steps around back that led to an extensive deck that was the entire length of the four car garage.

I took another deep, cleansing breath before I got out of my car; trying to compose myself and my nerves. Angel pulled into the garage next to my car and got off his bike. I watched him. He had this little smirk on his face as he leaned his bike gently over and dismounted. Helmet off and he ran his fingers through his dark hair. He took off his leather vest, folded it and laid it across the seat of his bike. His body is on full display for me now. His black tee shirt was tight across his chest, shoulders hard and bulging. Long, thick arms and strong hands. Angel had a large frame and a small waist, stomach as flat as a board. Thick, capable legs wrapped in loose fitting jeans and heavy black boots.

"Nice place." he said casually. He walked out of the garage and admired the main house and the opulence surrounding him. It was eerily quiet; almost two in the morning; and the stars were plentiful.

"Uh, thanks. It's my mom's house. I live upstairs; in the guest house." I pointed above my head. I felt silly for having to explain that I still lived at home. I'm 27 but in my line of work, I wasn't exactly in the money-making business. "The door's around the side."

He walked over to me, ran his hand down the length of my arm and laced his fingers with mine. "I know it's crazy that I still live at home, but my job is like 70% volunteer work and my mom really supports that. I guess I'm lucky though; I love my job and my mom loves that I can play house sitter here since she pretty much lives in the city lately." I unlock the door and head up the flight of stairs to my domain.

Angel

I follow her up the stairs to her place. And it's overwhelming being out of my element here in a damn mansion; but I'm quickly snapped out of that thought because Alexa has a skirt on and I can see up her skirt and her tight ass as we go up the steps. "So, what does your mom actually do to live in a place like this?" I ask. I'm definitely curious but more so just want to see what I've gotten myself into.

"Oh, she is the District Attorney." Alexa said casually as we walked into her house. Shit. I knew this girl was too good for me. I'm a fucking criminal at the god damn District Attorney's house. However fucked this situation is; it doesn't stop me from following Alexa into her kitchen. Her place is nice. Super clean and open. Giant windows from wall to wall and glass doors that open up to the deck. A couple of rooms off to the side and a family room with white couches and desert photographs hanging on the walls. Me and my dark jeans and shirt were a direct contrast to everything in this place. Alexa was the light and I was the darkness that was about to descend upon her.

Alexa seemed pretty nervous. She took off her jacket and slipped her shoes off at the door. "Should I take my boots off?" Before she answered, I knelt down and untied the laces and slipped my boots off.

"Do you want anything? Water? I don't have any beer;

umm...." Alexa moved to the fridge and grabbed two cold bottles of water. I thanked her and cracked open the water, drinking half the bottle in one go. I couldn't take my eyes off of her. With bare feet and leaning her elbows on the kitchen counter; she looked so innocent and beautiful.

"There's tons of stars out tonight; do you wanna come outside with me?" She led the way to the deck and opened the door to the cool night air. I didn't speak much; I took in everything that was Alexa and let my eyes roam her body. I noticed her nipples peeking through her shirt and felt my dick stir to life. She leaned on the railing; softly biting her bottom lip, head tipped up the night sky. My hand brushed away a few strands of hair that blew around her face and stoked my hand down the length of her hair and onto her back. I stood close enough that I could smell that sweet coconut and lemon scent that I found irresistible on her.

I couldn't take not tasting her lips for another second. She was so much smaller than me; I stood at 6 foot 2 and she felt so fragile in my arms. I dipped my head as I tipped her chin up towards my face and I softly kissed her plump lips. I felt her breath hitch and a soft, almost silent moan escaped her throat. When I pulled back, her eyes were heavy with lust and I knew if I didn't take a step back; I would have pulled her body against mine and taken her mouth hard and not stopped til she was gasping for air.

"Sorry, I've been thinking of your lips for a week and..." I smiled and her cheeks flushed and she licked her bottom lip. She shivered a little so I stepped behind her and wrapped my arms around her body. Both quiet for a second we listened to the distant howling of coyotes.

"Angel, where do you live? I feel like I don't know that much about you," she asked.

" I live in town, my brother and I rent a house on the west side. It's close to the clubhouse." I didn't want to go into details that the house we rented was a one bedroom shack where I slept on the sofa. It had everything we needed; we didn't have a reason to complain. Besides, we spent most of our time at the club or doing runs in the middle of the night for the DLs.

"And do you work? I mean, like besides what you do for the MC?" I know she was curious about how bad of a criminal I was or wasn't. I didn't want to delude her into thinking I was a damn pussy cat but I had to watch what I told her especially knowing now who her mom is.

"The MC takes care of what we need. We don't really speak about what we do for Los Demonios. But I can say that the guys; my brothers, are my family and they're not all bad." I knew I was skating around her question. She had an unconvinced look on her face.

She spun around in my arms to look me in the face, she placed her hands on my biceps and I couldn't help but lean my body into hers. "I know you're not a bad guy, Angel, the way you look at me tells me there's more to you than you'd ever let on." She smirked and furrowed her brows, still trying to figure me out.

Alexa

We talked and laughed for a while. He was easy to talk to actually. Angel's voice was soft and soothing when he spoke to me and he humored me by answering all my silly questions. He never made me feel pressured or uncomfortable. Being with Angel felt easy. For once in my life; I felt like me. I didn't need to impress him or talk his ear off; I didn't need to helplessly flirt with him to win his attention; he was here in the moment with me. It started getting colder out and standing out in the darkness was making my eyes sleepy.

"Let's go inside, ok?" I took him by the hand and we walked into the family room together. He closed the door behind us and grabbed my arm and gave a soft yank back towards him. I turned my body to him and he wasted no time to pull me into him. Sinking his lips once again onto mine. But it wasn't soft this time. It was needy and hot and I couldn't help but run my fingers through his hair as his hands traveled down my back and squeezed my ass cheeks. His kiss was all suction and warmth and I opened my mouth to allow his tongue to caress mine. He tasted insane. We kissed and explored a bit with our hands. I ran my hands over his hard chest and down across his shoulders then smoothed my way back up through his hair. He groaned into my mouth when I gasped for air in between kisses. My body was pressed hard against his and I can feel my nipples harden under my shirt. I was too aware of the wetness between my legs and I took deep breaths to calm my erratic heartbeat.

We kissed as he walked me backward to the kitchen island. When my body stopped at the counter; he grabbed the back of my thighs and hoisted me to sit on the counter. Legs spread with his body between them; he stood back to admire my skirt hiked up around my hips exposing my black lace panties to him. Angel looked at me like he wanted to devour every last piece of me and I loved it. He grabbed the back of his shirt collar and pulled his shirt over his head; granting me an unbelievable view of his bare chest and six pack. His abs were lean and hard with a beautiful V that dipped into his jeans. A tattoo of the Los Demonios Locos emblem inked over his heart and he had full sleeve tattoos down both arms. He took my mouth hard again. Painful but amazing bites to my bottom lip as he took a handful of my hair and tugged back so my face and neck were exposed for him. He kissed up and down my neck while his hands roamed my bare thighs freely.

Angel

Alexa looked like a goddess spread for me on top of the kitchen counter. Her head was back and she was panting hard with my tongue licking the sensitive skin of her neck, making my way back to her lips. I can almost feel her heartbeat thump quickly under my lips while my hands roamed up her thighs, teasing the intimate crease of her groin where her black lacy panties were. Her breath hitched and she placed her hands on my chest pushing back ever so gently so she could look at me.

"Angel, go slow with me, okay?" she whispered.

I may have put the night into overdrive when I took my shirt off. I hate to say that I've grown accustomed to fast girls in my days of hanging around the MC. With those girls; it was a no holds bar, take it and leave it type of situation, that I used to take full advantage of when I first patched in.

"Sorry, of course. You're so beautiful. It's driving me crazy seeing you like this for me." I put a hand on either side of her face and her eyes warmed to mine. I kissed her gently and she held me there; waiting for both of us to slow down our breathing and racing hearts.

While keeping my eyes on hers; my one hand traveled down her chest, slowly feeling her round breast in my hand. I felt her thighs squeeze around me and her mouth parted with approval. I massaged over her breasts and pinched her tight nipple in my fingers. I was rock hard and couldn't help but grind my pelvis into hers as she moaned softly and wiggled her ass on the counter. My other hand was still on her face; I wanted to watch her expression so that I knew if I was taking things too far. But she didn't stop me. I ran my thumb over her lips and she softly sucked it and licked her lips. She pushed into my body harder, trying to gain some friction on her clit that she was rubbing on me unconsciously. I ran my hand up her thigh and finally over her clit. She was so wet for me; I could feel it through the thin material. She moaned as I rubbed her over and over in lazy circles. "Does this feel good?" I whispered into her ear. "Should I stop?" I knew I was teasing her; she didn't want me to stop.

"It's so good, don't stop Angel." my name came out of her mouth in a deeper lusty sound and it only made me want to make her speak my name more. I breached her underwear feeling the soft wet skin of her pussy and she gave a sharp inhale and grabbed onto my biceps to steady herself.

"You're so fucking wet for me. I want to make you come all over my hand." I rubbed harder and then slower making her pant and moan for me. Then I gently eased inside of her and a soft moan escaped her mouth. She was so fucking tight. "Fuck Alexa; you're so tight. Baby come for me, that's it... yes." She was breathing hard as I fingered her harder and ran my thumb over her clit at the same time. She brought her lips to my neck and started to kiss and lick down to my chest; her hands rubbing over my stomach and clawed up my back as her body started to shake and shiver. "That's it baby, come for me. You're so fucking beautiful." Her legs and body went tense as I felt her pussy start to convulse around my finger and she came so hard; her body flooded with goosebumps and she dug her nails into my back.

I didn't take my hand away until I felt her body loosen up and she felt limp and defeated in my arms. I kissed her over and over and held her in my arms until her strength regained.

"You're going to ruin me; aren't' you?" She asked with a lazy smile. I returned her smile and she giggled, "that's ok. I think I like it."

"We should get you to bed." I picked her up off the counter and set her back down on her shaky legs. "Would it be ok if I stayed? I can sleep on the couch if that's ok?" Her eyes were sleepy and her body sated as she took my hand and led me to her bedroom.

Alexa

"You can stay, but maybe you can stay with me? In here?" I said nervously. Was I taking it too far now? It was nearing four o'clock in the morning and I just wanted to crawl into my bed and dream of how wonderfully delicious Angel just made me feel. His hands felt so good on my body and regardless of how sleepy I was; my body was buzzing with excitement. He stood in the doorway and ran a hand through his hair. Would he be able to just *sleep* next to me? I'm sure he was contemplating that very notion.

"You can sleep on the couch if you want but the morning sun will wake you up in about two hours." I made my way to the bathroom quietly shutting the door behind me. I wanted to at least wash my face and brush my teeth and slip into some pajamas. I chose silky pink shorts and a white tank top; piled my hair on top of my head with a scrunchie and smoothed some lotion over my skin. I haven't slept next to a guy in at least 5ish years. I didn't remember what the sleepover etiquette was.

I walked out and was surprised to see Angel laying on my bed; still in his jeans and laying on top of the covers. I had to giggle. It was like we were in high school again; afraid one of our parents was going to catch us. I crawled into bed next to him, sliding under the covers.

"If I got under those blankets with you in just my underwear; I wouldn't be able to hold myself responsible for not touching you all night." Angel quipped. He rolled over, propped up on his elbow facing me and played with the loose ends of my hair, fingertips slowly tracing down to the side of my face and brushing over my lips. He leaned up and kissed me ever so gently and whispered, "goodnight Alexa."

Chapter 4

Alexa

I stirred awake; fluttering my eyelids over my bed only to see Angel's sleeping body next to mine. Still in his jeans; still on top of the blankets. His one arm pulled over his eyes and the other hand rested on his lower stomach. I watched his chest rise and fall as my eyelids started to close again. When I was just about to drift off; the scent of fresh coffee filled the air, making me sit straight up in bed. I know I didn't program the coffee pot last night with everything going on! I glanced over at the alarm; 9:45am. Then I heard a rustling sound in the kitchen and I bolted out the door. Sarah. She's the only one who would raid my kitchen on a Sunday morning.

"Jesus! You scared the shit out of me!" I whisper-yelled at her and closed the bedroom door behind me.

"Were you still asleep? Miss morning glory herself?" She asked in disbelief. "Josh went to the gym and he has no food in his house. And boy do I have shit to talk to you about!" Sarah hopped up on the counter; sitting cross-legged; curling both hands around her coffee cup.

I fumbled around the kitchen for a minute trying to get my bearings and trying to figure out how to explain that Angel was asleep in my bedroom! I knew I wasn't awake enough for this conversation so I reached for a mug and poured myself coffee and inhaled the sweet aroma deeply. "Huh? What are you talking about? What shit? I was just with you like 8 hours ago."

"Ugh so we had just gotten home and were about to head to bed when freaking Randy was pounding on the front door. He was so frantic and drunk that when Josh opened the door for him; he damn near fell into the house." Even though I kind of knew where this story was going; I loved Sarah's stories. She was so animated when she spoke and everything was so much more exciting coming out of her bubbly mouth. "It took like ten tries for Randy to get the words to not slur together in one big clump... but apparently your super hot motorcycle man gave him quite a bit of shit last night for him touching you? Did Randy touch you? He said Angel told him that he was going to break his face or something!" Sarah burst out laughing; probably remembering how stupidly upset Randy must have been to go pounding on Josh's door.

"Actually, I told him I would break every bone in his hands if he touched Alexa again." Angel stood in the doorway of my bedroom; arms crossed over his chest with thick forearms on display.He was fully clothed and looking slightly amused by us gossiping. Sarah gasped at the sound of his voice then slowly turned to me with a devilish grin on her face.

"Oh, hi! Umm..sorry; I didn't realize you weren't alone." Sarah shot dagger eyes at me and mouthed 'oh my god'.

"Uh, it's ok, we um, I just... it got really late and I told Angel he could crash here." I know my face was beet red and once again I was stumbling for words as my embarrassment took hold of me. Angel strutted over to me; kissed the side of my head sweetly and took the coffee cup out of my hand, took a small sip and returned it back to me.

"Wow, ok... well I'm gonna take my coffee to go and get out of yalls hair. Angel, very nice to see you this morning," Sarah gestured a small nod and a big cheesy smile, "Alex, yea... call me later! Oh and I want to know what the hell happened with Randy last night.. So call me when you can fill me in on that." With that she jumped off the counter, gave me a quick tight hug and headed out the door.

We both watched quietly as Sarah made her quick exit. "Coffee? Are you hungry; I could make you something?" I didn't know what to say. I guess I slept off all my bravery last night. I was back to being nervous and shy around him.

"Coffee would be great, thanks." Angel sat at the kitchen counter watching me move around my kitchen.

"I never did thank you for what you did about Randy last night." I sat down next to him; looking down into my coffee. Angel's voice was still sleepy sounding and his hair was that perfect mix of sexy-messy from sleeping. "He was out of line; he's never done anything like that before."

"Listen, I know what people assume when they see the vest and who I'm with and what we are; they think I'm a hot headed asshole. But Randy was completely fucked as soon as he touched you." Angel sipped his coffee. The house was quiet. "I should probably get going though, gotta meet up with the guys." Angel drained his cup and stood up to grab his boots. "When do I get to see you again."

Butterflies filled my belly again thinking about more time with Angel. "Oh, umm.. My week is a little crazy with work but if you want to meet up for lunch or something?"

We made our way back down to the garage, Angel getting his helmet and vest on. "Lunch sounds good." he started up his bike and the rumble was so loud I could feel the vibrations through my body. "Tomorrow?" Before he got on his bike he pulled my body close to his, possessively grabbing the sides of my waist; my hands smoothed down the front of his leather vest. Then he grabbed the back of my head, he kissed my lips sending chills through me making me dizzy with want.

When he pulled away with a sweet smile, a breathy, "yes" was all I could muster.

He walked back to his bike, mounted it and before he pulled away and said, "ok; tomorrow. I'll pick you up." and with that he was gone.

Chapter 5

Alexa

Monday mornings at work were always busy. Tons of paperwork to file and calls to make to local vendors and political leaders for assistance and support. Constantly updating figures and databases with the influx of children entering the country. It wasn't until Tim; he was in charge of news briefings and press for the children's charity, came into my makeshift office at the shelter to let me know that Angel was waiting outside, did I realize it was already 12:30pm.

"Hey Al, there's someone outside looking for you. Tall, tan and gorgeously wrapped in leather." he stated batting his eyelashes at me. Tim had a different boyfriend every other week and always heckled me about my lack of dating. "Who is he? He looks slightly dangerous which makes me even more interested in who he is and what's going on!" Tim stood cross-armed in my doorway unwilling to budge until I gave him some details.

"His name is Angel. And he's taking me to lunch." I deadpanned, ignoring his nosy questions; while I picked up my purse and glanced at my reflection in the computer screen, calming the stray curls that slipped out of my messy bun.

"Well, I hope you're eating him for lunch! Yum!" Tim laughed at his own joke and walked back into the reception center.

I walked out of the building to find Angel waiting patiently on a bench in front of the shelter. Since it was a children's shelter; they didn't let anyone in that didn't work there or have an appointment. He looked just as hot as he did on Saturday night. His hair was combed back and neat, jeans and dark work boots, and a snug fitting army green long sleeve tee shirt under his leather vest. His elbows were resting on his knees and when he looked up at me, my heart melted with that smile that he gave me. When he looked at me; it's as if he was seeing the best thing in the world. His whole face lit up and his eyes gleamed; and those soft lips with just the hint of a devilish grin.

"Hi. I hope you weren't waiting long?" I walked up to him as he stood to meet me. I was wearing cute strappy black heels, a tight fitting black pencil skirt that hit right above my knees with a silk white blouse tucked in. Simple make up and my hair in a curly messy bun. I had a meeting with the mayor later in the afternoon and of course I wanted to look nice for Angel.

"You look beautiful." Angel breathed me in. We got a couple glances from people walking on the street. Him wearing his motorcycle club colors definitely brought about some attention but I tried to not show that on my face. I wasn't blind to what I was getting myself into with him; but I owed it to myself and to him to form my own opinion. I know I needed to start asking him the tough questions about what he did if I was going to continue to see him. I just didn't want this to end before it even had a chance to begin.

Angel

"There's this little restaurant around the corner that has the best empanadas you'll ever eat. My friend's mother's place. You game?" I wanted to take her hand in mine but I refrained. Alexa seemed a little shy and we were in front of her workplace. I wanted to be respectful of her boundaries. She nodded her head and we began walking down the street. I was used to the glares and nasty comments from people on the street when they saw the emblem on the back of my vest. Even though we had a dark side, the MC is about pride, loyalty and above all brotherhood. I never felt shame for belonging to Los Demonios Locos; they saved me and my brother from a shitty life.

"How's your day going? Do you always dress this sexy for

work?" I asked casually, opening the door for her as we got to The Desert Rose restaurant.

"Well, thank you for the compliment; and no, I don't usually get this dressed up. I have a meeting with the mayor at 3pm for a facility tour and well.. I wanted to look nice for you."Alexa blushed and her face glowed when she spoke to me. The restaurant was busy but when Senora Torres spotted me she made a show of pulling me to the counter bar and cleared two spots for us.

"Bien dia, Senora. Gracias. Como estan?" *Good day, ma'am. Thank you. How are you?* I asked as I gave her a big hug before introducing her to Alexa.

"Aye Angel. Que bien verte. Tan guapo como de costumbre. Y quien es esta chica preciosa? *Oh Angel. How good to see you. So handsome as usual. And who is this beautiful girl?* She shoved me out of the way to take Alexa in both her hands and admire her. Senora Torres played mother to many of us; always making sure our bellies were full and we often went to her for motherly advice.

"Soy Alexa, amigo mio." *This is Alexa, a friend of mine.* Alexa glanced at me blushing, allowing this woman to admire her from head to toe.

"Mucho gusto. Huele increible por aqui. No puedo creer que nunca haya estado aqui, solo trabajo por la calle en el refugio de los ninos." *Very nice to meet you. It smells incredible here. I can't believe I've never been in here before, I only work down the street at the children's shelter.* Alexa spoke perfect spanish as she put her purse down and settled into a stool at the counter. I guess I should have assumed she'd speak spanish.

"Gracias. Nos gusta que seamos como una joya oculta que la gente descubre. Por favor, dejame que te traiga algunos tipos diferentes de empanadas para que puedas probar todo!" *Thank you. We like that we are like a hidden gem that people discover. Please, let me get you a few different types of empanadas so you can try everything!* Alexa nodded excitedly and Senora Torres ran off to the back of the kitchen.

"You didn't tell me you spoke spanish." I said inquisitively.

"Mmmm, yea. My grandmother made sure of it. She raised me since I was about 5 years old. And of course, in my line of work, it's mandatory." Alexa sipped the glass of water that was placed in front of her. She had this simple way of surprising me.

"Your grandmother? What about your dad? You haven't mentioned him to me."

"Oh, um. I didn't really know my dad. My mom worked all the time and when she made partner at a law firm she worked at; my grandmother came to live with us; it was just really her and I. My dad, he lived in Mexico. I don't really know too much about him and my mom always made sure it stayed that way. My grandmother passed away my first year in college." Alexa looked sad as she spoke about her grandmother but when I placed my hand on her knee, she shook the words away and gave me a sweet smile and took my hand in hers.

"Anyway, so... what's on your agenda for the week? Anything exciting?" Alexa changed the subject quickly.

"We have some club business this weekend; so unfortunately I won't be around. I gotta head out on Thursday but I should be back sometime Sunday." I explained as a pile of empanadas were placed in front of us.

"Oh wow! This looks so good!" Alexa took one bite into the crunchy empanada; closing her eyes in appreciation. "Mmmmm, this reminds me of my grandmother's cooking. So delicious." I couldn't help but laugh as she smiled dreamily with a mouth full of food. "What kind of business do you have to do? Or should I not ask that? I'm so sorry, I'm just curious; I know you said you can't talk about the MC stuff."

"Uh yea. Nothing we can't handle." Being vague was easy but it bothered me that I wasn't sure if I could or should even confide in her. At least not until I know her intentions for being with me.

"Is it dangerous? She asked cautiously.

"You don't have to worry about me if that's what you're wondering." I brushed her cheek with my thumb and she leaned into my hand. It was the first time I actually dreaded making a run for the DLs. We needed to cross the border into Mexico for negotiations and check on the suppliers for the drugs we collected for the gun trade. Guns were a necessity for Mexican rebels and well, Americans thrived off of the drugs we got as payment. It was usually a smooth operating business but with the border being breached more and more; there was a lot of heat on us to pull off a covert operation.

"Uh huh. Well maybe one day you'll trust me enough to talk to me about it?" She raised her shoulders with a questioning look yet completely sincere. "Well, maybe you can come over on Sunday? I can make dinner." Alexa peeked up at me as she snagged another empanada.

"Yea. That will work. I'll call you when we get back into town. I can hide my bike in your garage again." I know I was being sarcastic; but I wanted her to know that the reason behind me parking in her garage didn't escape me. I knew she was concerned about her mother finding out I was with her. I gave her a smirk and laughed. She looked a little surprised by my candor. "It's ok Alexa, I get it. Not something you want to advertise to mom right now." I gave her a playful wink before I dug out my wallet to leave money on the counter.

Alexa

We walked back to the children's shelter; this time sneaking through an alley to avoid the food truck lines that were now lining the sidewalks of downtown. I felt really bad that Angel realized I was nervous about someone seeing him at the house on Saturday. I took Angel's hand and laced our fingers together. It felt so good to feel the warmth of his skin. He had this way of always making me feel at ease. I slowed to a stop and held tight to Angel's hand as he turned to face me.

"Listen, I'm sorry about the garage thing. I should have just told you that outright. But my moms pretty intense and I know she'd go ballistic judging you and making assumptions. I just want to figure this out for myself. See if this is something I can handle." I gestered between him and I. "I like you. And I want to spend time with you without worrying about what everyone else has to say about it."

Angel stepped in closer to me and I backed up so I was leaning against the brick wall. His face was serious, eyes trained on my mouth as he licked his lips and caged me in on either side of my head with his strong arms. "I like you too, Alexa. I'm not saying I'm not a bad guy but I could never be bad to you." His lips found mine and his body melted into my body. As we kissed I felt his hard length press into my stomach and he slowly felt his way down to my ass, squeezing and pulling me tighter to him. My heart raced in my chest and I pulled him into me; holding onto either side of his vest. When he kissed me like this; hard and full of lust, the whole world melted away.

Chapter 6

Sarah sat on top of the kitchen counter as I prepped dinner for Angel and I. I was making steaks on the grill; roasted potatoes, a salad and I had ice cream for a sweet dessert. I spent the day cleaning my place and Sarah helped paint my toes as we gossiped. It was already 4pm so I had about an hour before Angel got here.

"So, are you going to have sex with him tonight?" Sarah eye balled me as she sipped her iced tea.

"Jeez! I don't know. No. I... uh... I don't want to rush things; I really like him." I told her as I tossed a cucumber slice in her direction.

"How old is he anyway? I don't think I asked you that yet?" Sarah had asked me a million questions after she walked in on us that first morning. After Angel had left, I ran upstairs and dove directly back into my bed. For one, I was exhausted but really; I wanted to breathe in the sheets where he slept. I layed on his pillow and closed my eyes thinking about the way he touched me. I felt invincible when I came while he was fingering me. Just that sexy way he talked to me; watched my face as I came. It was so intimate and I loved him talking dirty to me. I've only had sex with three guys; and let's just say... it was all very *vanilla.* I was always a reserved type of girl; I had the same boyfriend throughout high school but we broke up when he went to college in New York. And two boyfriends in college; one I met in statistics class and the other in business law; if that tells you anything. They were both really sweet guys but there just wasn't too much that held my interest.

"He's 36. And before you make your usual Sarah comments, I don't care that he's 9 years older than me." I said maturely as I stuck my tongue out at her.

"Ha! Ok, okay... age doesn't matter anyway when you're that hot! But! But.... this whole motorcycle gang thing? Alexa... how bad is bad? Ya know? I'm just looking out for you. I don't want to see you involved with any of the Los Demonios shit. And your mother would kill you. And then maybe kill me for not stopping you." Sarah got serious with me. I know she was looking out for my best interest. Angel could very well be an angel but his motorcycle club was anything but.

She hopped down from the counter now, all 5 foot 7 of her peering down on me as she held my hands. "I know. I'm gonna see if he'll talk to me about the MC more. Maybe see how bad things are or how involved he is? There's something in his eyes that tells me, he's not completely invested. That the MC was more of an obligation?"

"Hmmm. Well, good luck. And try to figure that out before your mom catches wind that there is a hot motorcycle hunk in your bed!" Sarah kissed my forehead and gave me a hug. "Ok.. I'm leaving. Have fun! Use protection. And call me tomorrow!" She was giggling to herself as she left and I couldn't help but laugh too and shake my head.

I headed to my closet; picked out a cute and comfy bodycon tank dress. It was soft green cotton and paired it with a white lace thong and matching balconette bra. Before I jumped in the shower; I texted Angel, gave him the gate code to get into the development and told him to head up the back deck stairs when he got here. And, sheepishly; I added that the garage door would be open for him.

Angel

I parked my bike in the garage like Alexa had asked. It definitely made me feel better that she admitted to why she wanted to hide me away for now. And to be honest; I wasn't ready for the heat her mom would bring down on me or my crew for dating her daughter. I left my cut on the bike and headed around to the deck steps. The mouthwatering scent of dinner cooking and knowing I would be all alone with Alexa made me more than just hungry.

The run Roman and I just finished went well but not without some flaws. We crossed the border into Mexico in un-marked civilian trucks. But it was what we found on the other side that caused us some drama. The rebels had a shipment of drugs ready to go and negotiations went well. Except, for the fact they wanted us to smuggle their people back with us into the U.S. in return for a few kilos more of cocaine added to our usual payment. Things got heated. We knew there would be no way for us to enter the U.S. again with illegal immigrants without being yanked out of our trucks and when we declined the offer; the Mexicans threw a fit and a brawl broke out. Pressures in Mexico were high. And getting their people into the U.S. was becoming a priority, almost as much as the guns we supplied them with. After some fist to face conversations; we left peacefully with a promise to help them in the near future through some of the illegal tunnels. That sort of operation was better left to the presi-dent and higher seats of the Los Demonios. My hand was busted up pretty good and I had a few scratches on my ribs; but other-wise we left unscathed.

As I got up to the deck; I could hear Alexa humming in the kitchen and pots and pans clanging together. The glass doors were open and the lighting was low and sexy. Alexa had her back to me at the kitchen sink; humming and swaying her hips to a slow rhythm. I stopped in the doorway to watch and admire her. She was so petite and beautiful; innocent and painfully good-hearted. There were many times when I thought about her and I together and believed that maybe I should let her go. Don't let her get mixed up in my lifestyle, my crimes or in my history. But to see the sexy curve of her hips, strong lean legs and tight ass; I couldn't stop myself, I needed to be selfish.

"Can I help?" I asked as I started towards her. She gasped as she spun around to face me. Before she got a 'hello' out, I dove into her lips, pulling her towards me with my arms around her waist. She kissed me back hard, breathing me in and letting me take her weight as I leaned her back in a slow dip. Her hands ran up the sides of my arms and into my hair and then back down again.

"Well hello there." She had the biggest smile for me. So genuine and sweet. "You're right on time. I'm gonna throw the steaks on. You do eat red meat, right?" she asked with a wrinkle of her nose.

"Mmmhmmm. Looks great. I can do the steaks for you if you'd like?" I took the plate of steaks from the counter and headed out to the barbeque. Alexa made me feel at home. It was hard not to feel insecure in this mansion of a house but Alexa was so easy going. It all felt right. I flipped open the lid and placed the steaks on as Alexa came to stand by my side.

"Oh jeez, Angel, what happened to your hand?" She went to grab my hand to examine my cut knuckles and bruises but I quickly pulled my hand back and stuck them in my jeans' pocket. "Not gonna tell me, huh?" She gave me a little side eye and a slick smile. "I'll get it out of you eventually. You *can* talk to me, ya know. I promise I'm not big on judgement. I'll just listen and nod." she let out a sigh and turned back to the kitchen tending to something that was in the oven.

We sat down to dinner and I thanked her for cooking. "Did your grandmother teach you how to cook?"

"Yea, she always had me in the kitchen. Cooking, laughing together. She'd watch me do my schoolwork and make me snacks. We had the best conversations in the kitchen. She was originally from Mexico City. She came to America when she was a teenager. And man could she cook." She spoke lovingly.. her eyes drifted out the window with a hint of sadness.

"You miss her." I stated.

Her gaze drifted back to me, "Yea. You would have loved her. She was a free spirit, loved to have fun. She told the best stories of growing up in Mexico. The parties her family used to throw were my favorite. Nothing was ever too serious with her.

She took everything with a grain of salt. And she always saw the good in people; even if it were buried down deep."

"Sounds a lot like you. You know; what you do is incredible." I kissed the tips of her fingers and held her hand in mine as we talked. "And your mom? Are you guys not close?"

"It's not that we're not close; we are. She and I are just different but cut from the same cloth. We both work really hard and have very high expectations of ourselves but she's... how can I explain this... she's hardened. She's laser focused and I think she's forgotten that there's more out there. She lives for her job and everything else is lined up after that. I love my job; but I want more out of life." Alexa gets up to start cleaning up the dishes. "When my grandmother came to live with us; it felt like more of a free pass to get out of parenting me. My mom showed up late at night, bogged down with files and I was lucky if I saw her on the weekends. Now, we meet up maybe once a week for lunch." She shrugged her shoulders and gave me a simple smile. Maybe Alexa and I had more in common than I thought? Maybe she'll understand the path I had to choose to survive and protect my brother?

"What about you? Your family?" Alexa asked cautiously.

We walked over to the couch and sat down. Alexa curled her legs under her as she sat facing me. "Well, um, my mom died when I was little. 6 years old. I don't remember too much about her. Her name was Elena, she had green eyes and dark hair." Alexa saw that I was fidgeting with the hem of my shirt and she let her fingertips slide down the length of my arm to put her hand over mine in support. I think she knew that this was hard for me. I never opened up about my family; there was never a point. "My pops was a dead beat, you know.... never around. He left me and my brother alone to fend for ourselves most of the time. Our neighbors helped out a lot. When I was 18, he got thrown in jail. And we haven't seen him since."

"Angel, I'm so sorry. That must have been really hard on you and Roman." She looked at me with sadness in her eyes but not pity.

Alexa, holding my hand, took a deep breath and wiggled herself until she was almost in my lap. The next question made her nervous and it showed. "So, um. When did you join the Los Demonios?"

"I was 25." I breathed out deeply; searching my mind to figure out how to get the words out. I never told anyone what had happened to me. I didn't need to. My brother and my MC family already knew everything about me so there was no need to speak of the shit that I've been through. But I wanted to tell Alexa. Let her see the real me and let her decide whether she wants to be with me. I knew if I lied to her; this thing brewing between us would never even make it off the ground. She was too smart for that and she deserved better. "I dropped out of school to take care of my brother when I noticed my dad was coming around less and less. I started working at a motorcycle shop doing grunt work, cleaning, answering phones and picking up parts. Mack, the owner, started letting me help around the shop more. He taught me how to take the motors apart and put them back together. I had a knack for it. I loved rebuilding these machines; seeing them come alive in my hands. The shop started doing mods for the local MC. Los Demonios Locos. Slowly the guys started bringing their bikes to the shop; they'd hang out and we'd talk. What I didn't realize was that Mack was allowing the DLs to store weapons in the basement of the shop. The door was always pad locked and I never asked questions. Mack got a big cut from them to keep his mouth shut and eyes on the shop. They had a good system going. The DLs paid for the parts, we installed them and we took care of their machines for free." Alexa studied my face as I told her my story.

"But something happened, I'm guessing. Something bad. To you?"she asked. Alexa was very perceptive. I took her legs and laid them across my lap. Allowing myself a second to gather the courage to keep talking.

"Well, I was at the shop all the time; I practically lived and breathed motorcycles. Mack was coming in less and less. So it was up to me to open the store. One Wednesday morning,

I opened the shop; I was there alone so I just went about getting my work list started on; when the police came busting in through every doorway. They were screaming for me to get on my knees; guns pointed to my head. The next thing I knew, I was face down on the cement floor with cops on my back, slapping handcuffs on me. They walked me outside to put me in a squad car. Then a whole team of cops started coming out of the building with crates of weapons. Guns of every size. Bags of them. Boxes upon boxes of ammo. And I was the only one there to take the fall. I watched in disbelief. My life literally flashing before my eyes. My head swam as all eyes were on me, pointing at me. Before they drove me away, I noticed the boys of Los Demonios peeking out of the other shops on the street; watching their merchandise being taken. They saw me being ripped out of the shop; taking the fall for them. I learned later that Mack was gone. The guy was nowhere to be found. He disappeared. The police naturally assumed I had everything to do with the arsenal in the basement and I got two years in prison. My sentence was reduced due to circumstantial evidence. Not one fingerprint on those guns belonged to me. But the whole time; I never said who they belonged to. I kept my mouth shut because I knew if I didn't; I'd be dead in a second."

"So when I got out of prison; my brother was waiting for me with a couple of the brothers from the DL. I thought they were gonna kill us both. But what I didn't know is that while I was in jail; they took in Roman, made him one of their own, took care of him for me in appreciation for me keeping the silence. At that point; I joined too. Not that I really had any other choice."

Silence hung in the air between us for a long time. Alexa's head was down; processing the story I just laid out for her.

"Thank you." she said quietly and sincerely. "I can't believe that happened to you. It must have been horrible.

"Yea." I laughed to lighten the mood. "I don't recommend jail. Not for pretty little thing like you." I teased. I ran my hands up and down her legs. Her smooth silky skin felt good and reassuring under my touch. She wasn't pulling away; I hadn't frightened her away, yet.

Alexa

I felt terrible that Angel looked grift stricken while telling me his history. Waiting for me to judge him or ask ten million subsequent questions. I loved that he was opening up to me. So much of him was a mystery to me. It felt great that he was learning to trust and confide in me. Telling me about the guns and his jail time was a big time risk knowing who my mom was and that it might just be the thing to break things off with him. I don't know why it didn't scare me more. Angel excited me in ways I never knew a man could. He made my heart ache and race all at the same time. I wanted to know everything about him yet I feared what he would tell me. Inside I knew he was a little broken; but aren't we all? Growing up I lacked a real mother's love and support but found it in my adoring grandmother. Angel grew up without any love at all but found the support he needed in the motorcycle club. He looked to them as his only family and it gave him purpose.

"You know what I think?" I asked playfully; sending my hips over onto his lap so I could straddle him.

"I'm afraid to ask." Angel responded as he held onto my waist.

"I think you're really a great guy, trapped in a really hard life." I place my hands on either side of his face; studying those beautiful brown eyes.

"Trapped." Angel thought for a second. "More like settled. I guess. I've come to terms with how my life has played out up until now." His firm grip on my waist made my sex throb and I found myself slowly moving on him. Grinding down on his hard length underneath me.

"Until now? What's changed. What do you want?" I asked as my breathing turned into panting as I was unapologetically finding friction between my legs.

"You." he breathed out as our lips crashed and he wrapped

his arms around me, holding me still as he thrusted up, rubbing his cock between my legs. He felt so hard and huge even through his jeans. I pushed my breasts against his chest as he kissed down the side of my neck. Angel lifted my cotton dress above my hips and slowly up and off my body. He sat back on the couch to admire my body. My chest heaved and my lips parted watching him look me up and down like he was going to devour me. His hands explored my hard nipples and slid down my stomach, his thumb landing at the top of my clit. I was soaking wet for him and as he rubbed my sex I tilted back for him, placing my hands on his knees so he can feel more of me. My body ached for him.

"Fuck baby. You look so good. God, I want to taste this pretty little pussy." He licked his lips and I almost came right there. I never had someone speak to me like this and it was throwing me over the edge. "What do you want? You want to come on my hand or my tongue?" He stopped rubbing for a moment; long enough for me to moan from the loss of contact. I felt like I was going to burst. I was nervous to say the words. That I wanted his mouth on me.

"Your tongue." I whisper-moaned. I bit my lip waiting for his reaction. But I didn't have to wait long when he grabbed me by the ass and hoisted me off the couch with him. We kissed and licked until we got to my bedroom; where he laid me down on my back. He grabbed the back of his collar and took his shirt off. I laid on the bed, waiting for him to touch me again; my knees together and hands on my stomach; I felt so vulnerable.

"Spread your legs for me baby." His hands slid down my thighs, slipped his thumbs around the sides of my panties and pulled them down my legs and off. He spread my legs wide for him. I was so open for him. I felt myself start to shake with nerves as I watched him bite his bottom lip while looking at my most intimate parts. He started kissing at my knees working his way down the inside of my thigh. "You're beautiful." He teased the area around my clit and opening; kissing up my stomach and then my lips. I felt his warm hand start to caress my wet opening and he slowly fingered me; my back arching off the bed. His eyes

51

met mine and I was drunk with lust. "Does this feel good?"

"Yes." my voice came out shaky and quiet.

"Do I make you nervous?" Angel asked as he pulled down the top of my bra to expose my nipple to him.

"I'm, I'm… just not that experienced." I don't know why I even blurted that out. I was nervous. The things Angel was doing to me; I've never felt before. I've never felt like my body was on this roller coaster ride; about to come at any second.

His mouth sank down on my breast, sucking my nipple hard making me moan out loud. "I'm going to make you feel so good. I'm going to lick your sweet pussy til you come." With that he descended to my sex. First lightly licking and softly kissing. My hands found his hair and I couldn't help but hold him in place as my head spun with an impending orgasm. Then he was eating my hard, his tongue felt like heaven as he lapped at me and gave teasing bites to my clit. When he sucked hard on me I felt the explosion in my body. My legs grew tense and threatened to squeeze shut and I gripped the bed sheets under me trying to gain some stability. I came so hard, I felt my body shudder and shiver for what felt like minutes.

I felt weak and zapped of all my energy as Angel climbed up next to me in bed. He pulled me close to his body and brushed the sweaty hairs away from my face. His eyes were soft chocolate and his lips turned up in a satisfied smile. I entwined my legs with his; his rough jeans mixing with my bare legs. I was surprised when he slowed things down and laid next to me.

"You're beautiful when you come for me." Angel whispered as we slowly started kissing me. I tasted myself on his lips and tongue but it didn't bother me. The sweet, salty taste mixed with Angel was euphoric as his hands caressed my breasts. I ran my hands over his stomach and thick biceps; exploring every inch of his upper body. He was so lean and firm everywhere; being naked in his arms felt so good.

"Angel" I said with warning when things started heating up again.

"Shhhh; its ok. I want to take my time with you. I'll never

hurt you or do something you're not ready for." he cooed in my ear. The fact that he didn't want to rush to sleep with me was overwhelming. That and impressive being I just spent the last hour rubbing and grinding against him.

Chapter 7

Angel

I woke up to an empty bed. It was 5:30am on Monday morning. I didn't mean to spend the night again; but with Alexa's half naked body curled up against mine; I couldn't bring myself to leave. My eyes roamed over her room; looking for evidence as to where she would have gone. I know she has to work today; so maybe she was getting ready. I sat up trying to rub the sleep out of my eyes and tame the raging boner I had this morning. I had a mean set of blue balls last night after going down on Alexa; but I wasn't about to rush her into having sex with me. I wanted her bad though. Just to see her body quivering under mine last night sent my dick into overdrive. I'm not even sure how I didn't come in my pants.

I can hear the faint sound of groaning and music playing nearby. I used the bathroom, then went to go look for her. In the bedroom down the hall; the door was cracked open and I can see Alexa on a spin bike working out. Her body was glistening with sweat and her strong legs looked amazing as she was pumping her legs to the music. I watched for a second before she realized I was standing in the doorway.

"Oh hey!" She panted as she spoke. "Good morning.. I didn't wake you, did I?"

"Well I heard this moaning coming from another room and I thought maybe I should come investigate." I said with a laugh. She wiped the sweat from her neck and chest with a towel but her legs never stopped. Her body was hard as steel as she worked out and my cock was hard just looking at her. "Do you mind if I use your shower?"

"No, of course! I'll be done in a few minutes." she replied. I turned to the hallway as I heard her turn up the music a bit louder as she pushed harder and faster on her bike. Now I understood why she had such amazing legs.

I turned on the shower and jumped in. The warm spray on my face felt amazing. I couldn't remember the last time I took a hot shower. I fingered all of Alexa's shower supplies. I used her shampoo that smelled like coconuts and body wash that smelled like her skin; fresh lemons. I closed my eyes and re-lived last night in my mind as I fisted my cock. I was so fucking hard for her. I stroked fast and hard with one hand; bracing myself on the wall in front of me with the other. The orgasm nearly knocked the wind out of me and made me weak in the knees. I needed that sweet release so badly but I still ached for her. I wrapped a towel around my waist when I was done and came out to the kitchen.

Alexa stopped dead in her tracks and ran her eyes up and down my body. She cleared her throat before she spoke, "Um, are you hungry; I'm making breakfast?"

"You don't have to do that. I don't want to make you late for work or anything."

"No, it's fine. I have eat after a workout like that; and I don't have to be at work for another two hours. I'm kind of an early morning person." Alexa said shyly.

"Yea, 5:30am is pretty early. But sure, breakfast sounds good. Thanks." I turned to go back into the bedroom to get dressed but turned back to tell her with a devilish grin on my face, "you look sexy as hell in that outfit all sweaty." I heard her giggle as I turned my back. Alexa was wearing tight black workout leggings and a powder blue sports bra that showed her hard nipples. Her hair was up with curls poking out all over and her body was glistening with sweat. If I hadn't showered already; I'd be right back in there jerking myself off again; looking at her right now.

I walked Angel down to the garage. I was dressed and ready for work in a pair of black jeans and floral boho top. He straddled his bike after putting his leather vest back on and fiddled with some of the instruments on the machine.

"I'd like to take you for a ride sometime. If you're not too afraid?" He put his helmet on and took my hand in his. Angel had a devilish grin on his face that I just couldn't resist.

"I've never been on a bike but I'd definitely like to try it out." I smiled. Angel always seemed to want to make future plans with me before he even left me. I loved that he was looking forward to spending more time with me.

"Cool. Just let me know what day works. I can pick you up from work or something." He started the loud engine and I loved what the deep gurgling of the exhaust did to me. It bubbled up excitement and danger; curiosity and lust in me; just like Angel did.

After a sweet kiss goodbye; I stood at the front of the garage as Angel drove away; gracing me with the sweetest smile that left me feeling like I was on cloud nine. Just as Angel made the turn out of the driveway, two black Escalades pulled up to the house. Shit.

There's no way my mother didn't just notice a motorcycle leaving the house. The rumble of the throttle alone practically woke the neighborhood. The cars pulled up the circular drive and parked. My mother was the first one out; and she was marching straight towards me.

"Hey mom!" I blurted out with a half hearted wave.

"Um, yea, 'Hi'; who was that guy on the motorcycle?" She initially looked curious and cautious as my mom's eyes searched mine for the truth. How very lawyer-y of her.

"Ummm… he's a friend of mine." I said matter of factly . I didn't want to let on that I was slightly panicking here. She was definitely schooling *her* panic and frustration. Just as I was about to answer her, her bodyguard, Ben leaned into her ear to whisper something.

I put my hands up in defense; already trying to ward off the impending bitch fest I was about to get with her newly given information from her bodyguard. "Mom, wait. Before you flip out, hear me out, ok. His..."

"Alexa! You're hanging out with a member of Los Demonios Locos? Are you crazy! And for Christ-sake, it's seven in
the morning; so he obviously was here with you last night." At
this point both bodyguards were staring me down and her assistant was pacing behind her pretending to answer emails.

"Jesus, Mom. Can we discuss this in private. I don't think
your staff needs to hear about my love life!" Love life? Oh my god,
what am I saying. She had me so frazzled and defensive I needed
to take a breather to get the words out correctly. I took her by the
elbow and led her back into the garage near my car.

"Alexa. You know how bad this can get. He's a thug; a criminal even." She looked exasperated.

"Ok, Mom." I took her hands in mine and pleaded my case.
"His name is Angel. And it's not exactly how it looks. We're just
hanging out, getting to know each other. He's not a bad guy. I
just.. I don't know.." I hung my head, defeated. I didn't know how
to defend Angel. He may very well be a criminal. Angel's greatest
downfall was the very thing that saved him.

"Ms. Ramirez?" Maria, my mom's assistant stepped trepi-
datiously into the garage. "You have a phone conference in 5
minutes. Do you need me to reschedule it?"

My mom shook her head at me, "No, Maria. I'm on my
way." She glanced back at me. "Alex, we need to talk about this.
Not only for your safety but you know how this is gonna look for
me." Mom started to walk back to the main house; her face sul-
len and pensive. " I'm going away this weekend for the holiday;
Sonoma. Maybe you should come with me. Get away for a little
bit?"

"Thanks mom, but I can't. I have work and you know I
don't really drink." My mom looked disappointed with my answer but gave an understanding nod. "Sarah and I are having
some friends over Saturday for the Fourth; I hope that's still ok?"

"Yea, it's fine." She hurried away as Maria handed her her
phone. "I'm only here for the day, Alexa, call me later to talk?" a
demand; not a request.

"Sure thing." I got in my car and made my way to work. A million thoughts ran through my head: Will my mom ever understand. Will she ever accept Angel. Did Angel see my mom pull up to the house. Will he ever speak to me again. Is Angel going to run from this knowing who my mother is. Am I putting Angel at risk. Am I putting myself at risk. Ugh. My head was spinning by the time I pulled into the shelter's parking lot. It's Monday. Mondays were the busiest and I needed to focus on work. That and how to handle my mom when I call her later.

Chapter 8

Alexa

It was 3 o'clock and I hadn't stopped all day. I processed in 30 more children that came over the border since Friday and I had to scramble to transport them to our partner shelters a few towns over. I just sat down at my desk when my cell buzzed in my back pocket. *Mom's Office.* Great. Just what I needed right now.

"Hey mom."

"Oh, Alexa. This is Maria. Your mom is in back to back meetings until the end of the day; but she asked me to arrange dinner for you both tomorrow night if you're free." There was a long pause as I contemplated having to talk to my mom in person about Angel. "Alexa? Is that ok for you; shall I book a reservation at the Patio Bar for 6:30?"

"Oh, yes, sorry Maria. That'll be fine." I said defeated. Some days it really made me upset that my mother rather book time with me through her assistant than just send me a text.

Dinner with my mom came faster than I was prepared for. I haven't heard from Angel since he left the house Monday morning and I was beginning to worry. Did one simple glance at my mom's entourage scare him away? I went to the restaurant right from work; my mom's car picked me up so that I didn't have to drive into the city. My mom knew how much I hated to parallel park. I wore a long red floral maxi skirt and short white tee shirt and jean jacket. My hair was down in soft waves and I had gold hoops in my ears. My mom was already seated at a table with her bodyguards sitting adjacent. She was fiddling with her phone when I walked up to her.

"Hey mom."

"Hey." my mom didn't get up to give me a hug; she rarely showed much affection to me, even less so when we were out in public. I bent to kiss her cheek and sat beside her. If I wanted her to hear me out about Angel; then getting her pissed off at my defensive position was not the way to go. Much like the attorney she is; she always wants to hear all the facts in a calm, clear manner and I thought if I appealed to her softer side; she'd go easy on me.

The waiter came over to hand us our menus and take our drink orders. My mom ordered a very expensive glass of wine and I ordered sparkling water with a lime twist.

"So how is work going? I heard that the Children's Shelter downtown has been at max capacity for over a month now?" Leave it to my mom to go straight for the work conversation.

"Yea. We're really taking a big hit right now. I've been running around like a chicken trying to find spots at nearby shelters. It's getting harder and harder."

"I spoke with the mayor recently and he said you've done a wonderful job with the sponsors and volunteers." She added as the server came with our drinks and took our food orders.

"I'll have the Chopped Mexican Salad with Cilantro Lime dressing." I requested and my mom ordered a petite filet mignon with side roasted potatoes. "Umm, yea. The mayor has been in for a tour and we've been getting a lot of support from the neighboring restaurants and hotels. Right now, we just can't wait for the government to supply these children with the basic essentials; so these donations from local companies are our lifeline." She nodded in agreement as I dreaded her next question. But I cut her off before she had a chance. "So, Sonoma? That's nice you're getting away. Are you going with anyone?"

"Yes. I need a break for a few days. The city will be shut down anyway. No court, no calls. Not like I won't be working on the plane; but it's better than being stuck in the city. I'm taking a few of my girlfriends with me. You remember, Sylvia and Rosie? I used to work with them." she asked.

"Oh yea. I do. That's really nice. I didn't realize you still spoke with them."

"Mmmhmm, well our paths cross every now and then in the courtroom, so... it'll be nice." my mom answered a few text messages as she spoke.

"When will you be back in town?" I asked cautiously. Internally I wanted to get the 'Angel conversation' over with so I can stop fidgeting in my seat.

"Monday night. You said you're having a party at the house? Sarah taking the reins on that?" I knew she meant that as if I would never initiate a party on my own.

"Yea, she's pretty excited. Last she told me, she was able to get some fireworks out in the desert to go off at midnight for us. But don't worry; she'd never make it get too out of hand."

"Haha, sounds like fun. Who are you inviting? Remember to give security a list, please." She gripped her wine glass in her hand and I knew she was about to strike.

"Mom, just ask. Ok, is Angel going to be there? Right? I don't actually know. I haven't asked him."

"Listen, Alexa. I've never been one to tell who you should be hanging out with, you've always been very careful and respectful of my position. But, Al, really... what am I supposed to think!" She leaned in close, her voice lowered and she had daggers in her eyes. "You know damn well who Los Demonios Locos are and what they do; then you bring one home with you? Are you insane? And please don't just tell me that he's a nice boy and that he's in love with you or some nonsense." She rolled her eyes at me and was very flippant and snippy. I thought for sure she would have laid into 'my responsibilities and he's a criminal' speech. Instead, she was making me feel foolish and immature.

Dinner was served and I sat quietly and pushed around my salad. My mom took two work phone calls and we were interrupted three times from people passing by saying hello to my mother. I clammed right up with my mom; I searched my head for a new angle. Something to convince her to listen to my side of things. But somehow she took the wind right out of my sails.

How is it she said three things to me about Angel and shut me up faster than I could say *mom*. I guess that's why she's the D.A.? The waiter came over to drop off our check when my phone dinged with a text message.

Angel: Are you still at work? I just passed your car in the parking lot.

Me: I'm at dinner with my mom in the city; her car picked me up.

Angel: Wanted to see if I can take you for a ride?

Me: I'm leaving in a minute... I should be back to my car in about 20?

Angel: I'll be waiting.

Before we got up from the table; my mom took my hand firmly, "I'm sorry that we got interrupted tonight; but Alexa; you need to use your head about this guy. He's bad, he's not good for you. He may very well be dangerous. You're a smart girl. I know you'll do the right thing here. And I don't need to tell you how this will look if the media gets a hold of it." And that was it; her closing statement. It was about her image. How things would be perceived if it got out I was associating myself with a gang member.

"He... his name is Angel. And I understand your concern. We're just friends and his 'gang'(yes, I used air quotes) is a part of this city and downtown regardless of what we like to think of them. I'm not stupid; and I promise to take your advice into consideration." I stood from my seat and kissed her goodbye and made my way to the awaiting car.

Angel

I parked my bike and I grabbed a coffee from the food truck that was parked out on the street. I hadn't avoided Alexa on purpose the last day and a half. I just wanted to give her time to deal with her mom. I saw her mom's SUV come barreling down the road; looked like I left in the nick of time. I actually was half expecting a 'I'm sorry but we can't see each other' text from Alexa. I had no idea that she was with her mom tonight and I was pretty freaking happy she still wanted to meet up with me after eating dinner with her. Maybe things went well? Maybe her mom didn't notice me Monday morning; or more specifically my MC colors on my vest.

A few minutes after I finished up my coffee; a black Audi sedan pulled into the lot to drop off Alexa. The overweight, balding driver got out of the car and opened Alexa's door. I stood back in the shadows until he pulled away. Alexa sat in the front seat of her car, quickly fixing her hair and popping gum into her mouth. I strutted up next to the car and tapped lightly on her window.

"Jesus Angel! You scared the shit out of me." She whisper-yelled and got out of her car. She didn't hesitate to push her body up against mine and finger the hem of my leather vest before rising up on her toes to give me a light peck on my lips.

I laughed into her lips, "yea... you look terrified." She gave me a little slap on the chest and blushed.

"Funny. Where's your bike? I thought maybe you'd given up on me?" She peaked over her shoulder looking around.

"I parked it behind that truck. Didn't want the ace driving you back here to report me to mommy." I gave her a small dig. Really I was trying to test the waters; see what her mom voiced about me over dinner.

"Ugh; let's not go there. I had enough of my mom for one night." Alexa said as she flipped her hair over her shoulder. She looked beautiful tonight. Her skin glistened in the moonlight and the tiny sliver of stomach I saw peeking out from the bottom of her tee shirt made my dick hard just thinking about getting her naked.

"Well then; I won't ask. Ready for a ride? Let's clear out that cluttered mind of yours." I took her hand and walked her back to where I was parked. I can see the relief in her eyes when I didn't press harder about her mom. I handed her my spare helmet and started my bike.

"Thanks! Can you help me with the strap?" She tilted her chin up so I could adjust the buckle. She looked hot in a bikers helmet. "Shit. Um, I'm wearing a long skirt."

I sat on the bike and looked at her predicament. "Just pull your skirt up your thighs; no one will be able to see you." And she did. She wrapped her legs around my bike and I felt her strong thighs tighten around my legs. She wiggled until I felt her warm center at my back and she wrapped her arms around me. It felt so right.

"Just tap my arm if you need me to stop or slow down, ok" I explained as we pulled out of the lot. As we eased onto the highway; I felt Alexa hold me tighter but she never let on if she was scared. I can see her in my side mirror that she had her face up to the sky; watching the stars twinkle above our heads. The lights of downtown faded as we made our way out to the desert.

After about a half hour; there was a pull off that we stopped at. It was an open lot; used sometimes for small desert concerts or trade shows. There were picnic tables and bleacher seating under some lights. Alexa got off the bike and adjusted her clothing. I helped her with her helmet and we walked down to the nearest picnic table. We both sat on the top with our feet on the bench; searching the stars for answers. It was a beautifully quiet night and the air was warm.

"Did you like it? I wasn't going to fast for you; was I? I asked her.

"No, no.. I actually loved it. It felt so... sooo.. freeing. I always kind of wondered what the fascination was with bikes. What made the ride so much more enjoyable for bikers, ya know? But I kind of get it. The bike drowns out the outside noises and all there is, is the road in front of you and your thoughts. It's really pretty refreshing." she gazed at me with a small smile and I could see the reflection of stars in her eyes. "And well it doesn't hurt to be on the back of a fierce machine with a hot man." She laughed and blushed. I loved it when she blushed. She was so often sweet and gentle and when she pushed herself out of her comfort zone was when I got to see the real Alexa. She had an internal energy that drew me to her; aside from her kind heart and beautiful face. I laughed at her compliment.

"Hot man, huh? You're pretty gorgeous yourself, you know that." she leaned her head on my shoulder as I spoke. "I'm just gonna ask. Ok? I'm gonna assume things went sideways with your mom?"

Alexa didn't bother to pick up her head when she answered; shielding her face from my view. "Hmmm. Well, it wasn't awesome. Obviously she knows. She was informed by her bodyguard after they pulled up; as to who you were affiliated with. But you know what was strange?" She looked at me now, her eyebrows furrowed. "She seemed more concerned with me falling for a guy like you. She made me feel almost foolish; like I didn't know what I was getting myself into. Rather than mad that I could be associated with a member of Los Demonios. I mean, of course she mentioned the dangerous aspect and if the media got a hold of it..." Alexa was rambling a bit, trying to talk out her frustrations about her conversation with her mom. "I don't know. I'm sorry to put you in this position. But I did tell her that I was going to make this decision on my own."

"Alexa. I'm not going to pretend that I haven't done bad shit. The M.C. does some bad shit. But I would never involve you in that. That's my burden to carry. I will separate the two every way that I can. Sometimes I hate that I'm not a different person. That this life chose *me*." I stood up and paced, my frustration getting the better of me. I know that I should let Alexa go; but it was killing me even thinking about it. "Maybe we shouldn't see each other?"

"I don't want that." Alexa shook her head feverishly. "No, Angel, that's not what I'm saying and I'm not just going to roll over because my mother says to. I'm 27 and I am perfectly capable of deciding what's best for me. And right now; I choose you. I *feel* something for you." She came to stand in front of me with both hands on the sides of my face. "I think you feel it too. You know, growing up... everything was so perfectly timed and so strategic. My college, my job; all so convenient for mom, respectable. I never made waves, never. She never allowed it. And I never fought it either. And finally, when something like this; you and I; comes around. Why does *this* feel so damn right?" At Alexa's last word, I grabbed that back of her head and smashed my lips into hers. Our lips moving over each other's, not able to get enough. Our tongues colliding and sliding against each others'; tasting, caressing. I pulled her into me with my hands on her ass and her hands in my hair. My hard length throbbed between us as Alexa sucked on my bottom lip. We kissed until we were both breathless and needy. A couple of trucks passing by blew their horns at us making us stop and laugh.

"And you thought that I'd be the bad influence." I teased her. I held her in my arms for a few more minutes as we both stared off into the dark lonely desert. "We should get going." I resolved.

"Ok." We walked hand in hand back to the bike and started the ride back to her car.

Alexa

My head felt like a tornado of thoughts by the time we got back to my car. Maybe I should have censored what my mom said about Angel; but I just wanted to be honest with him. I wasn't being stupid. I knew damn well what I was getting myself into. I had done my homework on Los Demonios Locos and searched the news archives to see what kind of trouble they have been into in the past. I even went as far as to look up Angel Torres in the police articles. I found his arrest details and read the news articles associated with the investigation of the arsenal found at that motorcycle shop. After Angel had told me about his jail time; I had to see and read it for myself. The news painted Angel out to be a poor street kid that got mixed up in gang business. They never once mentioned Los Demonios though. What seemed like an open and shut case went sideways when the investigating detectives couldn't come up with any circumstantial evidence. But the wonderful justice system the way it was; Angel had already served 2 years before the charges were dropped and released. I did happen to find an associated article where the body of Mack Andrew Miller, the shop owner, was found in the desert nearly two years later. He had one gunshot wound to the back of the head; no suspects or evidence supporting an arrest was discovered.

As I readjusted my clothing and smoothed my now tangled mess of hair; I was sad to be leaving Angel. The more time we spent together; the more it felt right to be with him. We were electric together. The whole world seemed in balance when he was near me.

"Oh, don't forget I'm having a Fourth of July party at the house on Saturday. Well; Sarah is making me, but that's besides the point. Umm, I'd really like it if you came. Bring Roman or some of your friends! I really want you there."

Angel lightly kissed my lips, "I'll be there if you want me to be." he replied as he opened the car door for me.

"Thanks for the ride Angel. See ya soon?" I asked as I watched him slowly back away from my car.

"Yea, sweets, I'll see you soon. Good night." he said with a nod.

The rest of the work week flew by. I had to get volunteer coverage for the holiday weekend. Most of the regulars already told me that they wouldn't be in town. The few of the staffers made a rotational schedule so that the shelter was covered. I was finishing up for the day when Sarah breezed into my office.

"Hey doll! Ugh, what a day, right?" she plopped down in a chair beside my desk.

"Tell me about it. It's been swamped this week."I sat down with her and fisted my coffee that I had yet to drink from this morning.

"I'm so ready for Saturday; it should be a lot of fun." Sarah had planned everything, from the catering to the fireworks at midnight. We both agreed on the guest list; roughly 30 of our close friends and some family. A lot of the kids we went to school with were in town for the holiday so we were probably going to have a lot of drop bys. Sarah started jotting down a list of last minute things to do when she started tapping her pen nervously.

"What? You do that when you have to tell me something bad." I asked with a slick smile.

"Um, well, not bad. Well, um." she trailed off.

"Sarah, just spit it out, what?" I peeked up at her with one eye as I finished an email for work.

"Randy's coming." Sarah spit out.

"What? Come on man, are you serious? Why? Who invited him? You know Angel and Roman are coming!" I half pleaded and half yelled at her.

"I know, I know. Josh slipped about the party and Randy went into a whole monologue about how sorry he was and that he just wished that never happened. Josh said he sounded pretty sincere and said that you'd probably be cool with him coming as long as there was no drama." Sarah explained.

"Damn it Josh. Well, I mean that's all fine and good but I don't remember getting an apology from Randy. Did Josh mention that Angel was going to be there? The last thing I need is those two getting into a fight at my house." I explained, shaking my head.

"Yea, I'm pretty sure Josh told him that you and Angel were still seeing each other. I think it'll be fine though. There will be plenty of people there and I'm sure Randy will be on his best behavior. Oh, and are you still cool with Josh and I staying in the main house overnight? I don't want to worry about getting back to your place in the morning for clean up duty." Sarah jotted down a few more details.

"Yea, no problem. I appreciate the help." I got up from my desk and started to gather my belongings to go home. "Okay, what time are you coming over tomorrow? I think catering said they'll start their set up around 4. We just have some decorations and the lawn games to set up really. Everything else should be pretty easy. I'm going to stop at the store on the way home and grab some extra pool towels and things."

"Cool, let me know if you think of anything else too. I'll be over around 3? Is that ok?" Sarah asked as she grabbed her purse and things too.

"Yup! Sounds good to me." I said as we started making our way out of the building. I gave her a kiss goodbye and made my way down the street. There were a few shops down mainstreet that I wanted to check out.

The first store was a cute home store; they had beach towels and I found some really cute Fourth of July themed beach balls and pool floats. Across the street was a swimwear store so I headed there next. I had plenty of bikinis but I wanted something cute and special. I browsed the hundreds of tiny string bikinis; some with sequins and fringe, bikinis in all colors and thong bottoms until I found the perfect one. It was a strappy maroon bikini; the top laced up at the back and the bottoms were cheeky with strappy details at the waist. And it didn't hurt that the color matched Angel's bike perfectly. His motorcycle was mostly black and chrome with a maroon gas tank and fenders. I also grabbed a black lace sarong with crochet tassels for a cover up; I hated just walking around in a bikini. Just when I was about to check out; I breezed by the men's wear and decided on a whim that I should pick up a couple of men's swim shorts. Just in case Angel and Roman didn't bring a bathing suit with him. I used my best judgement for size and then grabbed three pairs; one all black, one black and grey and the last black and blue. It's always better to be prepared.

I finished my shopping and headed home. I wanted to clean up my area then head over to the main house and make sure everything was in order. I knew everyone on the guest list; but it didn't hurt to stow away breakables and lock my mom's office and bedroom. After a quick once over of the house and pool area; I emailed the caterer for confirmation and sent the housing development's security a list of guests and mine and Sarah's contact information for any questions or issues.

It was late when I finally got in the shower and threw on some comfortable pajamas. I wanted to get a good night sleep so I could wake up and get a good workout in before Sarah came over to help set up. I texted Angel when I finally settled into my bed and put on some tv.

Me: Can't wait to see you tomorrow.

Angel: Can't come soon enough

Me: Is Roman coming with you?

Angel: Yea, and my boy Taylor, if that's ok. He's cool. Pretty sure you met him at the bar last time.

Me: Yea! Of course! Work was hell today.. Im exhausted.

Angel: I could come over and help you fall asleep ;-)

Me: Mmmm.. tempting. But I need to get my beauty sleep for tomorrow.

Angel: You're already beautiful.

Me: If I knew we'd just cuddle; I'd say yes. But I have a feeling I won't be able to keep my hands off of you.

Angel: Not a bad problem to have.

Me: Stay with me tomorrow?

Angel: yes.

Me: Maybe more than just cuddle??

Angel: hell yes.

Me. LOL…. Good night Angel

Angel: Good sweets.

I slept in a little and had a kick ass work out. If I was going to be prancing around in a bikini most of the day; then I wanted to feel confident and amazing. I did a 45 minute spin bike sesh and followed up with abs. I made myself a delicious spinach and ham egg omelet and washed it down with a hot cup of coffee. Sarah texted me and told me she'd be over earlier; around 2, so she can get ready here after setting up and helping with the pool floats I told her I bought. I definitely needed the girl time with her; I wanted to tell her what went down with my mom and how things are going with Angel.

Before I knew it; Sarah was pulling up to the house so I ran down to the driveway to meet her. Her car was filled with red, white and blue balloons and bags full of streamers and noise makers. We got started right away decorating; tying balloons to the deck and lounge chairs. She bought little pool floating lights for night time and we draped the streamers from some of the trees and umbrellas. My mom's backyard looked festive and inviting; and we were sweating and exhausted by the time the caterer's showed up.

"Ok, the caterers are all settled in the main house and are setting up; they said they have everything under control." I plopped myself in a pool lounge chair and chugged a bottle of water.

"Oh good. Ok, it's 3:15; let's go shower and get dressed now so we can relax before people get here." Sarah perked up and was already out of her seat. We headed up to my place and Sarah used the guest bath and I jumped into my shower. I shaved and lotioned every inch of my body; applied minimal makeup- water proof of course; and left my hair in natural soft waves down my back. I threw on a cute tight white tank dress and strappy sandals; I'll change into my bikini later when people start going into the pool. Sarah finished up too and looked adorable in her powder blue skater skirt with white tank top and tan sandals; her hair up in a pony.

Josh and his buddies were piled into his Land Rover and a few other cars pulled up behind him. They made their way through the house and out to the pool area where Sarah and I were getting drinks from the bartender we so thoughtfully hired last minute.

"Hey good looking!" Josh gave Sarah a big sloppy kiss and me a hug. "Alex, I haven't seen you in a bit, heard you've had your hands full." He gave me a knowing wink. Josh introduced me to some of the guys that came with him as they helped themselves to keg beer. I was making some small talk with a couple girls that I knew from school; when I glanced over to see Randy come out of the main house. He was with two friends of his; the same guys that were there the night at the bar when he had that confrontation with Angel. I quickly turned away from Randy and tried to busy myself with the caterer that was firing up the BBQ.

"Hey Alexa." Randy tapped my shoulder lightly.

"Randy." I replied coldly.

"Listen, I know I should have stopped by or something to apologize to you. I feel like a dick for what happened at the bar." he muttered but he was busy glancing over my shoulder at some of the girls sitting by the pool.

"Is that your version of an apology?" I asked smugly.

"Alex. You know as well as I do; you're way above that guy's paygrade. I mean, we all slum it sometimes; but that's just shooting too low." Randy laughed.

"Randy, you're a dick, you know that?" Randy's eyes snapped to mine at my comment. "But listen, I will take into consideration that you only see dollar signs when you look at women and that you're as deep as a puddle. But let's just agree that it won't happen again. We've known each other a long time and I've never given you reason to think that I was interested in you or that you need to meddle in my life. So let's just squash it for today, ok? Angel will be here shortly and I will not have any drama here. So if you can't handle me 'slumming it' then you can just leave." I verbally back handed him but he kept his eyes schooled and his mouth in a tight line. I was mad that he was still such an asshole to me but I just wanted to agree to disagree and be done with this conversation.

"Damn. Ok. Yea. You do you I guess; and I'll go do that hot blonde over there." Randy laughed in my face and sauntered off in the direction of the girls.

Chapter 9

Angel

Roman, Taylor and I rolled out from the club to head to Alexa's place. I gave Taylor a quick run down of the deal with Alexa's mom and to play it cool around her friends. Taylor was mellow; he's been in the club for almost ten years; a pretty boy gone bad after he spent his late teenage years in juvie and 5 years in prison for assault with a deadly weapon. He was one of the quiet ones, never started shit outside of the MC; kept to himself even though he had the girls flocking to him with his blonde hair and blue eyes, boy next door look. Fortunately I knew better than to cross him; they say it's the quiet ones you should look out for and in Taylor's case; you'd be correct. If given the motivation; he's deadly and vicious- street smart and cunning; a great asset to Los Demonios.

Roman was all too excited to come when I mentioned the party. Roman was the opposite of me; goofy, outgoing and loved to party. He loved the MC life; party all day; danger at night. He thrived off intimidating others when it came to representing our MC. He had no remorse for the crimes we committed; he was raised in violence and chaos. Roman would never know a 'normal' way of life and wasn't interested in finding out.

Alexa texted me the code to the garage door earlier in the day. Said if I wanted to park the bikes in there; it was my choice. Other than to hide them from security; it worked well to park the bikes out of the blaring sun. Nobody liked to burn their ass cheeks on a hot leather seat. We walked through the expansive main house. The place was insane. White walls and leather couches, huge kitchen, stone floors and minimal decor on the walls. You could tell the house wasn't lived in much or if it was; they sure knew how to keep it clean.

"Damn son, this place is legit." Roman added as we made our way out to the pool area. I gave him a quick elbow to the ribs while I scanned the backyard for Alexa. We stuck out like a sore thumb. The three of us, in our Los Demonios Locos leather vest, tattoos running down our arms with jeans and boots on. Everyone else was either in bikinis or board shorts. A couple of the people stopped their conversations to look our way as we headed for the bar. Alexa spotted me from across the pool; she was talking with a couple other girls. She looked amazing. Her tanned skin against that tight white dress; hair was down in natural soft waves. She had an athletic body that I fucking loved with legs that were meant to ride me.

She strolled up to us with a huge smile on her face. "Hey guys! I'm so glad you all came!" Alexa looked nervous with her hands on her hips. She didn't lean in to kiss or hug me; I'm sure she didn't know what to do in front of the guys.

"Hey. You remember Roman. And this is Taylor." I gestured to the guys.

"Hey Roman," She gave him a hug. "Taylor, nice to meet you." She shook his hand. "Well, help yourselves; whatever you want to drink and the food is all inside. Um, Josh and Sarah are here somewhere and I think you might remember some of the guys from the bar." Alexa came to stand next to me. I looked down at her with those beautiful lips and I couldn't help but lean down and give her a quick peck on the lips. She didn't hesitate to meet my kiss or pull away; she just beamed with that smile of hers.

"Ugh jeez. Well baby girl; I hope there's some single ladies here that I can flirt with. And shit if it isn't hot as hell out here." Roman goofed as he surveyed the girls that were sitting at the poolside.

Alexa laughed, "Ha! Yes, Roman.. I'm sure you can find some cute girls to talk to. And, OH! I have some board shorts in my place. I grabbed a few just in case someone forgot their bathing suits; if you want to go swimming. Angel can show you." she gestured to me.

"Oh man! Good looking out!" Roman replied.

"Angel, can I talk to you for a sec?" Alexa asked quietly. She walked me around to the hot tub area; it was down a small walking path and hidden behind a row of hedges.

"What's up?" I asked, guarded.

"Listen, it wasn't my idea. But Randy is here. I didn't think he'd really show up, otherwise I would have told you sooner. Josh had mentioned it to him and he acted all butt hurt and apologetic. But when he showed up early he was just a complete asshole." My jaw ticked as she told me. I wouldn't put up with anyone being an asshole to Alexa and I had already warned Randy. There were no second chances in my book. "I asked him to just squash things and told him if he couldn't handle himself that he should just leave. He hasn't said anything else to me and before you get upset with all this, I just hope that we can just steer clear of him tonight?"

I took a deep breath to steady my temper. Alexa has a point though and there was no way I was going to cause a scene at her home. But I'd be lying if I said I wasn't going to keep my eye on him. "Don't worry, I won't do anything. As long as he keeps his hands and eyes off of you." I put my hands on either side of her small waist and breathed her in. She was like sunshine and sex rolled into one.

"Thanks Angel." She tipped her head up so that I could kiss her and I did. I kissed her hard, holding her body tight against mine. My hands naturally slid down to her ass as I caressed her body while she moaned into my mouth. We laced our hands together and walked back up to the party where the music was loud and people were everywhere.

Sarah and Josh stopped us to say hello and we talked for a bit. Taylor and Roman found a pack of hungry blondes to talk to by the pool who were intrigued by their vest and patches.

The party continued on. Randy was sure to stay on the

opposite side of the property from me and my boys. He gave a few glances our way and I was sure to show him that I was watching him. We ate some food and mostly sat off to the side and I watched Alexa mingle with her friends. When she caught me watching her, she'd throw me this sweet little smile; her face would blush a bit and I couldn't help but smile back.

I sat talking with a few guys that we played pool with that night at the bar when Alexa came and sat on my lap on the lounger I was on. "I'm gonna go throw a bathing suit on, ok?"

"Ok sweets. Need help?" I whispered into her neck, giving her goosebumps.

"Mmm, maybe you could help take it off of me later?" She whispered with her lips grazing my ear. My dick was instantly hard and I knew she felt it by the smirk on her face. She gave me a second before she got up so I could calm myself down but it was no use around her. I wanted her too badly.

Taylor, Roman and I got into playing a game of flip cup when Alexa came walking towards me. She was wearing a maroon string bikini with a short black wrap around her waist. Her tits looked amazing, her bikini top just on the border of too small and those legs looked long and lean as she came to stand next to me.

"Fuck. I mean, you look fucking amazing." I stumbled. She blushed and when she leaned into my arm I could feel her warm tits brush against me and I suddenly wished we were very alone.

"Thanks. You gonna come into the pool with me." She asked.

"Yea, I'll go throw some shorts on and be right in." I said as I finished up my beer.

I left Roman and Taylor to the drinking games; they were getting shit faced. Thankfully Alexa told them to crash in the main house tonight so I wouldn't have to babysit them.

Alexa

When Angel and Roman made their way out of the guest

house in board shorts; I think the whole party stopped to stare. They came down with just shorts on; tanned skin and tattoos on full display. Both brothers had their Los Demonions Locos emblem, thorns and flames surrounding a skull with devil horns with roses for eyes, tattooed over their hearts. While Angel had full sleeve tattoos on both arms; Roman had a Phoenix covering his entire side, from under his armpit, wrapping around his ribs and disappeared below the waistline of his board shorts. And to top it off; their bodies were perfection. Angel was tall and lean with every ab muscle on display and that perfect V that dipped into his shorts; thick forearms and biceps and rounded shoulders. Roman was a bit shorter than his brother; stocky and thick, but equally ripped. Angel made his way over to me in the pool and I couldn't wait to put my hands on him.

Sunset had come and gone and the night was becoming darker and quieter as some of the guests started to leave or make their way over to the firepit to relax. Angel and I had played under the surface of the water with each other; casually toying with the strings of my bikini top and I kept skimming the surface of Angel's board short waistline. Sarah and Josh were cuddling by the fire and Roman was half passed out on a lounge chair when Taylor came stomping up to the pool side with Randy in his grips. It looked like Randy already received a punch to the face; his under eye swelling and bruising by the second. Taylor spent most of the evening hanging back, drinking and watching some of the girls compete for his attention.

"What the fuck is this?" Angel spit out. Before I got the words out to speak, Angel jumped out of the pool and got into Randy's face.

"This punk here thinks it was a good idea to take some pictures of you and your girl. I found him sneaking around the backside of the pool and showing the pictures to his douchebag friends." Taylor explained as he pushed Randy down to his knees in front of Angel. Roman heard the commotion and was on his feet and at Angel's side in seconds. The rest of the guests looked on quietly, cautiously.

I got out of the pool and stood next to Angel, searching Randy's face for answers. "Randy, what the hell is going on? Give me your phone." I demanded. Taylor had already taken the phone from him and handed it to me. I quickly scrolled through the pictures and found over a dozen pictures of Angel and I, kissing or talking and then some pictures of us in the pool together; as well as pictures of Roman, Taylor and Angel sitting around the patio. "What? Why would you do this? What's going on?" I asked confused and frustrated.

Angel watched over my shoulder as I held out the phone. "What the fuck you gonna do with these pictures, huh asshole?" Angel bent down to Randy's face that was now full of panic and disgust.

"Nothing. Nothing. I was just going to hold on to them. I don't know why, I'm sorry. I'll fucking erase them, ok." Randy's voice shook as he turned his head to glare at me with ice in his eyes and back at Angel.

"Yea, you're going to erase them alright." Roman stepped up.

"Ok. Guys. Let's just calm down for a second, ok." I placed a hand on both Angel and Taylor. Taylor's face was stone. His eyes were cold and mouth frozen in a sneer. All the guys were looking at me now. I knew that I had the say in whether they beat Randy's ass or let him go. Randy deserved the black eye but I didn't want to promote more violence towards him on account of me. "Randy; why did you take these pictures?" I demanded.

"I don't know." Randy shook his head; frustration and hate laced his words. "Alexa, you don't belong with this guy. It's not right. You should be with me." he shot at me and then back at Angel who looked like he was going to lose his shit.

Angel picked Randy up off his knees grabbed him by his throat and spoke quietly into his ear, "If she wanted to be with you then why the fuck am I here with her. I told you to stay the hell away from her. Now, you better watch your fucking back, boy, because you just unleashed a world of hell on yourself." Angel tossed him back into Taylor and Taylor shoved him to the ground. There was an audible gasp as Randy hit the floor of the patio.

"Get the fuck out of here." Angel said as he stood in front of me; blocking my view as he, Roman and Taylor stood as a united front and Randy scrambled to his feet.

"You better keep looking over that shoulder of yours, buddy." Roman laughed as he darkly threatened. "You just made yourself some enemies."

Randy's two friends walked him out of the party and left with him. I stood there with my head down, Randy's phone still in my hand; as the party resumed.

"What the hell just happened?" I asked to no one. Angel, Roman and Taylor turned back to look at me; they were calm and quiet.

"I'll take care of this." Taylor said as he took Randy's phone from me and pocketed it. Angel and Taylor shared a glance and a nod before Taylor announced, "I'm gonna head out, bro. Gonna check in at the club. I'll hit you up tomorrow." There were unspoken words in the looks in their eyes. I didn't want to think about what Taylor's plans were with Randy; but it was obvious he was thinking about following him. He gave me a quick nod and was out the door.

"Hey, are you ok? What was that about?" Sarah came to me, she wrapped her arms around me in a warm hug.

"Yea... I'm fine. Randy strikes again, I guess." I shook my head at her.

"Ugh. Alright. He took pictures of you guys? Why would he do that?" she asked me as Angel and Roman spoke to each other quietly.

"You're guess is as good as mine. He said that *he* wanted to be with me. But that just doesn't make any sense." I explained. Randy had more intentions for those pictures; I just knew it. He's a snake and I don't put it past him to do something really shitty.

"Well, it looks like your guy has got your back." Sarah gestured to Angel. "Don't worry about Randy; I'll get Josh to talk to him. He should be pretty freaked out that he got manhandled by

Los Demonios *twice* now! He's an idiot but he's not stupid."

Angel stood behind me now, with his arms around me. "Don't worry about it. We'll get it handled." he spoke gently in my ear. "Taylor's got his phone and he's going to just follow him around a bit; just freak him out."

"Randy will get his shit together after seeing Taylor on his ass." Roman joked.

I had a lingering bad feeling about all of this. I may have known Randy for a long time; but I didn't trust him. He always seemed shady and calculated. Things always seemed to bend to his liking and he definitely wasn't used to being told what or what not to do.

The 'boom's and flashes of colored lights exploded in front of my eyes as the fireworks were beginning. I grabbed myself a towel as Sarah announced that the fireworks were starting and everyone made their way to the edge of the patio. The fireworks were set off in the near distance for our viewing pleasure and exploded strategically over our heads. Angel sat down in a chair and pulled me into his arms. The night air cooling off and my nipples peaked from the chills that ran down my body. Angel's warmth surrounded me and pulled a towel over my legs as I cuddled into his chest.

Reds, whites, greens and blue explosions of light flitted across the sky in beautiful patterns and shapes. The bass of the explosions was so loud; it's all you could hear. Angel pressed his lips to my neck as his hands slowly caressed my bare thighs underneath the towel. Once again, he made everything and everyone else disappear when he touched me. I felt him harden under my ass and I melted into his kisses. Secretly and slowly, I rocked back and forth on his lap, teasing him as I felt his breathing increase in speed and his hands gripped my thighs and pulled me into him.

I glanced around, taking notice that there were only a few couples left. Sarah was wrapped up in Josh's arms and Roman was sitting poolside with his feet dangling in the water. Catering was slowly cleaning up their equipment and the DJ had wrapped up for the night an hour ago. I tilted my head up to whisper in Angel's ear; then took his hand and quietly led him up to the guest house.

I closed and locked the door behind us and then led him wordlessly to my bedroom. I turned to face him and the look in his face was ferrel, serious and hungry. He stalked to me, placing one hand on my face and one on my waist. His fingers slowly moved down the side of my neck and my back as he untied the bikini strings. My top fell to the floor but I stood unmoving; my pulse racing and wetness pooling between my legs. I wanted him. For everything he is and everything he is doing to me; I needed to feel him. With my breasts bare I closed the gap between us; feeling the heat radiate off of his body. We were nose to nose as our skin met. He looped his thumbs at my waistline and slowly pulled my bathing suit bottoms off of me, and as he rose back up he stopped to give me slow, wet kisses to my thighs, then my groin, below my belly button, my breasts and then my lips. We kissed slowly and passionately; our tongues feeling and sliding around one anothers'. My breath hitched as I felt his hands grab my ass and pull me firmly to his body; feeling his long, hard cock hitting my stomach.

"Alexa, I want to fuck you." Angel whispered into my ear with a deep lusty voice. His words alone had me squeezing my thighs together as a moan escaped my lips. He pressed into me until my ass hit the mattress behind me. "Get on the bed." He instructed.

I laid on the bed, my elbows propped me up to watch as he untied his board shorts and let them fall to the floor. His cock hung heavy between his legs; the head already dripping with precum. He was long and thick and mouthwatering. If he didn't touch me soon I might come just from anticipation.

He slowly stroked himself as he kneeled on the bed between my legs. Angel leaned down to lick my lips. "I want my cock inside of you so bad." He teased me as he kissed my breasts and gently bit my hard nipples. I felt his touch everywhere as my body grew more needy; on the verge of an orgasm.

"Angel; I feel like I'm going to explode." I breathed as I ran my fingers through his hair. He pushed one finger inside of me; slowly stretching me while his thumb teased my clit softly. "Angel." I warned on an exhale.

"Come, baby. You'll be coming all over my cock next." Angel promised as he added a second finger and pumped faster. It took seconds for me to fall apart as I shuttered under his touch while my orgasm rocketed through my body. He waited until my breathing came back to almost normal and pressed the thick head to my entrance. He slid up and down the slick opening; watching the whole time. I heard the rip of the condom wrapper and watched as he sheathed himself; using one long stroke. His eyes met mine as he slowly pushed inside; gentle and careful. I pulled my bottom lip in between my teeth and grabbed a hold of his arms when he nudged further.

"Breath Alexa. I need you to breath and relax; fuck you're so tight." Angel kneaded my breasts, pinching my nipples while pulling each one into his mouth. "That's it, yes, you feel so damn good baby."

He slowly pulled out and then slammed back in; knocking the air out of my lungs. I let out a loud moan as I fought to keep my eyes open to watch his body move over mine. Every muscle was tight and corded, and Angel watched the space where we connected with a sexy smirk. He filled me like I've never felt before; I was so full of him; I felt him everywhere.

His eyes gazed back at mine as he found a punishing rhythm. He pulled my leg behind his back so that there was no space between us. The base of his cock grinding down on my sensitive clit.

"Oh Angel... oh so good."

Angel

"Breath Alexa. I need you to breath and relax; fuck you're so tight" I slowly pushed into Alexa, filling her up and stretching her. "That's it, yes, you feel so damn good baby." Her muscles around my cock relaxed enough to fill her to the hilt and fuck if she didn't feel amazing. She held onto my arms, digging her nails into my biceps, as I moved faster in and out of her. I spread my knees wide on the mattress; pushing my body weight into her as she gasped for air. I knew I wasn't going to last long; I've never felt anything so tight, warm and wet like her sweet pussy before.

"Oh Angel... oh so good." Alexa moaned as she squeezed her thighs tight around my waist.

"I love the way you moan my name. Do you like me inside of you?" I leaned down to suck her nipples as she arched off the bed. My balls felt like bricks; so tight and ready to explode. I was unapologetically pounding her now and she was taking every bit of it.

"Angel, oh my god." Alexa called out at the same time I could feel her pussy start to pulsate around me, making my dick throb for my own release. She was so wet; coming for me as her hips bucked up against me.

"Fuck Alexa. You're so beautiful; I love when you come for me." I came hard as I smashed my lips into hers. Alexa was still panting hard; coming down from the high. My heart beat hard and fast in my chest as we both clung to each other. "Tell me you're mine, Alexa. Tell me that you don't want anyone else but me." I breathed into her ear as I caressed her face.

She didn't hesitate, didn't think, "I'm yours, Angel."

Chapter 10

Alexa

While Angel got up and cleaned himself off in the bathroom, I laid on the bed staring at the ceiling; still feeling Angel everywhere on and in my body. My head and my heart swam with emotion and excitement. I've never felt like this before. When Angel asked if I was his; I didn't hesitate. I wouldn't want it any other way. Angel brings out this hidden side of me. I feel more like myself around him. Everything is easy; there's never any pressure, nothing is expected of me. He has an ease about him; moving through life like he's already accepted the trials and tribulations that life has thrown at him. He makes me feel beautiful, normal. The last ten years since my mom's been in the limelight has made me reclusive. I threw myself into my work because that was expected of me; I never veered from doing the right thing because my mother and her success was priority. But when Angel is near me; he makes *me* his priority.

Angel saunters back to the bed; naked and beautiful. His cock again hard as looks down at my naked body sprawled out over the bed. He climbs in next to me and holds me tight to his front; we kiss over and over again becoming breathless. I slide my hand down his godlike abs and wrap my hand around his hard shaft and softly tease the tip of his velvety skin. He moans in response as I push him to his back.

"Alexa, your hands feel so good on me." He licked his lips as his fingers found my wet center once again. I stroked him softly, enjoying the pleasure that I was giving him. I was dripping wet again and I was on the verge of coming again when Angel grabbed my hand. "Baby, I want you to ride my cock. I need to watch you as you fuck me." I didn't think twice; I grabbed a condom from the nightstand and handed it to him. He rolled it on and I straddled his firm body and lowered myself onto him. His hands came to hold my waist as I threw my head back, feeling him deep inside me once again. "Knees up," he told me. I held my pace as he watched me glide up and down his thick length. Angel's eyes were glued to my body. I felt my body start to shake and shiver again; tremors ran down my spine when I felt him grow harder inside of me. He rocked my hips front to back as he sat up to meet my sweaty body. I threw my arms around his back; holding us together when he bucked his groin; coming inside of me as my orgasm spilled over the edge.

Angel pulled me on top of him; he was still inside of me as we came down from sweet bliss. I laid my head on his chest, listening to the thrumming of his heart as we both tried to catch our breaths. I didn't have words for what was happening between us, besides, my body was humming and sated and sleepy. I drifted off momentarily until I felt Angel lay me down on my side while he cleaned up the condom. The mattress dipped when he came back and I curled up on his chest; breathing him in. He kissed the top of my head and played with my hair until we both fell asleep.

I slept peacefully in Angel's arms all night; our legs twined together and his thick arms holding me close. I peaked my eyes open when I felt the warm sun on my face. We had fallen asleep with all the blinds open and the summer sun was relentless in the morning. The clock next to my bed read 7:23 AM but when I tried to sneak out of bed to use the bathroom, Angel's arms tightened around me and he pressed his hard cock in between my ass cheeks.

"Mmmm, you can't leave." Angel moaned. I giggled and wiggled my ass into him. I was wet already and throbbing from last night. Angel kissed my neck and my back as he snuck his dick between my legs. "Fuck, I can't get enough of you," he growled into my neck as he nudged his tip at my entrance. His hands were at my breasts and he was pulling me into him, greedy and ravenous. I lost his hands for a moment as he put another condom on and sunk into me. I arched my back, laying side by side, Angel took me fast and hard. I was so sweetly sore and deliciously wet; you could hear my arousal as he slammed into me.

"I'm starving." I announced as we laid in bed; the sheets a tangled mess underneath us.

"It's good to eat after a workout." Angel teased.

"Ok, shower, eat, and then clean up duty. Sarah and Josh will probably be up soon too." I got up and made my way to the bathroom to let the shower warm up. We showered together and stayed under the spray of water, kissing and exploring each other. Angel dressed in his jeans and tee shirt and I threw on a pair of soft cotton shorts and a white tank top and tossed my wet hair into a bun. I was just getting the coffee pot started when I heard a soft knocking at the deck doors.

Sarah peaked in, a worried look ran across her face when she saw me. My heart stuttered in my chest for a second; Sarah's happy-go-lucky attitude was non-existent this morning.

"Hey." I swung the door open.

"Hey, sorry Alexa. I didn't want to bother you this early, but." she wrung her hands in front of her.

"What? What's wrong? I'm sorry I didn't stick around last night..." I trailed off when she started shaking her head.

"Um, no that's not it. Um, Alexa. Have you put on the news yet? We were laying in bed and we started getting all these text messages. Haven't you checked your phone yet." She moved further into my space reaching for the tv remote. Angel came to stand with me with just as much confusion written all over his face.

"I haven't even looked at my phone." I scrambled as I tried to remember where I left it yesterday. I got to the kitchen island, where my phone was still on the charger and saw a slew of alerts. Five missed text messages from Sarah asking if I was up and ten from my mother; along with two voicemails from her and seven missed calls. Shit.

Sarah flipped to the local news. The headline read, "District Attorney Disgraced as photos leaked of daughter mingling with felon and members of local motorcycle gang".

"Oh. My. Fucking. God." Was all I could get out. I stood frozen in place as pictures splashed across the screen. Pictures of Taylor, Roman and Angel sporting their MC vests on the back patio of my mother's house; pictures of me sitting on Angel's lap and shots of us kissing in the pool. Sarah grabbed my cell from my hand and swiped through the text messages from my mom.

Mom: Alex, just got a weird call from a reporter- call me back ASAP

Mom: My assistant just called; said there's pictures of you circulating the internet?!

Mom: Call me.

Mom: I just tried calling you. Alexa. This is all over the news.

Mom: I'm sending security over to the house; what the hell is going on.

Mom: Alexa I told you this would happen. Call me the second you wake up.

The rest of the texts and voicemail followed suit. No doubt her assistants were all over this story and trying to beat off the reporters that were already lined up to get her story. As I stood with my phone in hand; more text messages poured in. This time from friends and co-workers. Angel spun me around away from the tv and took my face in his hands.

"Tell me what to do." He demanded. He looked on edge and furious, but worst of all, helpless. He didn't know what to do with this. It was different from his world where you solved problems by beating it out of people. I just shook my head trying to wrap my head around damage control.

"I don't know. I've got to call my mom." And with that, I withdrew from him and headed out to the deck to make the call.

It rang once before my mom picked up. "Alexa. What the hell is going on over there? Why haven't you answered my messages? Has security gotten there yet?" Her line of questioning made my head swim.

"Mom, I just woke up. Listen, I know who did this. I don't know what they're saying; but it's not as bad as it looks." I paced the length of the deck as I spoke.

"Not as bad as it looks! Alexa, right now it looks as though my daughter invited known criminals to my home and allowed herself to be photographed, in next to nothing, on top of some guy's lap!" She bellowed. "I want the name of the person who took the pictures, now. I sent private security over to handle any reporters that tried to make it onto the property. We need to issue a statement regarding the party and try to retract the pictures from the internet." My mom rattled off the list of things and I can tell she was pacing too. "Who was it Alexa?"

"It was Randy. He's been giving me some trouble lately, but Angel.." I admitted before she interrupted me.

"Angel? So this is about the motorcycle guy, huh? What are you thinking? Alexa, he's beneath you. He's a thug; a criminal even."

"No, mom, you don't know him! And Randy, Randy is being a complete asshole and starting all this trouble for me. Angel kicked him out of the party last night and..." my mom didn't want to hear me; she just plowed over my words.

"Alexa. I'm telling you right now. You need to get away from this guy and his friends. This doesn't look good for either of us. You think you're going to ride off in the sunset with this guy? Well, I'm telling you now, it won't happen. He's using you. He sees what you come from, the money; you're his meal ticket if he gets in trouble." She was harsh. Her voice dripped in a condescending tone and she made me feel like I was 16 again. I'm a grown woman! I won't allow her to decide this for me.

"Mom, I gotta go. I will figure this out. I'll go to Randy myself. I'll see you when you get back." I hung up the phone. When I turned around Angel was leaning on the door frame, arms crossed and guarded.

"Angel." I went to him.

"I heard what your mom was saying. I got you into this mess." Angel said, his face full of determination. "And I'm going to fix this. I just called Taylor; he's going to meet me at the club and then we're going to Randy's."

"Fine. But I'm coming with you." I deadpanned.

Chapter 11

Angel

While Alexa was on the phone with her mom out on the deck, I called Taylor and asked him what happened last night after he left the party. He told me that he ended up following Randy and his buddies to a nearby housing development. It was gated so he couldn't get in but he was able to watch the front of the house from where he parked the bike on the side of the street. He made sure Randy knew he was out there. Hiding in plain sight. Taylor told me that about 20 minutes after he got home; a car full of girls arrived at the house. No one else entered and no one left.

If we would have taken care of Randy last night; none of this would have happened. I was stupid to think he didn't already send those pictures off to someone else or emailed them to himself for safe keeping. Randy was a smug son of a bitch and I was determined to beat that smug look right off of his face. Alexa insisted she come with us to confront Randy. I promised her I would never get her involved with MC shit; but this was personal for her. I needed to set some ground rules for the guys; Alexa didn't need this to get messier than it already was.

"Alexa, you shouldn't go. What did your mom say?" Sarah asked. "This has gotten way out of hand. So what? Now you're going to jump on a motorcycle and help beat up Randy? This is nuts. Let's call a lawyer, or get the news to retract their stories, I don't know. You guys are only going to make this worse." Sarah pleaded. Alexa stormed into her bedroom to change her clothes and Sarah followed closing the door behind them.

"Ro, get your ass up and over to Alexa's." I called Roman, who was still passed out in one of the guest rooms in the main house.

Roman was over a few minutes later, groggy and hair a disaster. "What the hell, you sleeping in like this is a hotel or something?" I barked at him.

"Bro, I haven't slept that good since fucking forever; that mattress is the shit." Roman stretched as he made his way to the coffee pot. "What the fuck is going on here?"

I tossed my phone at Roman that had the photos and news feed already brought up on it. He swiped through the links I had up and realization crossed his face when he understood who was behind all of this.

"So, what? Now can we beat this guy's ass? I gotta eat first though. I can't break someone's face without having food in my stomach." Roman joked. He was forever making light of any situation; it's just how he dealt with things. The girls were still bickering in Alexa's bedroom when Josh joined us in the kitchen. He gave us a knowing nod and started rifling through the refrigerator. No words were exchanged. I knew Josh was good friends with Randy; so I didn't want to assume where his loyalties lay. And I sure as shit didn't want to tip Randy off in any way that we were coming for him. Silently we took out some fresh fruit and made eggs as the girls came out. Alexa was dressed in jeans and a black tee shirt, hair braided down her back and her eyes looked red and puffy from crying. She held her head high and didn't let on that she was upset. She poured herself some coffee and nibbled on an apple.

I looked between the two girls. Sarah looked put out but concerned and Alexa looked determined and pissed. I've never seen her this mad; so I didn't know what I should say to her.

"Alexa, I can call Randy... figure out what the hell happened. What he did was so wrong but I have a feeling you're hellbent on going over there with these guys and that will only cause you a load of trouble. You know who his father is and he'll pitch a fit if anyone touches his son." Josh pleaded with Alexa. I knew the conversation was directed more so at me and Roman. He wasn't stupid to think he could control Los Demonios or their actions.

"I appreciate that Josh but I'm done laying down and taking everyone's shit. He has no idea the shit storm he just unleashed for my mom. And I'm going to be on the receiving end of her wrath." Alexa said firmly as she set down her coffee and pulled on her sneakers.

We walked down to the garage. Sarah stayed quiet and told Alexa she would finish the clean up around the pool. Things were tense between the girls but I knew Alexa already had her mind set on confronting Randy. Before Alexa hopped on my motorcycle; Sarah gave her a big hug and told her to 'keep her head on straight'. We rolled out, Roman and Alexa and I; and it just felt right. Her on the back of my bike; holding onto my waist. She stayed quiet but I can tell her mind was going at a million hours an hour. We pulled up to the club; it was the first time I've ever brought someone there that didn't already belong there. The clubhouse was an old factory building that was kindly donated to us from the original owner. The building was used as a carpet factory and the owner was a member of Los Demonios back in the 60s. His business took a nose dive when he became sick with cancer; and having no other family of his own; he donated the building to our organization. It was a wide open space where we could park our bikes inside. The only office worked as our table room and basement used for private meetings both amicable and uncivil. Many beatings and bloodshed took place in the depths of the basement while the main floor had a lounge and bar, tvs on every wall and a small kitchen.

Taylor was waiting for us outside. We pulled up and I was ready to give Alexa the floor so she could lay out the plan; but she seemed nervous and distracted by her surroundings. "Taylor, did you see any security guards at Randy's? Any car patrols?"

"No man, it was just a gate with a security pad. Houses are spread pretty far apart, two cars in the driveway when I left this morning." Taylor said leisurely as he laid on the bike eating a breakfast sandwich.

"Alexa, this is your guy. What are we looking at here?" Taylor asked Alexa.

"Huh? Oh, um, Josh gave me the code to his gate and I don't think there's a guard posted up; just a patrol car at night." Alexa answered.

"Ok." I turned to Alexa lowering my head, "This is your call, ok. Either we go in and rip him out of his house or we can just be there to back you up. I'm good with whatever. But just know; if he touches you, it's game over for him."

Alexa swallowed hard then steeled her expression, "Let me talk to him, see what I can get out of him first. I don't want to make things worse. I want to know who he gave the pictures to and what he wants out of all this." She looked to each one of us for confirmation and she had it. Without another word, we mounted our bikes and rode out to Randy's house.

The code worked and we entered the development. Randy's house was one of the first mansions that you came to and made Alexa's mom's house look like a shack. The estate was older, spanish stucco with terracotta roof; circular drive and two, three car garages flanking the main house on each side. We pulled in and got off our bikes, placed our helmets on the seats. As we approached the door, Randy stepped out with two of his friends hot on his heels.

"Randy, I just want to talk to you. I don't want any trouble." Alexa stated. Taylor, Roman and I stood back; allowing Alexa to say her piece without triggering a fight with Randy and his guys.

"Looks like you're ready for a fight, to me." Randy deadpanned.

Alexa threw out her hands, "I just want to know why you'd do this? What did you have to gain by giving my name and photos out to the press?"

"Oh what so mommy doesn't appreciate your *new* friends?" Randy laughed.

Taylor, Roman and I took a step forward; my hands were

clenched at my sides and I was ready to pounce on this asshole. Randy eyeballed us with that stupid smirk on his face.

"Go ahead assholes, I've got security cameras and whatever happens here will be all on tape." Randy threatened.

Alexa turned back to us and her eyes pleaded for us to stand down. She stepped up closer to Randy, lowering her voice and crossing her arms over her chest. "Randy, just tell me why. Please."

I watched as Randy glared at Alexa, dipping his head so that their eyes were level with each other. "Alexa, I wanted you and you shit all over that. No one tells me no. No one. I made it clear that I had my sights set on you and instead you're wrapped up with a thug on a motorcycle. You made me look like an idiot at that bar." Randy's words sent shock waves to Alexa's ears as her face softened. Randy stood up tall in front of her now. "But now I figured I'm too good for you anyway. At least my mommy didn't get knocked up by some loser in Mexico. Maybe you take after your father after all? Maybe that's why your mom tucked you away into that immigrant shelter. Make you feel one with *your* people." Randy laughed in her face and his friends had joined in.

Alexa looked stunned and confused, "What are you talking about? That isn't true. I, I..." I grabbed Alexa's shoulders as she lunged for Randy. If anyone was going to make a play for him; it was me. She struggled against me.

"Oh man, you didn't know, did you?" Randy fanned shock. "That's why your mom wanted nothing to do with you growing up. That's why you'll never amount to anything. Because you're a product of a drunk one night stand with a mexican dirtbag."

While I held Alexa back with both her arms locked in my hands, she kicked out to Randy and connected with his chest, tossing him into his buddies. Rage took over his face as he went after her; lunging towards her only to be intercepted by Roman. Roman stood like a brick wall against Randy's futile attempt to push him away. I turned Alexa's body away from the scene that was unraveling quickly and caught a punch to the side of my face from one of Randy's punk friends. That was enough to set me off in a blind rage. I swiftly turned around and landed a left hook to the guy sending him flying onto his ass; while the other punk was trying to get in between Roman and Randy. Bad idea. Everything happened so fast. Roman pulled out the knife that was nestled in the sheath at his back as Randy and the friend backed off. Taylor moved in and gave a quick jab to the friend's nose, instantly gushing with blood. I grabbed Randy by his throat and pushed him down to his knees and stood over him with my fist cocked and ready. Just as I was about to connect with his face; we all spun around as the sound of shattering glass exploded in our ears.

Alexa stood poised next to Randy's Porsche 911. She had shattered his windshield with a large rock she found next to the driveway. The sight of her destroying the prick's car made my dick stand at attention; while all of our mouths dropped to the floor, Randy was trying to scramble out of my grasp.

"You crazy bitch!" Randy screamed out. "You're fucking done, you piece of shit!" I still had him by the throat; so I squeezed even tighter as he continued to lose his shit at Alexa; collapsing his air supply. He began to slap at my hand while we all looked on, shocked and proud of Alexa. With her chest heaving, and tears in her eyes; she walked back over to us.

"Let's go." Alexa said somberly.

We rode back out onto the highway; wordless. Taylor and Roman broke off and headed back to the clubhouse and I drove Alexa back to her house. By the time we got there; everyone had left and I was thankful for the quiet. Alexa dismounted, eerily quiet and her eyes so sad and thoughtful.

"Do you want me to come in?" I broached.

"Sure. I um, I just need to make some phone calls, ok?" She answered quietly.

This was like a whole different Alexa; almost detached and moving robotically. I sat on the couch while she paced the length of her deck, making attempt after attempt to reach whomever she was calling.

Alexa

Come on, Mom, pick up your phone. I dialed until finally my mother finally answered.

"Alexa, what the hell did you do?" She rushed out. "You know who I was on the phone with? Randy's Dad, Travis. You threw a rock at Randy's windshield? What has gotten into you?" I couldn't get a word in edgewise; although not at all uncommon for conversations with my mom, as she asked question after question without waiting for me to answer. "Did Angel put you up to this? You will get your ass over there and apologize before this thing becomes a freaking nightmare for me. Do you understand me? Travis said he was going to contact his lawyer for trespassing and assault!"

I put my head in my hands as the world started spinning out of control. "Mom, jesus, just listen!" I yelled until the line went quiet. "Mom, Randy sent those pictures to the press; he's the one who's dragging us through the mud."

"Fine. That's fine. I could have handled that, Alexa. I've already put into works getting the stories retracted. But this? This vandalism? Alexa, I told you that that man was nothing but trouble. Now look at what he's gotten you into? You need to stay away from him. Angel and the guys you went over there with are criminals. That MC will be your biggest downfall yet!" Her voice boomed in my ear.

"Yea, Mom? What was the first?" I asked, accusatory.

"The first, what?"

"My first downfall? If this is my biggest; then what was my first?" I looked up to the sky for answers. The phone went silent as I could feel my mother scrambling for her answer.

"Alexa. This needs to be resolved quickly. I'm on the first flight out in the morning. I have to be in the city but I'll call you." And with that, she hung up.

After that disaster of a phone call; I plopped down on the

couch, bringing my knees up to my chest. Angel was quiet with his elbows on his knees, staring at the ground; most likely waiting for me to broach the 'mom' subject. Truth was; I didn't even know what to say, what to think, about *any* of it. Heaving that huge rock into Randy's windshield was amazing. There's nothing like that surge of adrenaline and moment of absolute *not giving a shit*. And the look on all of their faces was pretty damn priceless. I felt helpless amongst the chaos, Angel shielding me to the brute force of his wrath. He pushed Randy down with one hand on his throat; a move I've seen him do before, making someone kneel before them was demeaning, degrading and pretty damn hot (in a good girl loves bad guy, type of way).

We looked up at each other at the same time, concern and fire in Angel's eyes. "My mom's got a handle on the pictures and the press. As for everything else, I don't know what to say." He searched my face for a moment before pulling me into his chest.

"I'm proud of you for standing up for yourself." Angel said quietly into my hair. "And I would be lying if I said I wasn't completely turned on by your bad assery." He quipped.

I giggled and leaned up to face him. He kissed me slowly and sweetly, taking his time to kiss one lip at a time and then parted my lips to slip his warm, sweet tongue into my mouth. We kissed as he pulled me on top of his lap, both leaning back into the couch. Before I could get lost in the moment, I pushed back on his chest and broke contact with his lips.

"This could get ugly for you." I warned. "Randy won't let what happened go. I'm actually surprised I don't have cops banging down my door right now."

"I'm not worried about the cops, the MC has a few in their pocket and technically I was defending you." Angel admitted.

"My mom has known Randy's family since we were kids, her and Travis had a 'thing' back in the day, after he got divorced. Travis called my mom to let her know what happened this morning." I informed him.

Angel nodded his head, understanding. "Um, the stuff that Randy was saying?"

I let his question hang in the air. I didn't know how to respond. Was it all bullshit? How could Randy know who my dad was when I didn't even know? "I don't know. I don't know my dad, and my mom's never told me about him." I answered solemnly. "My mom's coming home tomorrow, to the city, but I'm probably going to have to meet up with her at some point."

"Well then, we have today." Angel answered decisively.

Chapter 12

Angel

If we had the day to relax before Alexa's mom came home and unloaded a world of shit down on Alexa; we were damn well going to take advantage of it. Alexa stayed cuddled against my chest for a while; I could tell a storm was brewing in that head of hers. I tried my best to reassure her that I wasn't afraid of Randy or his family but I can tell she was worried. I grabbed her ass and stood up with her legs wrapped around my waist.

"Can we go for a swim? You could torture me in one of your little bikinis again?" I teased.

"Mmm... I think I can make that happen." She finally smiled. I set her down and she walked into her bedroom to get ready. I pulled on my boardshorts and ran a hand through my hair when she came waltzing out. Sure enough, she stood before me in a tiny little white bikini, strings hanging in bows at her hips; like little presents. Her tits perky and round in a skimpy little top that showed as much side boob as it did under boob.

"This torture enough?" She asked lightly.

"Fuck. Me." My mouth hung open. My dick stood at attention as she walked towards me. "Please tell me that you bought that just for *my* viewing pleasure." I asked, bringing my hands to grab handfuls of her ass as she pressed up against my hard on.

"I've had it; *but*, it's the first time I've been brave enough to wear it." Alexa giggled.

We walked down to the pool, I grabbed two beers from the cooler and set them down next to the pool before diving head first into the water. Alexa followed suit, jumping into the water with a small splash and resurfacing in front of me. The water felt amazing, washing us of the stress, even if momentarily. We played and splashed around in the pool; thankful for the privacy and laid out on the lounge chairs letting the sun wash over our tanned skin. We had talked and laughed about growing up and the ridiculous ways that Roman used to get in trouble as a kid. Alexa told me about college and how the most insane thing she's ever done up until now was when she and Sarah stole a golf cart from the security guard and drove down to the local BBQ joint when she was only 15. Alexa had tried pot for the first time and had a mean case of the munchies. The sun was brutal as I sat up to reach for my beer.

"God damn it's hot out." I commented. Alexa sat up looking at me, looking at her. I licked my lips as I saw her skin glowing under the desert sky. Alexa stood up and made her way to the side of the pool. Looking back over her shoulder at me, she reached behind her neck and untied the strings, then her back and did the same; letting her top fall to the floor. I sat up in approval; my hard cock straining against my board shorts. She looked back at the water as her hands simultaneously untied the bows at her waist and let her bikini bottom slide down her legs. Alexa stood in front of me, she looked like a golden goddess. But before I could get my hands on her, she dove into the water. I dropped my board shorts and followed her. She stood in the shallow end of the pool, just deep enough to cover the tops of her breasts and she waited for me to swim up to her before she wrapped her legs around my waist. My cock hard and throbbing between us. She kissed my neck and worked down my chest before she met my eyes again. I took advantage of the water and rubbed my way up and down her body, my hands exploring her breasts and thighs. Alexa's breathing was heavy and I pushed her body up against the side of the pool. Her hands came to my hard length as she played and rubbed me up and down.

"Your're fucking killing me Alexa." I groaned into her ear.

"Take me." She panted. She held my dick firmly as she rubbed it against her opening.

"I'll pull out," I rushed out just as I pushed into her. Feeling her bare was a religious experience, I was just cursing the lack of friction due to being in the pool. But hell if I was going to complain. She moaned out as she clung to my neck, widening her legs around me, pulling her knees up to her chest as I worked in and out of her.

"Oh my god, Angel. What are you doing to me?" She asked and pleaded as her head hung back and mouth open and loving it. I pumped her faster and harder, working for our release, her body starting to quiver around me. "I'm coming, Angel, oh my god." I crashed into her lips taking her moans into my mouth. I pulled out of her just in time to find my own release. Both of us breathing heavy, clinging and staring into each other's eyes, we didn't even hear the sounds of boots heading around the patio towards the pool.

With Alexa's back towards our intruders, I glanced up to see four cops making their way towards us. Alexa turned her head in surprise as I tried to shield her body with my arms and chest.

"Angel Torres, we need you to get out of the pool and come with us." The first cop announced. I recognized one of the cops that the MC had in their pocket in the past, as he eyeballed me with a wink and a nod. "Let's go, Torres. We were kind enough to wait until you two were done." The cop said as he dropped two towels at the edge of the pool for us. I pulled Alexa's towel down into the water for her so she could cover up. Her eyes were as big as saucers as she looked between me and the cops waiting. I jumped out of the pool, junk swinging and all, and dried off before putting my board shorts back on. As Alexa came to stand next to me, holding onto her towel, the front cop approached me with handcuffs in his hands.

"Don't worry, I'll be out soon enough." I promised her as I bent to kiss her softly. I turned around and placed my hands behind my back. "Call Roman for me, my phone's in my jeans pocket."

"Ok." She answered hearing the sound of metal on metal as the handcuffs clicked into place.

"Angel Torres, you are hereby under arrest. Let's head out to the squad car and I'll read you your rights on the way." The cop instructed. I nodded my head and took my last glance at Alexa.

Alexa

I stood in the middle of my patio; towel soaked and dripping into a puddle at my feet. I watched them take Angel from me without a single glance towards me. What about me? What about my crime? I wanted to scream out that it was me that smashed that asshole's windshield. But instead I just watched them whisk Angel away.

I made my way up to my house; dropping the heavy, wet towel at the door. I threw on a pair of joggers and tank and found Angel's phone in his jeans. Damn it; he didn't tell me the password. I set the phone on the kitchen counter; wishing at least Roman would call so I could tell him what happened. I paced for at least an hour. Made myself a salad and a hot cup of tea and waited some more. Only two hours had passed when Angel's phone started vibrating across the counter. I picked it up as it flashed 'Roman' across the screen.

"Roman? It's Alexa." I answered.

"Hey. What's up baby girl." Roman said leisurely.

"Roman, Angel got arrested. The cops came and took him from here. I don't know what to do. I tried to call the station; but they wouldn't tell me anything." I spoke at warp speed as my words were trying to match my racing mind.

"I know." Roman interjected.

"You do? How?" I said confused and shocked.

"Ah well, we've got a few connections down at the station. My guy called to tell me Angel's been taken into custody." Roman explained.

"Oh. Well, can I bail him out? What do we do!" I knew I sounded exasperated but I've never been in this situation. And I was really feeling guilty that this was all my fault in the first place.

"Slow down, Al, it's fine. I was about to head over there to go get him but he's gotta see the judge first. He should be able to get out of there in a few hours. Nothin that he can't handle."

"Okay. Do you need, um, money? You know, to bail him out?" I asked. I didn't want to step on toes but I wanted to help.

"Nah, he's being released. They're not gonna hold him for a little game of push and shove with ass bag." Roman teased.

"Oh, yea, I guess that's true. Roman, when the cops came; I was terrified they were coming for me too. I'm sure my mom has something to do with that, but I feel really bad I got you guys involved with all this."

"No worries. We've been into it way worse than this. Besides, you're Angel's girl now, right? We've got your back." Roman was a breath of fresh air. He was always so light on his feet, taking everything with ease; like nothing could bother him.

"Oh, well thank you." I said quietly.

"Listen, I gotta run, but do you want me to drop Angel back off at your place? His bike's still there, right?"

"Yea.. and his clothes."

"Ha, poor sucker is in lock up with board shorts. I'm sure that got interesting. Alright, I'll text Angel's phone when we're on the way. Shouldn't be too much longer."

"Thanks Roman." I set the phone down and felt relief wash over me. It was nice having someone watch out for me for a change. I decided to get in the shower and wait for Roman to text.

The hours ticked by slowly, this was the longest day in history. When the sky was starting to get dark, I decided I had to occupy myself with something other than binge watching mindless reality tv. I made my way over to the main house and I automatically steered myself towards my mother's office. I had a nagging feeling ever since Randy's divulging of who he thought my father was. Was there any truth to it? I guess growing up I never questioned it. As I got older, I assumed that my mother didn't know who the father was. She was always pretty closed off with me, she lacked that warm, cuddly motherly instinct that my grandmother more than made up for. My grandmother taught me the ins and outs of love and relationships; she made sure I learned Spanish and spanish culture. She was a proud American and did her fair share of community outreach when she was my age. She really shaped me into the woman I am today; compassionate and trusting.

I riffled through some of the office drawers; most files related to cases and investigations. She kept a locked drawer in the credenza that I always assumed was more work related files. I searched around for a key; emptying vases and turning over books and frames that were on her shelves. I was just about to give up when I leaned my head against the tall bookshelf filled with law books when a shiny keyring caught my eye. It was hanging on the side of a statue of Don Quixote; hanging off the horse's tail. It blended right in but so obvious at the same time. The key slid in the lock easily and the drawer opened. It was filled with files. I fingered through the tabs; most of the current cases I knew she was working on; banking files and some other personal files she kept with her credentials. And then there was a file that didn't have a tab on it at all. I pulled the file and sat cross legged on the floor and spilled the contents out. There were a couple of pictures, what looked like a hotel key with a plastic key tag and a big number 7 on it. A couple of movie ticket stubs and a concert pass. The concert pass was all in spanish; the same with the movie stubs. I picked up the pictures next. The first was a very faded picture of a girl sitting on a blanket, her hair dark and wild; tight jeans with a black tank top. She was wearing sunglasses that covered most of her face and I looked closely to see if this could be my mom. She was smiling so big with her head cocked to the side. I wondered who it was she was smiling at? The next picture is what left me breathless. It was my mom for sure. Dark hair pulled into a ponytail, with a white, boho lace dress on. She was standing wrapped in the arms of a man. Tall, handsome, tanned skin with jeans and a button down shirt. He was kissing the top of her head and she was smiling into his chest. My heart squeezed and my vision blurred. I stared for a long time. Memorizing her smile. A smile that I have never witnessed myself. I flipped the pictures over in my hands; nothing written on the back. No dates, no names. Nothing. Could I assume that this man was my father?

I put the file and its contents back as the phone in my pocket started to vibrate. It was Roman.

Angel: It's me, on the way back to you.

It was Angel. He was out and on his way back here. I cleaned up and waited for them in my driveway. Roman pulled up in an older F150. Angel got out and rounded the truck, stopping to say something to Roman. I gave Roman a small wave and he winked back at me before he drove away.

Angel walked up to me, looking exhausted and hungry in his bare feet and board shorts. He was quiet as he kissed me and we went upstairs to my place. During my tortuous wait for him to be released, I did a load of laundry including his clothes.

"If you want to shower, I washed your clothes. And I ordered pizza and salad; should be here in a few." Angel was quieter than usual and nodded before heading into the shower.

"Thanks. You didn't have to do all of this." The pizza arrived while he was in the shower and he came out of my room in clean clothes and bare feet, looking and smelling like a new man.

"It's fine. It's the least I could do." I shrugged.

"You don't have to feel bad, Alexa. I know damn well you were scared to shit thinking they were hauling you in too. I'm relieved that it was just me." Angel admitted as we sat down to pizza.

"Yea, at first I thought it was a mistake, maybe they meant to take me too. But as the hours passed, and nothing happened, I realized that my mom probably smoothed things over with Travis. I'm sure I'll get an ear full when I see her. But why did they release you? I mean, not that I'm insanely thankful."

"One of the cops that were here earlier clued me in as soon as they stuck me in holding. Said the video from Randy's house got deleted somehow and they had nothing to hold me for, other than Randy's bruised ego. You see, Taylor's a pretty ingenious tech nerd. Surprise, surprise. He was on top of that the second we left Randy's house. Since Randy called and made the report with the police; they had to at least arrest me. But even the judge said there's no evidence, no case." Angel smirked at me with a mouth full of cheesy pizza.

I giggled at his cheesy grin. "Ahhhh, I see. Very resource-ful," I praised.

"Alexa, as much as I do not want to leave you tonight; I have to go to the club. Gotta answer for my whereabouts today. Club likes to keep tabs like that." Angel admitted on a sigh. "You gonna be ok alone?"

"Yea, I'll be fine. I'm just glad you're out and ok. I have to be at the shelter early tomorrow anyway, maybe I'll just go to bed early."

We finished up our pizza and Angel helped me clean up. I walked him down to the garage, hand in hand. I didn't want to let him go. I missed him enough today.

"I know you got a rough week ahead of you, with your mom and all. Just call me. Let me know when I can see you again." Angel got on his bike, and pulled me into his arms for a sweet kiss. I nodded as I watched him leave, again.

Chapter 13

Alexa

The week passed by in a fog. I spent most of my time in the shelter talking to the children and checking on supplies. I avoided the glances and stares from my co-workers and the whispers behind my back. The stories were out of the news; but the damage had already been done. It was already Wednesday and it's been radio silence from my mom. The end of the day couldn't come soon enough; I had been putting in ten hour days and going home and throwing myself right into bed. I had texted back and forth with Angel but he's been busy with club business. I ducked into my office at 6 o'clock; hoping I'd get a few spare moments with Sarah. She's been just as busy; the holiday weekend backed up our in-processing and it has been all hands on deck.

"Hey" I surprised Sarah who was checking emails on her laptop.

"Hey!" She jumped up to give me a big hug. "Before you say anything; I want to apologize for not being a good friend this weekend. I mean, I was trying to be a good friend but it was a really bad situation." She scrunched her nose waiting for my response.

"No, stop. Don't apologize. The whole thing was so insane. It could have been so much worse; I'm just glad things seem ok right now."

"Well, I heard that Angel got arrested. Is that true?" she probed.

"Yea. It's fine though. They released him that day; the evidence seemed to just vanish in thin air." I wiggled my eyebrows. "And besides, Angel didn't do anything but defend me. I was the one to smash Randy's windshield." I added absentmindedly. I forgot that that little bit of information wasn't public knowledge.

"You what!!!!!!" Sarah whisper-yelled.

"Um, yea." I covered my face with my hands; peeking through my fingers at her.

"Alexa!" Sarah rolled her desk chair back laughing so hard she had to hold on to her sides.

"Well you took the news better than my mom." I teased.

"Oh my god. I could only imagine what Miss District Attorney had to say about her little heathen." Sarah said wide-eyed.

"Ugh, it wasn't good. But, apparently she smoothed things over with Travis, Randy's dad. I haven't heard a thing from Randy or anything. I thought for sure the cops were coming to arrest *me* when they barged into the patio on me and Angel." My face turned red because I haven't told Sarah yet that I had slept with Angel. But I'm sure the look on my face was saying it all.

"Wait. Back up. I know that look. Ok. No. We can't have this conversation here. Let me finish up this email and let's go grab dinner down the street. And you better *spill*, girl."

"Okay, okay. I'm done. I haven't eaten dinner yet this week. Ready when you are." I gathered my bags and laptop and waited for Sarah.

We walked down the street, there were a few cute restaurants nearby but we settled on a sushi joint a few blocks away. They had bistro table seating outside and it was a beautiful night. We ordered a few different rolls to share and I was thankful that we were somewhat secluded so I can dish on my details.

"Ok. Talk." Sarah demanded. Her chin rested on her palm as she batted her eyelashes at me.

"Um, ok. Where should I start?" I asked.

"Start at the beginning! Where you two snuck off during those fireworks. Don't think that I didn't notice." Sarah giggled.

"Mmmm.. Well, we snuck up to my bedroom, and..." I trailed off, blush creeping into my cheeks and I felt a warmth between my legs just thinking about Angel being inside of me.

"Jesus, Alexa, he must have a magic penis or something. I've never seen you so flushed!"

"Oh my god, Sarah. He's amazing. The sex was freaking hot. I've never felt something so insane before." I gushed.

"He's huge, isn't he? I bet he is. And I hoped you guys were safe." Sarah sipped her water as the food was being delivered.

"He is big; and thick. I was so sore the next morning." We laughed together.

"Well, good for you! I'm glad you're getting some good sex finally! So what happened when the police came for Angel? Did you freak out?" Sarah asked.

"Um, well.. We were in the pool." I let that hang for a second, then looked up at Sarah as she was sticking a huge sushi roll in her mouth. "Having sex. When the police walked onto the patio." I smirked as she coughed and sputtered around her food. Her eyes bugged out of her head.

"What!!! No. You're lying. Oh my god. That is so embarrassing." She slapped the table, making a few people turn towards our direction.

"Mmmhmmm. Yup. We were naked. Thankfully the one cop dropped towels at the side of the pool so I could wrap one around me. Angel got out of the pool, naked. Then he dried off, put his board shorts on, so that they could arrest him." I explained, shaking my head with a small smirk.

"Badass. That's actually hilarious. So then he got released right away?"

"Yea. Roman picked him up and brought him back to my place since all his stuff was there."

"Roman's sweet. I got to chat with him a bit at the party." Sarah blushed a little when she spoke Roman's name.

"Yea Roman is great. He's got that easy-go-lucky attitude. You could tell he really loves his brother too. They seem really close." I sat back and watched Sarah school her features when I spoke about Roman, maybe she just thought he was cute.

"He's so funny too. And that body... holy shit." Sarah giggled.

"Sarah! Oh man, if Josh could hear you now." I teased her.

"Um yea, Josh and I kind of got into it about me hanging out with Roman. I promised him that I was just trying to make him feel welcomed, but Josh thought I was flirting with him." Sarah finished up her dinner and we both sat back in our chairs and let the cool desert breeze hit our faces.

"Oh. That kind of sucks. I can't imagine Josh getting mad at you; he's always so sweet. Anyway, let's get going, I have another early start tomorrow. This jobs' gonna kill me." We put some money on the table and held hands as we walked back to our cars. Sarah and I were close. More like sisters. I trusted her with everything and we neve judged each other.

We got to her Jeep when I let go of her hand and crossed my arms over my chest. "Sarah; Randy said something to me. Actually, it was pretty much the reason that I smashed his windshield in the first place."

"Oh god. What did *he* have to say?" Sarah stood with her back on her car and searched my face.

"He, um, he said he knew who my father was. Not like his name, but said that he was a guy my mom had a one night stand with in Mexico. He was so nasty; started saying how my mom didn't want anything to do with me and that I would never amount to anything." I looked down at my feet, his words bringing back so much hurt and questions.

"Alexa." She cooed and she wrapped her arms around me. "First, you don't even know if Randy was telling the truth. And second, Randy's a piece of shit. He would have said anything to set you off and start a fight with Angel." Sarah spoke softly into my ear.

"I know, but I went looking in my mom's office." Sarah pulled back so she could look at me. "I found some pictures. And a hotel key and ticket stubs from places in Mexico. I think Randy's right." I admitted.

"Okay. Well if he's right; then it probably came from his dad. But, not about the part about you. You're fucking amazing, and beautiful, and kind hearted and AMAZING." Sarah smiled.

"I'll have to work up the balls to ask my mom about it. I still haven't heard from her yet. She said she wanted to talk to me about all this crap. Gave me the full speech about how Angel is bad for me and that he'll be my downfall, blah, blah."

"Al, listen. Your mom's a smart lady. But she's a very different person than you. I know you had a tough upbringing with her and she's not the most understanding woman. Yes, there's aspects of Angel that worry me and I want you to be careful. But, you're a grown woman; and need to decide that for yourself." Sarah offered. I gave her another big hug.

"Thanks, Sarah. Alright, I'm outta here. I'm beat. Thanks for listening. I'll let you know how it goes with my mom; when I finally hear from her." We parted ways. Sarah was in the city offices for the rest of the week; so I know the rest of my week I'll be on my own in the office.

Angel

As soon as I left Alexa's on Sunday night; I got called into the table room at the clubhouse. It was never good getting a text from the President; telling you to get your ass to table ASAP. I pulled up and Roman and Taylor were already outside waiting for me. They got the same texts and were dreading being called to the carpet. The three of us walked into the table room quietly. The Prez already seated at the head of the table with a bottle of Jack in one hand and a joint in the other. The President, Rey (spanish for King) had a smirk on his face and only spoke one word as we stood in front of him. "Talk."

"I was arrested this afternoon. I roughed up a kid that was giving shit to my girl." Roman raised an eyebrow when I referred to Alexa as 'my girl'. I asked Roman and Taylor to come with, because they were at a party with me when this punk was causing some trouble." I explained briefly and precisely. Rey didn't appreciate long, drawn out emotional stories.

"And were you charged?" Rey asked, cocking his head to the side.

"No. The evidence vanished into thin air." Taylor inter-jected.

"I see." Rey stood. "When you involve our club members in your own personal battles, it needs to be cleared through your brothers and approved by me. You know this, Angel. This girl you're walking around with. She's the daughter of the fucking D.A." His voice boomed and he narrowed his eyes at me. "What the fuck are you thinking? Or are you only thinking with your dick. She's a hot piece of ass but you're skating on thin fucking ice here."

"I know. I've made it clear to her that she's not to be involved with my club business. She understands. She's good." I stutter out.

"Right. And we're just to believe that? You fuck the D.A.'s only daughter and you don't think your President will just say, 'yea, Angel. Good for you'. How do you know she's not telling her mother everything about you; about us? I'll tell you one thing Angel; the cops or the fucking D.A. start sniffing around here; I'll have your fucking head. I know you're good at keeping your mouth shut; you proved that over ten years ago. But don't think I will just let this slide." He paced as I stood, knowing that now was not the time to open my mouth to argue. "You better watch it with this girl. She better be fucking worth it. Now get the fuck outta here and you better keep your head low. You don't need an-other arrest."

We walked out of the office, quiet and emotionless. Taylor broke off to go get himself a beer and Roman and I walked back out to our bikes.

"That was fun." Roman joked. "Fuck man, you had to know Prez was gonna come down on you about Alexa. Shit's just not a good idea."

"What's not a good idea? Alexa? Man, you don't get it. She's it. She's fucking amazing." I stood up against the brick building, staring up to the night sky.

"Yea? You fuck her last night?"

I looked over to Roman, the smirk on my face saying it all.

"Yea, that's what I figured." Roman laughed. "That pussy's got you under a spell, alright."

I elbowed Roman and laughed along with him. "Man, we were having sex when the cops walked into the patio area at Alexa's. We had just finished when their fucking boots made me look up."

"What. Sick man. They get an eye full?"

"Yea. We were naked. I got out of the pool with my dick swinging in their faces before they slapped cuffs on me." We both let out a big laugh, Roman patting me on the back. "Jesus man. I'd do anything for this girl. Seriously. I don't want to give her up." I confided in Roman. He only had one other girlfriend that I knew about. A girl named Jessica that he dated for two years until he found her on her knees in front of one of our brothers is Los Demonios. Roman couldn't do shit to him because he was one of the officers and would kill him if Roman caused any trouble.

"Well man, all I can say is, use your best judgement here. Prez will kill you if this goes south. Make sure she's worth it." Roman punched me in the shoulder before he headed back into the club. Roman spent most nights at the club drinking and shooting the shit with the guys.

I went back to our house, I was exhausted but I still had too much adrenaline coursing through my body. I looked around at the shitty house with the equally shitty couch I slept on and with my frustration, I decided to clean up the place. I spent the next three hours throwing out trash, emptying the recycling bucket and washing down the kitchen and bathroom. The place still looked like a shack but at least it was clean and I felt a little better. Roman was a slob to live with; I still don't know why I ever agreed to let him have the bedroom as I stripped off my jeans and shirt and laid out on the couch. I finally drifted off to sleep as Roman came stumbling through the front door. He grunted as he made his way to the bedroom and passed out.

The week went by quickly, thank fuck. The club was busy with increased runs to Mexico for pickups and deliveries; the

Prez called on more of the brothers to do tunnel runs with the prospects and of course I drew the short straw. Tunnel runs were the absolute worst. It was exhausting and disgusting. The tunnels were dark and the air quality sucked; the prospects almost always complained the entire way and we had to carry the merchandise back with us in heavy bags. By Thursday morning; after pulling three all-nighters in a row; I was dying to get back to my house, shower and pass the hell out. I was at the club finishing up a meeting when all hell broke loose. A handful of us were seated at the round table going over numbers and money when the door slammed open and five armed guards came rushing in. We all went stock still, casually looking up, showing no fear; when nobody but the District Attorney Sonya Ramirez waltzed through the front door, eyes locked on me. Her heels clicked loudly as she came right towards me.

Chapter 14

Angel

"Angel Torres." She hissed as she stood before me with hands on her hips. Sonya Ramirez was a short thin woman. The only thing that Alexa shared with her mother was her honey brown eyes and skin tone; Sonya had skinny legs with large fake breasts and enough botox to rival most LA actors. Dressed in her version of a power suit; she stood before our table, eyeballing each of the guys. I nodded my head in her direction as Prez came out of his office looking madder than a hornet.

"I need to talk with you. Now. Can we step outside of this pig pen." She was already walking out of the door before I could answer her. All the guys turned in my direction. Prez eye balling the fuck out of me. My chair scraped loudly across the floor as I stood and made my way outside. The armed guards stayed in the doorway watching for any trouble as I walked over to where Ramirez was leaning against her black Escalade.

I stood in front of her, hands gripping the collar of my cut and cocked my head to the side with a disinterested look on my face. "What can I help you with, District Attorney Ramirez?" I said lazily; as if I didn't already know the hell she was about to try and unleash on me.

Her back went rigid as she leaned into my personal space; finger pointing in my face. "You're going to listen to what I tell you right now. You *will* stay away from my daughter starting now. I will not have you or your band of thugs corrupt her or her friends. If I find out that you or your brothers go near her, contact her or even breathe her name; I will make sure to bring down the wrath of hell upon your little organization. Don't fool yourself into thinking I don't know what you do here. I will destroy your operation and take down every one of you criminals for gun trafficking and drug distribution. The *only* reason I have not raided and shut down this hell hole is because right now; the city has its hands full of migrants flooding our streets and I don't have enough manpower to deal with your petty shit right now." She was panting now, face red and I can see the determination in her eyes.

"I think Alexa is old enough to make her own decision, yes? What makes you think she'll stay away from *me*?" I growled. Alexa was the one person in my entire life that made me feel like someone worthy of a life, a future. And I wasn't going to give that up easily.

"You listen, and you listen good, Angel. If you so much as touch her I will have the DEA breathing down your neck faster than you can blink. And we all know that with your record, I'll make sure to put you and your brother away for life. You'll be a caged animal and I'll be the one to throw away the key." Sonya snarled. There were raised voices and shouts coming from inside the club when one of the guards shouted out to Sonya to wrap it up.

She turned her back to me as she put her hand on the SUV's door handle. "I care about her." My voice cracked and I dropped my hands to my sides. I knew I wasn't going to change her mind but I needed her to understand that I was more than just a criminal in her eyes.

"You care about her." She said, mocking my tone. She opened the door but before she jumped in she gave one last punch to the gut. "The only thing you care about is what's between her legs. I know you. I know your type. You'll ruin her and destroy her career. Alexa isn't made for this life. She's made for so much more. So much more that you, Angel, will *ever* be able to give her." Sonya got into the SUV and shut the door in my face. The guards drew back from the building and got into their vehicles, Sonya's driver starting the engine back up.

The SUVs sped out of the parking lot; leaving me standing there watching. Fuck. A million thoughts raced through my mind, but first I knew I had to face Los Demonios about what the hell just went down.

"Angel! Get your fucking ass in here." Prez shouted from the doorway. Fucking great.

Alexa

It's Friday morning and I can't remember when I've been more excited about the weekend. In the past; I've never been one of those people racing through the week so I could party on the weekends; but now that I've got something or someone to look forward to; I cannot be any more anxious. My alarm is about to go off and I'm dreading another long ass day at work but I decide to get up and get on my spin bike; start the day off with a bang. I always look forward to my workouts. They just get my head straight; give me that huge boost of energy and I just feel so good afterward. I just started with a slow warm up, peddling my feet with a smooth and comfortable pace, adjusting my music when my phone starts buzzing wildly on the bike mount.

Mom: *Alexa, we need to talk.*

Mom: *Meet for lunch today. Market Street Bistro at 1 sharp; I have a meeting at 2:30.*

I stare at the messages with dread filling my belly. It's not very typical of my mom to schedule her own lunches; let alone not even ask me if I was free. This seemed demanding. I could already sense her bad mood. Wonderful.

Mom: *I'll send my car for you.*

My head starts to fog over with the millions of things that she'll probably have to say to me today. All of a sudden I felt like my work out just wasn't going to cut it today. I didn't hear from Angel yesterday; I texted him to say that I missed him. He may just be busy with the club or something but I had this nagging feeling in the back of my mind. I started to peddle faster, started to feel my adrenaline pumping and energy flowing through my legs as I worked on my defenses that I could use against my mom. I wasn't going to let her just railroad me today. I tapped out a text to Angel.

Me: Hey! Hope everything's ok...didn't hear from you yester-day. Mom just texted me-meeting her for lunch today.. Fun fun.

I finished up my work out; my legs burning with that wonderful post spin pump. I was sweaty but felt good; felt confident. I checked my phone before jumping in the shower; no response from Angel. It was early and he was probably still asleep.

I got ready for work in record time; dressing in army green wide legged linen pants and a tight fitting black tee shirt. My car rumbling to life as I waited for the garage doors to open; I finally responded to my mom.

Me: Sounds good. Can't be late if your car is picking me up. :-)

I tried not to sound like a smart ass; but hey... maybe it would give her a chuckle. I sent another message to Angel; I missed him and was hoping we could spend some more time together this weekend.

Me: Hey, sorry if this wakes you up. Want to see you this weekend? Got plans?

I was really hoping Angel would have already asked to make plans with me for the weekend. I pulled into work and for the first time dreaded being here. I loved my job; but I just felt like I wasn't doing enough anymore. I didn't feel challenged or that I made enough of a difference in these childrens' lives. But, I picked my head up as I entered the building and counted down the hours until I had to meet with my mom.

It was 12:50 PM and I was just grabbing my bag and heading out of the building so that I 'wouldn't be late' for my mom's car when Angel finally texted back.

Angel: Sorry, I can't.

And that was it. I stared at the phone screen like I couldn't read English. That's it? 'Sorry, I can't'? That's all I get?

Me: Oh, ok. Do you want to grab dinner tonight? Miss you.

Ok, I sounded a bit pathetic; but I did miss him and this just didn't *feel* like him.

Angel: No.

What the hell? Okaaaaay. My stomach flip flopped inside of me just as the black SUV pulled up at the curb. I got in wordlessly as I just kept staring down the phone in my hand; hoping he'd call or message something else. I threw my phone in my bag when it became apparent Angel wasn't going to elaborate and watched the town blur by my window.

Of course my mom was already seated at her favorite table, sipping mineral water and typing away at her phone. She barely picked up her head to acknowledge me when I sat down across from her.

"Hey mom."

"Alexa. Thanks for coming." Oh shit, she was sounding very 'lawyery' with her eyes trained on my face; her lips in a tight line.

"Nice to see you too." I said sarcastically.

"Alexa, cut the crap; you know I'm not very happy with you right now." She nodded at the waiter to come over to take our order.

"I'll have the Cobb Salad with house dressing. And please make it quick; I'm short on time today." My mom said to the waiter as he scrambled to take her menu from her and look at me.

"Oh, um.. I'll have the same." And I handed the menu off. "Jeez, if you're that busy, this could have waited til you came home." I suggested.

"I'm swamped, but no, this can't wait any longer." She barked out.

I sat back with my arms crossed. I already dreaded anything that came out of her mouth and I felt my defenses rise as my arms prickled with goosebumps.

"I want you to go to Travis's house and apologize to Randy. I already paid for the windshield and thanks to you; I had to beg Randy to not press charges against you for destruction of property and assault." I sat with my mouth gaped open. "Not a word, Alexa. I can not believe that you even allowed this to happen in the first place. And you know damn well who started this." Our food came and the waiter scurried off after seeing the daggers we were throwing at each other.

"Fine. I will apologize. But you have to know that Randy instigated all of this. He grabbed me at the bar and it's been hell with him since. Angel was just…"

My mom interrupted me with her hand halting my words. "No, Alexa. I don't even want to hear his name. Randy is a spoiled brat but that is nothing new. Your time running around with those thugs is OVER."

"Mom, you can't tell me who to be with. I care about Angel. He's a good man." I raised my voice causing a few people to glance over at us.

My mom plastered a big smile on her face as she continued spewing her venom. "I will not hear of it. He will destroy you. And your career. He has nothing. He *is* nothing. You've done nothing but embarrass yourself and me. I will not stand for this." Her voice was low and menacing. I slunk back into my seat; not knowing how much further I could push her.

Just when I was about to push further the waiter arrived to check on us and our lunches. My mom shooed him away, asking him for the check.

"Mom, Randy was saying some stuff that I need to ask you about." She glanced up cautiously as she pushed around the salad on her plate. "He told me that he knew who my dad was. Said he was a one night stand; from Mexico?" My voice was small and timid; I had no idea how she was going to react to my questions. I've never been able to broach the 'dad subject' with her before; she was a professional at deflecting.

Her voice trembled with anger when she looked up at me, "Alexa, this is not the time nor the place for that conversation. If I had wanted you to know who your father was I would tell you. He was nothing more than a sperm donor; *that* is all you need to know." She threw down her utensils and pushed the strands of hair that escaped from her low bun.

"Fine. That's just fine." I said as I threw my napkin on top of my untouched salad.

"Alexa, I'm warning you right now. This ends here. And now. If I find out you're still associating yourself with those criminals; you better find yourself a new place to live; you're 27! Maybe it's time to grow up."

I had tears welling up in my eyes and a knot in my throat from her words. I stood up and grabbed my purse and left her sitting there by herself. I felt everyone's eyes on me as I stormed through the restaurant and pushed the doors open with more than enough force. I bypassed her waiting SUV and walked down the street. I didn't want to stop moving; otherwise the tears would spill over. After a few blocks in the wrong direction; I hailed a cab and headed back to work.

I sat in the back seat of the smelly cab with it's sticky seats and messaged Angel, again.

Me: Lunch was hell with my mom, can you talk? Can I see you?
Angel: Alexa, I think you and I ran its course. Probably for the best you just get on with your life.

That was it. The tears spilled over and I sobbed quietly in the back of the cab. Frustration digging a hole in my heart and mind. Angel was the first person that made absolute sense to me. He set my world spinning yet in complete balance. And I thought he felt the same way.

I got back to work and I put myself on auto pilot. I moved through the motions and at 5 o'clock I gathered my belongings and headed home. I drove in silence with nothing but my thoughts driving me crazy. Why would he do this? How could he be done with me? Did he just use me? Could I have been so blind and stupid? These questions swirled and twirled around in my mind right up until I pulled into the garage. All of a sudden, this house felt like a trap, a deep dark hole to bury myself in. I looked up at the massive lonely home in disgust and stomped up the stairs to the guest house. I guess that's all I was? A guest. A passerby that just fed off of the kindness of others. That's how my mother made me feel. A burden. Dependent. I didn't even stop at the kitchen, I dumped my stuff on the couch and went to my closet to change. I threw on work out legging and a sports bra and hopped on my spin bike. I blasted the music at ear piercing levels and closed my eyes and I pumped my legs. I never worked out twice in one day; but I needed something; a distraction to the thoughts driving me insane. My hands shook and the sweat dripped down my chest as I clutched the handlebars and peddled faster and faster; increasing the resistance until my legs ached.

By the time I couldn't feel my legs any longer and the tears started spilling down my cheeks; I had given up. My heart was pumping in my chest and I was breathless. I remembered the last time I was this breathless. It was when I was with Angel. When he touched me, the entire universe came to a screeching halt and all I saw was him and me. I felt sparks and fireworks when he was around me and when he was inside of me; I felt my body connect to someone on more than just a physical level. Angel filled me and stretched me and I loved every second of his hands on me. The heat between my legs and the swirling in my broken heart pissed me off. I was furious. Blindsided. I deserved more than his lame text message; even if he was a 'thug' like my mom loved to call him.

Before I even realized what I was doing; I was in my Dodge Charger flying out of my driveway and headed for the Los Demonios Locos clubhouse. My palms gripped the steering wheel, and watched my headlights fall upon the building and bikes that belonged to the MC. I had no idea if he'd even be here; but it was Friday night and there was a shit load of bikes lining the streets and girls scantily dressed roaming the streets. I double parked my car and slammed the door shut. I marched right into the building without anyone stopping me. I stood in the open space, eyes searching for a familiar face when they landed on Angel in the far corner.

He was sitting on the couch with a beer in his hand and a girl on either side of him. Before I lost my nerve, I took a deep breath and marched right up to him. I can tell by the look in his eyes that he was drunk. He slowly looked at me, starting at my feet and working their way up the length of my body. His nostrils flared and his eyes narrowed at me. He barely made a move, showing any surprise that I was standing before him. I eyed the girls on either side of him. The one blond had her legs draped over his lap and she leaned back with her tits almost hanging out of her tight tank top. The other girl had dark raven hair, wearing a bikini top and jean skirt. She had her hand around Angel's arm and was talking into his ear like I didn't even exist.

"I'd like to talk to you." I demanded. I heard some cat calls in the background when I remembered I was still dressed in work out leggings and just a sports bra.

"I don't have anything to say." Angel responded. His eyes were cold and detached. But his mask didn't fool me; behind those eyes were sadness and frustration that matched my own.

"Please. You owe me that much." I asked, crossing my arms over my chest as the catcalls and whistles didn't stop. Angel rose to his feet, and I noticed a gun shoved into the front of his jeans. His tee shirt was dirty and hair a mess and he looked like he hadn't slept in days.

"Outside." Is all he said as he walked past me, not even bothering to wait for me to follow.

He leaned up against the brick building, keeping his eyes on his surroundings instead of looking at me. "Can you tell me what the hell is going on?" I asked, pleading internally that I didn't turn into a blubbering mess.

"I told you. It's over Alexa. What don't you understand about that?" He was as cold as ice. His body tense and I can smell the booze oozing out of him.

"So that's it? You just fuck me and you're done. I guess I was just a piece of ass to you? Is that all it was Angel?" I asked as I grabbed a hold of his vest, directing his attention to my face.

"Yea." He closed his eyes as he answered me and I swear I felt my heart shatter into a million pieces.

Chapter 15

Angel

I saw her from across the room. I knew she would come. As sweet and gentle Alexa was; I had a feeling she wouldn't take my text messages laying down. I shielded my face as I watched her gulp a giant breath, square her shoulders and march over to where I was on the couch. I was exhausted, dirty and drunk and the two whores sitting on either side of me cared more about screwing a Los Demonios than if I was even breathing while they were doing it. I had no intention of doing anything with these girls but I welcomed their idea to cuddle up next to me; hoping Alexa would sniff me out tonight. I kept the gun on my waist for an added bonus. Alexa had to understand that I was a criminal. I was dangerous. And she shouldn't be with me.

When we walked outside I tried so damn hard to not pull her into my arms and beg for her forgiveness. A few guys were outside smoking and talking shop when I spotted Prez watching me. The look on his face told me that I need to cut and run from Alexa or there would be hell to pay. After the run in with Sonya Ramirez yesterday, Prez had pulled me in his office; one on one.

"You want to tell me what the fuck just happened Angel?" Rey spit out; he was furious with me.

"I know. I'm handling it." I dropped my head; I knew I had to end this before the Los Demonios got on my ass too.

"Handling it? How exactly are you handling it? The fucking DA just waltzed her ass into my club. Armed guards, Angel! You better get rid of this girl and fast before the club comes down on you." Prez threatened. I knew better than to test him; guys suffered his wrath for less bullshit than girl problems. He paced the length of his

office; Rey and I had a long history together and I considered him a friend but I took an oath to obey his rules and the club's.

My throat bobbed as I met his eyes. "I'll get rid of her. She doesn't belong with me anyway."

The silence hung in the air between us for a while. He wasn't dismissing me that easily. Rey went easy on me from the beginning. When I was arrested for the gun's back when I worked for Mack; the day I got out of jail, Roman took me to Rey. Rey welcomed me with open arms providing me with a roof above my head; money in my pocket. He felt indebted to me because I never even hinted to the cops that the Los Demonios Locos were responsible for the arsenal the cops found that fateful day. The DLs took my brother in; made him a member and protected him when I couldn't. I couldn't deny Rey when they proposed an offer I couldn't refuse; to join Los Demonios Locos. I had the brothers' respect from the get go and I never gave them any reasons to feel otherwise. Until Sonya fucking Ramirez made my world crumble before my eyes.

"You love this girl?" Prez asked me, hands on his hips and eyes boring into my soul.

"No." I lied.

"I'm gonna give it to you like this, Angel. You choose that girl; and you choose to hang up your vest. I'm not stupid, Angel. I know this life didn't choose you; you fell into it, face first. You've been a loyal brother and part of our family for a long time now. But I will not tolerate you bringing our organization to its knees over a pussy." Rey deadpanned.

"I got it Prez; my loyalty is to the club."

"Good. Now get out." Prez smirked as he dismissed me. I walked out of his office and went right for my bike. I needed to get some air and get my head on straight.

I leaned my back against the warm brick building as Alexa's sweet smell of coconut and lemons washed over me. I tried not to breathe her in; I knew it would break me. She searched my face looking for answers and I tried to look as disinterested as possible. She fired off her questions and I answered on auto pilot. I was hurting her, and it was killing me.

Her eyes filled with tears and her lip quivered as my eyes met hers. I needed to drive it home so that she got as far away from me as possible. I stood up, shifting my vest to reveal the gun at my waist and leaned into her face.

"Run back to your mansion Alexa. You don't belong in my world and I sure as fuck don't belong in yours." I growled at her. She stepped back, shock lighting up her face as a single tear ran down her cheek. I straightened my spine and crossed my arms over my chest.

Alexa bit her bottom lip and tipped her head up at me. Sadness and hurt but most of all anger in her eyes. "I hope you go to hell, Angel." That's all she said before she turned and got back into her car. Never looking back at me, she revved the engine and sped down the street.

I walked back into the club where Prez and Roman stood waiting for me. Prez handed me a beer and slapped me on the back, "Go get yourself laid, Angel. Take your pick." He laughed as he walked away. Roman's eyes met mine and in a silent understanding he put his hand on my shoulder; giving it a firm squeeze.

Alexa

I couldn't even see where I was driving to; the tears blurred my vision. But I ended up at Sarah's house. She had a little bungalow on the other side of town and I prayed that she was home. When I pulled up, the lights were on in the house. I pulled my body out of the car; I felt drained, exhausted both mentally and physically. Before I even reached her door, she swung the front door open with a concerned look on her face.

"Al? Are you ok?" Sarah took me in her arms without a word and just held me as the tears flowed openly. Sobs wracked my body and she pulled me into her home and shut the door.

"Alexa, tell me what happened. Oh my god, Alexa, you're shaking." She grabbed a blanket off the couch and wrapped me up as she sat me down on her couch.

"I'm an idiot." I shook my head as the words escaped me. I felt so dumb. I couldn't believe I allowed this to happen to me.

"No you're not. You're anything *but* an idiot. Please tell me what happened. Are you ok? Did Angel hurt you?" Her tone was defensive and motherly. She searched my now puffy eyes, taking both my hands in hers.

"He destroyed me." I whispered and hung my head. My head started to throb and my hands wouldn't stop shaking. "It's over. He doesn't want me." Sarah just held me and my eyes became so sleepy I couldn't even open them anymore.

"Lay down sweetie, I'm not letting you out of my sight." Sarah's voice was the last thing I heard before I drifted off to sleep.

When I peeked an eye open; it was morning. I was still wrapped up in a blanket and curled up on Sarah's couch. Sarah was curled up on the other end, blond hair strewn over the big fluffy pillows. I slept hard and dreamless. My head felt like a ton of bricks and my body was so sore. I stumbled into the bathroom and almost cried all over again as the evidence of puffy red eyes stared back at me in the mirror. When I got back out, Sarah was sitting cross-legged on the couch with sleepy eyes and hair pulled into a messy bun.

"Hey babe." Sarah gave me a lopsided smile.

"Hey." I mustered.

"I'm gonna make some coffee." She said with a yawn.

I followed her in the kitchen. It was small and sweet just like her. The buttery yellow walls were soothing and soon the smell of freshly brewed coffee filled the air. I sat with my legs curled up into my chest on the kitchen chair and Sarah placed a big mug of coffee in front of me. We both sat and sipped until the caffeine seeped into our bodies, waking us up.

"I'm all ears when you're ready." Sarah said quietly over the coffee cup pressed to her lips.

"Sarah, it was awful." I took a couple deep breaths as everything that happened yesterday came flooding back to my mind. "I met up with my mom yesterday. Let's just say I get why she's so cut throat in the courtroom."

"That bad, huh?" Sarah mused.

"Yea, and then some. So she did smooth things over with the windshield thing; but I have to go to Randy's to formally apologize." I explained.

"Well, you're not going there alone. I'll go with you."

"And then my darling mother decided to demand that I end things with Angel or she's kicking me out." I raised my eyebrows as Sarah gasped.

"That's pretty shitty. Jesus, you're not marrying Satan or anything!" Sarah exclaimed.

"Well, to her, Angel may as well be Satan. She said some pretty terrible things, although I wasn't all that surprised how cold and calculated it was. And I ended up walking out of the restaurant." I got up to grab a banana off the counter.

"Okay, so your mom's always been a cold bitch, no offense. What happened with Angel." Sarah said honestly. If anyone knew my mom's behavior; she did. She was always over the house growing up, Sarah spent just as much time with my grandmother as I did. Sarah had divorced parents; her mom was a realtor, catering exclusively to estates and mega homes and her dad was a Captain in the Marines. Sarah's mom was constantly dating losers that she pranced around Sarah and her dad was never home.

"Ugh, I lost my damn mind, Sar. I had texted him earlier asking to meet up and he just responded, 'no' and when I pressed him he messaged saying that 'him and I ran its course and that I should get on with my life'." I shoved the rest of the banana in my mouth; my stomach flip flopping from the thought.

"What the hell? Where did that come from? I thought you guys were totally into each other." Sarah watched me pace the length of her kitchen.

"Me too. I don't know; maybe I just was being stupid. How could a guy like Angel be interested in a girl like me? We have nothing in common and he'd be crazy to get into something with the DA's daughter in his line of work." I wrinkled up my nose, referring to his criminal activities with the DL soured my stomach. "I really fell for him."

Sarah came to push my hair out of my face, "I know, babe. I really thought he was the one for you. But maybe your two worlds just can't collide? Ya, know. Maybe he's saving you from a lot of heartache in the future." She kissed my forehead and turned to the fridge, digging around for some breakfast.

"Well, thanks for letting me crash last night. I barely even remember driving here from the clubhouse." I threw myself back on her couch.

"Wait! You went there? To confront him?" Sarah spit out with her mouth gaped open at me.

"Ugh, yea. Dressed like this, no less. I was so mad when I got home from work, I worked out and got myself so fired up- I drove over there and confronted him. He was cozied up with two sluts and couldn't even look me in the face." I threw a pillow over my face, remembering the skanky girls touching him made my blood boil.

"Are you serious. Shit. What an asshole." Sarah shook her head. I left out the part about Angel having a gun in his waist belt. I didn't need more of a lecture that he wasn't right for me.

"Wait, so why were you home? You're never home on a Friday night?" I sat up.

"Josh and I were arguing all week. I didn't feel much like seeing him last night."

"Shit, Sarah.. And here I am rambling on and on and you have shit going on with Josh." Sarah came to sit next to me on the couch.

"It's fine. We've just been bickering a lot lately; over the dumbest stuff. We've been together forever and I'm beginning to feel like he's never going to ask me to move in with him; he told me he didn't believe in marriage. Like what is that? Shouldn't I have known that about him like 5 years ago; not *now*?" she huffed.

"Josh? Not wanting to get married? That doesn't seem right. He seems like a family man. I'm sorry, maybe you guys just need a break or something. Or a good, honest talk about your futures." I suggested.

"Meh, we'll see. Let's just do nothing today. I think they're doing a Sex and the City marathon today?"

"Sounds good to me." Sarah and I curled up under a huge fuzzy blanket with our heads together on a big pillow.

"You don't think your mom got to Angel, do you?" Sarah asked after the second hour of our favorite series. "I mean, like, threatened him?" she asked skeptically.

"I don't know. I mean, I *think* Angel would tell me something like that rather than flat out dump me. I don't know." I couldn't even entertain the idea of such betrayal from my own mother.

The weeks started to blur altogether. Work, home, work, home. That was my routine. I spent the weekends doing volunteer work and hanging out with Sarah. She and Josh decided to take a little break and reevaluate their relationship. I guess it's hard when you've been dating the same guy since senior year in high school. She's been just as moppy at work as I have. Things at the migrant shelter have eased up a bit and I've been able to get more office work done. I love doing the volunteer work; I get more time with the migrant children and play games with them. I help the teachers with story time and crafts and have been on diaper duty for some of the infants that we have at the shelter. Some of the older kids tell me stories about how they've made their way into America; the long journeys they traveled on foot with their parents or alone. Some kids were even traded into the country in exchange for guns or drugs. And then dumped on the streets with nowhere to go. It's truly sad that these innocent lives are bartered with and taken for granted.

I haven't seen my mom since that terrible lunch date. She's in and out of the house but I just stay in the guest house. She seems perfectly happy avoiding me. Sarah offered for me to move into her bungalow with her but it's a tiny little one bedroom with barely enough closet space for her. I've been toying around with finding my own place; but I just lack the motivation. It's been a month since I've seen Angel and I still feel restless. I know we didn't even have that long together before he broke things off; but I miss that connection we had. It was so easy with him; natural. From being on the back of his bike to being in his arms; it just felt so right. Angel was able to bring me out of my shell; I wasn't afraid to just be myself with him and vice versa. I guess, too, I didn't realize how much my life was lacking before I met him. He brought excitement and happiness, I got butterflies every time I saw him or he touched me.

It was 11PM on Friday night and I sat alone in my house; cuddled under the fuzziest blanket I have. I tried to put on a movie but my eyes kept drifting to my kitchen island. I close my eyes and I can see myself spread on top of the counter with Angel between my legs. I remember the feeling of his hands roaming my body along with his heat and manly smell as my core clenches. I can still feel his bruising grip on my hip as we kissed and how his fingers traveled down and explored my thighs and clit. My heart begins to thump in my chest and I squeeze my legs together trying to pull myself out of my daydream. Damn it. I can't stop thinking about him. My bed, my kitchen, my shower; even the pool outside flashed with memories of him and me; how happy and free I felt when I was with him. How happy I thought he was. I shake my head and toss the blanket off of me; once again pacing the length of the house.

I haven't been sleeping well; I've doubled up on my workouts to tire out my body. Only when my body is truly exhausted do I sleep at least 6 straight hours. But I'm restless. Words from my mom float across my brain and invade my dreams; questions haunt me about my father distract me at work and make me irritable. And I just miss him.

I bought a bottle of wine the other night on the way home from work; hoping it would lull me to sleep, numb me; I grabbed a glass and poured a healthy amount for myself. I climbed into bed, stuck my headphones on and listened to 'ocean sounds' as I sipped wine until my eyes felt heavy and the room started to blur. A nightmare of Angel's firm body towering over me; he pointed a gun at my face, telling me to run as fast as I could away from him; sent me flying out of my bed. I gripped the side of my bed, steadying my feet and allowed my heart rate to slowly fall back to normal pace. I was sweaty and thirsty and my head ached already. I grabbed the bottle of wine that I left on the side of my bed and marched out to the kitchen. I dumped every last drop of wine down the sink and threw the bottle into the sink, watching the shards of glass splash against the metal and scatter across the counter.

I crawled back into bed; I knew it was pointless to try and fall back to sleep. I had a constant thumping in my head and my legs were restless. I decided to text Randy, asking him to meet up sometime tomorrow to get my apology over with. I knew at this point, it was stupid to hope he thought that I was actually sorry. I waited long enough so it seemed like I didn't give a shit but not too long that Travis whined to my mother that I hadn't made the effort. The sun had barely started to peak out over the horizon when I climbed my body onto my spin bike, praying that the natural endorphins would bring me some sort of happiness.

By the time I got out of the shower, I had a missed text from Randy.

Randy: Let's meet at the coffee shop downtown. How's 7pm?
Me: Ok.

Ugh. I was kind of hoping he would blow me off or say that he didn't want to ever see me again; because I would be very ok with that. I got ready for work in a mid length army green flowy skirt and white tee shirt and my hair in a high ponytail. It took effort to feel like wanting to look nice. The last few weeks; I showed up for work in jeans and tee shirt and got a few looks from the management team. Sarah was at my office today so I filled her in on meeting up with Randy.

"Damn, I can't come with you today. I told Josh I would meet him for dinner to talk about *things*." Sarah groaned. "Do you want me to reschedule?"

"No, no it's fine. It's just coffee, and at a public place. It'll be fine. I guess I do need to apologize, but really, I'm kind of hoping to ask him more about my dad and what he knows. If he isn't a complete dick, that is." I shrugged as I restocked some pantry items in our stock room.

"Ok, but just text me or call me if you need me. And I'll call you when I get home. And, Alexa, don't be too easy on him. You may have been wrong about the whole windshield thing; but what he did was a huge betrayal; we've all known Randy since we were kids and it was a whole new level of fucked up; even for him."

"I know. I'll just feel him out. I hope things go well with your dinner tonight?" I changed the subject. Sarah was definitely feeling conflicted about her relationship. The last few weeks proved that she needed some alone time and to reflect on the things she wanted out of life and a man.

"Thanks, yea. I'm not really sure what to expect. Would it be terrible of me to ask him for more time apart? I keep going back and forth in my mind if I even *want* to be in a relationship. I love him. But we've been together for so long; it just doesn't feel 'special' anymore. It feels, I don't know, expected? Does that make sense?" She rubbed her arms as she shook her head.

"I think it's natural to feel that way. And it's not like you guys have taken the next step and moved in together or even talked about getting married. I think that itself; would make me question a lot of things." I explained as I threw my arms around her.

"Alright; I'm gonna cut out early and hit the gym. I've been putting in so much over time, I haven't worked out in a week."

"Ok... I'll talk to you later." I went back to my office to finish up some charts and emails. Before I knew it; it was 6:30PM; so I made my way over to the coffee shop Randy was meeting me at. I walked since it was so beautiful out and walking cleared my head.

Chapter 16

Angel

It's been three weeks since I've seen Alexa. I can't get the look on her face out of my head. The way I leaned into her, scaring her. Her eyes travelled down to the gun and back at my face with fear and disgust. I hurt her with my words. I needed her to think I was using her and threw her back to her own world; and it worked. I haven't heard from her or her mother. Although I know that Sonya Ramirez was keeping tabs on me since her little outburst in the club. I've seen a few men sniffing around the streets where the clubhouse is; following me while I'm riding around town. I don't dare even go over to *her* side of town. I've been keeping to myself during the day; and at night, I'm at the club's will. I've been pulled more and more to oversee transport down in Mexico. There's been a lot of heat on the border and more patrol. The Mexicans are getting restless; asking for more and more guns and trying to barter with their own people as payment.

Roman and I are partnered up during our club duties; without him, I think I'd go nuts the last few weeks. He's great at letting things not get the best of him, his laughter is infectious and he knows how to give it to me straight when I feel like my head's up my ass.

"Bro, why don't we get you drunk and laid; there's gotta be a few club bunnies that you haven't had the pleasure of screwing, right?" Roman elbowed me as we sat drinking coffee at our shitty house.

"It's 8 o'clock in the morning. How are you thinking about getting drunk when you have barely been sober for 6 hours?" I grunted over the black liquid that I held tightly in my hand. The club was burning me out. We were out all night making runs and then partied till the sun came back up. Roman loved this life; the danger, the woman, the fear; all of it. If anyone was meant for club life; it was Roman.

"Man, you're in a shit mood." Roman slid his chair back with an annoying screech as he stumbled toward the fridge. "I'm just saying, Angel, you gotta get over this girl. She's fucking with your head. You should be happy the fucking D.A. is off your ass and Prez isn't going to slice a finger off for bringing trouble into the club." Roman scoffed.

He's right. Prez had all right to take one of my fingers for bringing heat to the club, the brothers were pissed after that fiasco. But I've kept my head down and volunteered myself for the extra runs to the Border; so I've put my time in to making it right. I need to forget about Alexa. I dream about kissing her beautiful lips; it's so real I can almost smell her when I wake up. I've deliberately taken rides out past the Migrant Children's Shelter, hoping for a glimpse of her. I miss her small body against mine. Her sweetness and innocence; the way she never looked at me like I was anything but her equal; until I made her. After she walked away from me that last time; I jumped on my bike and just rode. I rode until my ass hurt and I could barely hold my handlebars anymore.

Roman broke me out of my daydream with a smack to the back of the head. "Angel, damn, are you hearing me?" My eyes snapped to his. "Shit's going down at the club, Prez called a table meeting. Get your shit together." I drained my coffee and slammed the mug on the table.

We got to the club and backed our bikes into the building; the street was where the prospects and younger club members were made to park. There were already a lot of men standing around; hushed conversations and the club bunnies were forced to wait outside. Typically, most table meetings were closed off aside from higher ups; Prez, and the VP, and their officers but Rey asked Roman to join them today. Roman was next in line to be an officer; he had a head for business and negotiations. The brothers and I along with the club prospects milled about until Prez entered the Table Room and the officers filed in afterwards. Table meetings were known to last anywhere from an hour to all night if shit was hitting the fan.   I worked on my bike while I waited; it always cleared my head when I focused on my machine and made sure it shined like the day I bought it. I sprayed down the chain with lube and checked the spark plugs for any wear and tear or cracks and damaged wires. By the time I got done and started to polish the chrome; the boys were coming out of the office; Roman and Taylor were walking directly toward me.

"What's up." I asked as I stood. Taylor was an officer; an asset to the club with his technological abilities and his mean as shit disposition. He's killed plenty; he proved his loyalty to the club by single handedly taking down a rival club that was pushing into our territory by buying up some of the downtown bars. Taylor made sure that the money from their offshore accounts got locked up by Homeland Security investigations for money laundering.

"We got some business to deal with up north; a club called The Serpents are stepping on our toes. Trying to steal our trade with the Mexicans by smuggling their people over the border as an extra bonus for more drugs. We're riding out there to have a little chat with their mules." The mules are what we refer to as the actual guys that move the product from Mexico into US territory. "Word is they're using the old El Mexicano tunnels; so we're going to drop by and have a little chat." Taylor explained as he pointed between the three of us.

"Be ready at 7. It'll take a few hours to get there." Roman added as he shifted from one foot to the other. Taylor walked away, he was a man of few words.

"You good, bro?" Roman asked, looking over my bike.

"Yea, whatever the club needs." I responded on auto pilot.

We drove out to the tunnels just as the sky was starting to get dark. Taylor passed out in the backseat of Roman's shitty F150. We left with a small arsenal that we hid in a long compartment under the bench seat in the back. We had intel about a house that had a secret passage way down into the tunnels; we'd have to bribe whoever lived there for access; but we knew it was the only way to intercept the Serpent's mules. We got to the house around midnight and parked the truck alongside the road. It was off the beaten path and looked abandoned. With the three of us armed, we made our way to the house and sure enough it was vacant. We searched for the passage door and found it underneath the shed's floor out in the backyard. We descended the creaky wooden ladder and waited. After an hour, the sound of crunching dirt and footsteps grew closer and closer to our position. We didn't know what kind of men we'd be encountering but we were ready.

There were only two guys, small in stature, dragging a heavy duffle bag down the path of the tunnel. They froze when they saw us standing in their way. They had with them two Mexican teenage looking boys that looked exhausted and scared. Taylor approached the Serpents with a gun in his hand and a knife in the other. We needed them to understand that the encroachment on our territory was not going to be permitted. Roman backed up Taylor as I grabbed the two kids from running off. If we needed to send the Serpents a message, this was the only way to do it. The two mules tried to fight us off and pleaded with us to let them pass or their President would kill them; we explained who we were and why we were there.

"Tell your President that this is your official warning to back off of the Los Demonios Locos territory. We know about your smuggling people into the US in order to sway negotiations with the Mexicans to cut off our supply." Taylor held the one Serpent by his dirty leather cut as he towered over him and easily outweighed him by fifty pounds. Their mules were nothing but prospects; probably their first run-in with an opposing MC. The other guy watched on and before Taylor could release his friend, he tried to pull a knife on Roman. I let go of the two teenagers and reached for my gun, aiming between the two Serpents as Taylor and Roman unleashed their strength and brutality against them. Blood sprayed across the dirt ground and Taylor's knife dug into the one guy's side. Roman has his guy pinned underneath him, already submitting. But just as Taylor pulled his knife from the guy's side; his other arm flew up at Taylor's head with a gun. I fired. The body dropping in front of me pulled me back to reality that I had killed the Serpent.

"Thanks." Taylor mumbled as he wiped the blood off the side of his face. Taylor's face was calm, nonchalant as he wiped the bloody knife on the dead guy's pants and Roman positioned the other living Serpent on his knees before us. "You want to live or die." Taylor asked him.

The Serpent's eyes were as big as saucers and yelled, "Live, live!" Roman yanked him up onto his feet and grabbed him by the throat as Taylor approached him.

"Ok, well since a verbal warning didn't do the trick, maybe we'll just send you back home with a dead body to make our warning stick real good." Roman quipped.

We didn't bother going after the two teenage kids that probably ran all the way back to Mexico. We took the Serpent's drugs and decided to stuff the dead Serpent's body into the duffle bag and make the remaining Serpent drag the bag all the way back to our truck. We deposited them both at their waiting truck that was in the middle of the god damn desert and made our way back home.

"You god man?" Roman asked as he dozed on and off while I drove us back to the clubhouse. I was quiet after killing the Serpent. Blood stained my jeans and boots and I felt dirty and wanted to get a shower. Taylor worked on some shit on his phone in the back seat.

"I'm fine. Tired." I responded quietly.

"You know, bro, Prez had asked if I thought you wanted to be brought in as an officer soon. Along with me, by my side." Roman admitted. Taylor's eyes met mine in the rear view mirror. "What you did tonight will be in your favor; if you want in."

"Are you ready for that level of shit?" I asked Roman. Roman loved the club life but there wasn't a lot of structure in him. He was smart as shit and was a good talker; that's why Prez needed him here for negotiations; but Roman lacked the discipline it took to be an officer. He was always joking around; never too serious about the crimes we committed.

"This is my life, man. I've never known anything else but the club. I'm ready for it. But I'd like it better if you were by my side." Roman said seriously. I nodded my head but remained silent as we rolled back into town.

It was just before 8AM and the traffic was light as we drove back to the clubhouse. We were down the road from the Shelter again and I was hoping Roman didn't notice and give me shit for taking this way into town. I slowed down for a red light ahead as I spotted a girl walking down the street. Her hair was warm brown and lay in soft waves down her back. She was wearing a light pink skater skirt, jean jacket and sneakers. The guy next to her had his arm around her shoulders and they seemed to be in deep conversation. The guy was a skinny punk with tight fitting khaki's on and a blue polo top. As I came to the stop behind a BMW at the light; both of them glanced over to my truck. And when my eyes connected with Alexa's; I felt my heart stop. She blinked at me and then over to the guy with his arm around her and her mouth fell open. Before I knew what was happening; I slammed the truck in park and jumped out and ran across the street. My hands were on his throat in a second as I pushed him down to his knees in front of me and connected my fist to his nose. Blood squirting everywhere including Alexa's white sneakers.

It happened so fast; so when I heard her screaming; I didn't even realize she was on my back trying to pull me off of him.

"NO, no Angel, no, stop. Please!" Alexa screamed over and over. She pulled at my vest and tried to yank my arms away. The world came back into focus when I turned to look at her face. She had tears in her eyes and she was frantic. "What are you doing? Stop! This isn't what you think?" She begged as she put her body between the guy and myself.

I stood as I heard gasps and screams from all around me and Roman yelling at me to get back in the truck. He was behind the wheel now with the door open for me to jump in.

"What the fuck, man! I'm not with her! I like cock. You fucking asshole. You broke my nose!" The guy was covered in blood, his nose dripping onto the sidewalk in front of him.

I stood unable to speak. I couldn't take my eyes off of Alexa and she couldn't take her eyes off of me. Her face filled with disappointment and hurt. For the first time; I felt ashamed. I looked down at my bloodied hands as the sounds of sirens nearby, jump-started my brain again. I turned and walked away from her; got in the truck and Roman drove off.

Alexa

"Hey Randy." I said as I sat across from him at the coffee house.

"Hey." He raised his eyebrows as he scanned my body up and down. I don't know if he did it just to set me off or if that was his usual obnoxious behavior. But I chose to ignore it. I came here to apologize and see if he would tell me more about what he knows about my dad.

As soon as I sat, a waitress rounded the corner and stopped at the table to ask what I'd like. "I'll just take a decaf cappuccino with almond milk."

"Decaf?" Randy hitched an eyebrow.

"Yea, I don't need any more reasons to have trouble sleeping." I offered. He shrugged his shoulders like he couldn't be bothered to care about someone other than himself. I looked around and scanned my surroundings. A lot of people on dates from the looks of their body language and a few people sipping coffee and working on their laptops.

"So, ok, well obviously I asked to meet up so I can apologize. I really just want to put this whole thing behind me." I blew out. Randy didn't bother looking up from the cell phone in his hand until I called his name. "Randy. Did you hear me?"

He gave his phone a small toss onto the table and finally met my eyes. "Yea, sorry. Um, well thanks for finally getting around to apologize; it's only been like a month." He said sarcastically.

"Yea. I've just been slammed with work and everything." God he was being a complete prick.

"Smash anyone else's windshield, lately?" Randy asked snidely.

"No." I deadpanned. This was going nowhere.

"Okay. Sorry. I'm being a dick." He laughed and put his hands up in surrender. "Things got out of hand and let's just let it be that." Randy placed his hand on top of mine. As much as I hated it there I felt better that he admitted that he was just giving me a hard time.

"You with that guy anymore?" Randy asked as he licked his bottom lip.

"No." I looked down at the table and slid my hand out from under his. "We're not together anymore." I could feel Randy studying my face. When I looked back up and took a sip of my coffee, he leaned in, lowering his voice.

"How about a date." He asked quietly with a raised eyebrow and biting his lip. When Randy smiled, he had the cutest dimples. He was classically handsome. Strong jaw and bright blue eyes; he had a nice body; almost six foot tall with a lean build. His blonde hair tossed in that effortless messy look and had just enough stubble to make him seem gruff and manly. It was too bad that the second he opened his mouth; all his good looks got washed out by his shitty stuck up attitude. The guy was in love with himself and thought very little of women besides wanting them to put out.

"No." We both were startled by my abruptness. "I mean, Randy, that's just not a good idea. I don't really think I'm your type." I was flustered and frustrated that this is what coffee was coming down to. He thinks he can guilt me into a date. So, I tried the 'it's not you, it's me, tactic.

"Aww, come on Alex. We've known each other forever. Our

parents were into each other, maybe we can follow in their footsteps." Randy said, grabbing ahold of my hand again.

"Randy, my mom broke it off with your dad because he was cheating on her left and right!" I was shocked and tried to pull my hand away again, but he had a good grasp.

"Alex, your mom's a busy woman. She just wasn't giving enough attention to my dad." Randy leaned back as he explained that my mom wasn't putting out enough, so casually to me.

I decided to deviate. "Wait, so I need to ask you; being you know more than me. What else do you know about my dad. What did Travis tell you?" I leaned in trying before he lost interest in what I was saying.

I lost his attention as he watched a couple young girls enter the coffee shop. They were giggly and happy with their short skirts and crop tops.

"Randy." I smacked the table with my hand. His head snapped back to mine.

"What? Jesus." He said annoyed.

"Randy, I really need to know what you know about my dad. My mom's never told me and I can't get it out of her. We're not exactly on speaking terms." He looked pissy as I begged him for answers.

Cocking his head to the side, a smirk grew on his face. "Have dinner with me tomorrow night." He asked as he flashed me his dimples.

"What?" Jesus, here we go.

"Dinner, Alexa. Dinner. You owe me that much." Randy smirked and leaned back on his chair with his arms behind his head.

"Tell me about my dad." I countered.

"Dinner. Say 8ish; I'll come pick you up. Where something cute." He rubbed his chin and looked at me as if he was picturing me naked.

"Damn it Randy." I crossed my arms over my chest and sat back on my chair. I was pissed.

"Oooo… there's that fiery temper again. Glad we're not

standing in front of my car." He laughed darkly. "Listen, you want info; I want a date. With you." Randy smirked as he brought his coffee up to his lips, draining the cup.

"Fine. One dinner, that's it, Randy. I don't really even know why you're interested in me. We have nothing in common; we've known each other for forever." I said emphatically.

"Oh Alexa. I've had a hard on for you for years. And you know; the best way to get over someone is to get under someone new." My jaw dropped as he said that last part. Who the hell did he think he was. I sure as shit wasn't about to sleep with him; I could barely stomach being in the same room as him.

"Forget it Randy; you're a sleazebag." I stood up, speaking louder than I probably should be in a coffee house. "You're a fuck boy. You have zero personality and zero respect for women. I wouldn't go on a date with you if you paid me. Now I apologized for my part of what happened and that's all I owed you." I dug into my purse for a few bucks to throw on the table for my drink. A five dollar bill and some change rattled on the wood table as I looked up and saw people staring at the scene I was causing. "From now on, stay the hell away from me. Don't speak my name, don't show up at my house, don't talk to my friends. Just go on with your pathetic life, living off of daddy." His jaw clamped shut and I could see the muscles twitching as he grinded his teeth. No one had the balls to speak to him this way. I ripped my purse off the back of the chair and stormed out into the warm night air. Gulping breaths as I stomped all the way back to my car.

I got into my car and pulled my cell out of my bag. I was fuming mad. To think that I even considered going out with him just so he can try and feed me bits of information about my dad. He probably didn't even know anything else. I'll just have to figure this out for myself. Maybe I can hire a private investigator. Or worse; maybe just confront my mom once and for all. I tapped out a text to Sarah.

Me: Furious. Coffee was pointless; Randy=douche bag
Sarah: I'm having an equally shitty night. I'm coming over.

143

Wow. I guess things didn't go well with Josh and her dinner. I drove home feeling defeated and agitated but Sarah always knows how to talk through our frustrations. She has the personality that even if things were falling down around you; you left the conversation feeling just a tad bit more positive and refreshed. That's why she kicks ass at her job. Being an Occupational Therapist; Sarah processes information in a way that makes it more manageable; digestible. And then she takes pieces of your troubles and spins them into a positive experience. I truly love her like a sister and I don't know what I would do without her.

By the time I pulled into my driveway; she was already there. She was laid out on the couch with her arm over her eyes. I dumped my bags and purse on the floor and she didn't even budge. I kneeled down on the couch beside her and peaked under her arm. Her face was wet with tears and her bottom lip trembled.

"Babe, what happened, tell me." I said in a soothing voice.

"He met someone else." She sobbed out.

"What!" I snatched her arm away from her face so I could see her eyes. "What the hell."

"Mmhmmm. He didn't want to tell me at first. He just wanted to end things. But I could tell he was hiding something." Sarah sat up and reached for a tissue to blow her nose. "Al, we didn't even make it into the restaurant. This all happened in the damn parking lot."

I came to sit next to her on the couch; we sat knee to knee as we both stared off into my quiet house. "What did you say? Is this why he needed the break? Was he cheating?" I asked her.

"I don't know. First it started off with, 'hey maybe we need more time to figure things out'. We both agreed we were enjoying our alone time. But then he got all twitchy and said that maybe it was better if we just ended things on a high note instead of us fighting and hating each other. He was acting so strange. So when I pushed further, Josh blurted out that he met someone." She sobbed louder and the tears flowed freely. Never in a million year would I think Josh would cheat on Sarah; he idolized her. "I couldn't even say anything when he told me he met someone. I just stood there dumbfounded. He said that he met her a while ago; she works at the same college. And they started spending more time together in the last two weeks. Josh says he hasn't touched her; not like it really matters. He wants to be with her, not me." I held Sarah in my arms and waited until she calmed down.

"Oh sweetie, I know this is the last thing you want to hear; but maybe it was for the best. You said you were enjoying being a part. Maybe this was the best way things could have ended. I know hearing him say he's into another girl, hurts. But maybe it's just time. Time to move on?" I patted her back and the tears slowed and her hiccups started to subside.

"I know. I just didn't expect it to hurt so bad." She blew her nose again and rubbed her red, puffy eyes. "We hugged and it felt weird to walk away from him. I just got in my car and drove away. That's it. The end." Sarah said numbly.

"We'll get through this. Hey, at least we'll be single together. That's a first." I said lightly. She half laughed as we hugged.

She shook her head and took a deep breath, "Tell me about fuckwit. I knew he was going to be a complete asshole."

I told her what happened at the coffee house and about me storming out; she laughed but couldn't believe the balls on him. I still couldn't believe how he talked to me. But it was over with. One more chapter behind me. We both took showers and I lent her some comfy pajamas. We had work the next morning, she had to go to the city office; but we spent the night binge watching scary movies until we passed out on the couch. I knew with her by my side; I'd never feel completely alone and everything was going to be ok. For the first time in about a month; Angel didn't creep into my mind, the nightmares stayed away and I got a decent night's sleep.

I woke up the next morning; crept off to workout as Sarah snored lightly on my couch. By the time I was done; she had showered and had a towel wrapped around her body. Her eyes were puffy from all the crying last night, but she had a light smile on her face and renewed determination.

"You mind if I raid your closet? I don't have time to run home and change before going into the city."

"Yea, of course. Just not my pink skater skirt; I'm wearing that today." I shouted as I got into the shower. I finished getting ready for work and came out to a fluffy omelet and apple slices. Sarah was a morning person like me; and she loved breakfast.

"Ooo.. thanks. You didn't have to make me breakfast." I clapped my hands together.

"Well, just a thank you for last night. And, you're getting kind of skinny. You working out too much?" Sarah cocked her head at me, taking in that my outfit that was a little loose on me.

"Ugh, I've been doing two-a-days on the bike. I can't sleep unless my body is exhausted." I admitted as I shoved the apple in my mouth.

Sarah plopped down next to me at the kitchen island with her own omelet. "You miss him?" She stated more than asked.

"Yea. I can't stop thinking about him. It's everything from the way he looked at me, to the way he felt. How easy he was to talk to." I shook my head trying to push the images out of my head. "I miss him. I feel like we ended way before we even got started."

I got to work and put my purse away, turned on my computer when Tim came knocking on my office door.

"Good morning Alexa." Tim was always so cheerful. It was a shame we didn't get a chance to hang out outside of work. Tim worked a second job as a bartender in the city.

"Hey." I said with a yawn.

"Man, late night? You look like hell." He leaned on the door jam as he eyed my sleepy face.

"Ugh, yea. Didn't get to sleep til late and thanks. I love hearing that I look like shit." I giggled.

"Well your outfit is cute. But maybe some coffee will perk you up? Wanna run out with me. I could use a latte before I start back to back meetings in an hour." Tim offered. There was a cute coffee stand just down the street.

"Oh yea. That sounds like a good idea. Let me just grab my wallet." I bent to pick up my bag.

"I got you girl. You can fill me in on some of the gossip I missed out on about your hot motorcycle guy." He locked arms with me as we left the building.

"Oh. Angel? We're not together anymore. After the whole photo incident; it just didn't work out." I left it hanging. I wasn't in the frame of mind to divulge all my drama. Besides, I knew Tim was just fishing for gossip. He slung his arm over my shoulders as we walked down the sidewalk. The smell of fresh coffee permeated through the air, making me have a little bounce in my step.

"Well, listen, I have a really cute friend I can set you up with. He's a regular at the bar, works in stocks or some shit. But he's hot and loaded." Tim spoke excitedly; trying to set me up on a date.

We were just about to reach the coffee stand when I heard screeching tires next to us. I looked over at the street in time to see an F150 slam on their brakes at the traffic light. My eyes locked on the driver's; it was Angel. He looked pissed. My feet froze to the spot and my body went rigid. Tim, not even paying attention to the traffic, kept talking. The whole world stopped as I watched Angel's dark eyes and hard body stomp out past the honking cars and before I could react; he had Tim by the throat. The force of Angel pulling Tim away from me had me stumble a few steps back, knocking me off balance. I watched in horror as Tim clawed at Angel's arms, stunned and confused. Angel pushed him down to his knees and in one quick, effortless motion; Angel's fist connected with Tim's nose. Blood erupted from his face, spraying my white sneakers and splattering on my pink skirt. It happened so fast but felt like slow motion.

I didn't even realize I was screaming. I yanked on Angel's vest and arms to try to get him to stop. Tim was on the ground now, holding his face with one hand and trying to block Angel with the other. Noises went muffled and I felt like my head was being held under water when Angel finally looked back over his shoulder at me. His eyes dark and lips curled up in a snarl. He smelled like man, and sweat and leather. That split second our eyes connected had my tears dripping down my cheeks.

I heard Roman's voice yelling out to Angel as sirens started to ring out in the near distance. Angel stood before me; anger and sadness in his face. I stepped back away from him, my hands up to guard myself against the insanity that just played out before me. And then he was gone. My attention turned to Tim as I knelt down on the ground trying to pull him up to standing. He looked woozy and light headed from the amount of blood that came out of his nose. There were people standing all around us; a woman offering a handful of napkins; others with their cell phones out, probably trying to call the police or take video.

"Oh my god, Tim." I had him by the shoulders when he finally got the bleeding under control.

"Just don't Alexa." He snapped out. It felt like a verbal back hand as he stepped back away from me.

"I'm, I'm sorry." Was all I could stammer out. Blood covered his shirt and the swelling in his face seemed almost immediate. He turned his back to me and walked back to the shelter.

I stood on the sidewalk with the blood drying into a dark red splatter pattern beneath my feet, watching Tim walk away from me. My body still not connected with my racing mind. People just stopped and stared. No one offered help. No one asked if I was ok. I looked down at my bloodied sneakers and forced my shaking legs to walk back to the shelter. When I entered the building; there were whispers and people talking in huddles; eyeballing me and pointing. I kept my head down as I ran-walked into my office, grabbed my belongings and snuck out the back exit that led to the parking lot.

Chapter 17

Alexa

"I'm sorry but we're going to have to let you go." That simple sentence rang over and over in my head. When I got the phone call about three hours after I got home from the office; I didn't even try to fight it. I was nodding my head; even though my boss couldn't see me; and offered them no remorse; no argument, not even a single word as the founder of the Shelter asked me not to return to work. He explained sternly and decisively that it was in the best interest in the safety of the children and employees in the shelter that I be let go from my position immediately. He explained that he would have Sarah box up any belongings I had in my office and human resources will be in touch with the termination paperwork.

I sat on the edge of my bed. Numb. The images of this morning danced in front of my eyes over and over. I heard the screaming; the pleading; the begging; now realizing it had come from my own mouth. I close my eyes and I can still smell the blood and sweat. I sat in my day-nightmare for a long time.

I glanced down at my clothes and slowly started to peel off my sneakers, skirt and top. I had dropped my jean jacket and purse at the door. My clothes fell in a heap as I dragged myself to the shower and turned the water to 'hot'. I needed to burn today off my skin. I needed to feel something; because right now; my head was in the clouds and my body ached. The water washed over me as the steam filled the room. I cleaned the speckles of blood off my legs and arms. And then I washed again. I let my head fall back to the cool tiles as the bubbles circled the drain and my eyes became sleepy. I toweled off quickly, not even bothering to get dressed; dove under my blankets and closed my eyes.

I woke up to Sarah on the side of my bed, trying to shake me awake. I felt groggy as I looked out of my window. It was night time. I sat up, covering my bare breasts as Sarah pushed back my messy hair away from my face.

"Hey." She said quietly; like she was talking to a child.

"Hi. What time is it?" I asked, my voice raspy from sleep.

"Um, it's 8:40 PM. Did you sleep all day?" She asked as she sat down on my bed. "I texted and called when Roger called me in to clean up your desk."

"Oh." I looked around. My surroundings finally coming into focus. "I don't have my phone, it's in my bag."

"It's ok. I let myself in. Um, here, let me get you a tee shirt." Sarah got up and went into my closet; pulling out an oversized Bon Jovi Band tee shirt and a pair of soft cotton shorts.

I pulled the tee over my head and wiggled into my shorts. I rubbed my face and gathered my insane bed hair into a messy bun. Instead of Sarah pounding me with a million questions about today; she simply got into bed with me and snuggled into the pillow. We didn't need to talk. She saw the pain in my face.

"What did Roger tell you?" I asked quietly after a good amount of time passed and I was more awake. Roger Miller was the founder of the Shelter; a true pilgrim of the community and friends with my mother.

"Well. He called me and asked me to come down to the shelter. I was just finishing up a meeting so I got there as soon as I could. The place was so quiet. No one would look at me as I walked into Roger's office. Obviously he couldn't go into details but said that you'd be let go due to some external issues." She rolled to her back and stared at the ceiling. "I think I got everything. You never really kept much in the office besides your water bottle and extra sweater." Sarah let out a sigh.

"A couple of girls stopped me on the way out to my car; filled me in on what happened. Did Angel really do that to Tim?" She whispered as if saying it out loud would catapult me into tears.

"Yea. He did." I breathed out. "Sarah, it happened so fast." I propped myself up on my elbow. "And when he finally stopped; he looked at me and the entire world stopped spinning. He looked so mad. And sad. Tortured."

"Did he say anything to you?" Sarah sat up and looked at me with her eyebrows furrowed.

"Nope. Roman was there and he was shouting at Angel and that was it. He was gone before I could even open my mouth." I stretched my neck, cracking it left and right. I must have been sleeping tightly curled up because my entire body was sore.

"Fuck." Sarah let out and fell back to the mattress.

Angel

The truck sped away from the intersection. I beat my fists into the dashboard and until Roman threw his arm across my chest yelling at me to stop. Taylor was on the phone, trying to find out if the police were on our ass as he looked left and right out of the backseat windows. I looked down at my hands, I had blood all over them and my knuckles on my right hand were split open.

"Fuck man, what the fuck." Roman bellowed as he made a sharp left turn down an alley towards the clubhouse. At least we got off the main road in case the truck's description was called into the police. Roman slammed the truck into park once we got to the dead end section where the clubhouse sat.

"Angel. Talk." He demanded.

I hung my head in my hands and just breathed for a beat.

"I'mma go in. Make sure no one called in your description to the police. I'll let you know if I hear anything." Taylor said cooly as he got out of the truck and went inside the club.

Roman just sat looking at me. The air between us was thick with unanswered questions.

"I just lost it." I said almost to myself, shaking my head. I stared out the window watching bikes come and go. No one else was taking notice of us sitting here.

"I lost my shit when I saw his arms around her. She looked happy; and I couldn't handle it. I saw fucking red, man." I glanced at my brother's unjudging eyes.

Roman nodded, understanding the pain I was feeling. "I know bro. But, you beat the shit out of that guy. In the middle of the street." He said with a laugh.

I went to put my hand on the handle to get out of the truck when I looked back at Roman rubbing his hands down his face. "I'm gonna head home. I'm exhausted and I smell like shit." I grunted.

"Alright, I'm not far behind you. I could use some sleep. Be home in a bit, I'll just check in with Prez." Roman agreed.

I got on my bike and rode towards home. The cool morning air gave me some energy back but the images of Alexa's scared and disappointed face kept flashing in my head. The last thing I wanted to do was hurt her. I wasn't even sure if I knocked her down. Did I scare her? Did I break the guy's face? There was so much blood. When the guy yelled that he 'liked cock', it didn't even register until now that I've seen him before. At Alexa's work. They must work together. I made a fool out of myself. I went crazy when I saw another man touch Alexa. She's mine. I want her to be mine.

I slammed the front door closed behind me when I got home. The house was a pig sty once again, garbage covered the kitchen counters and Roman left dirty pots on the stove. I stripped my clothes off; not wanting to deal with any of it. My shirt was splattered with blood and sticking to my chest and stomach.My jeans and boots were caked with dirt from the tunnels. The last two days were intense and it was starting to make me feel crazy. I ran the water in the shower; the water never reached above lukewarm. I stood under the spray and ran my hands down my face, closing my eyes as Alexa plagued my mind along with the man I killed in the tunnel replaying over and over. I braced myself on the walls of the shower and hung my head and let the water wash away my sins. I pushed the image of myself holding the gun and splattering that guy's brains all over the sides of the tunnel, out of my head and focused on Alexa. Her beautiful face and her sun kissed skin. The fresh smell of her hair and her plump pink lips. I washed my body and stroked my hard dick slowly. It was almost painful. I missed her hands on me and her tight, sweet pussy. I fisted myself faster and harder as the water became chilly and let out a loud growl as I came all over the sides of the shower wall. I felt some of the pressure in my balls and chest release but nothing would take away my heart ache over her. I wrapped a towel around my waist and went into the bedroom. Fuck Roman, he can sleep on the couch when he got home. I kicked the sheets off the bed and I was asleep before my head even hit the mattress.

Alexa

I tossed and turned all night. I regretted sleeping all day; but my body just refused to get up and face reality. Sarah had stayed with me until she was sure I wasn't going to do anything crazy like show up at Los Demonios Locos clubhouse or anything. I watched terrible reality tv reruns until 3AM and finally popped a Tylenol PM and waited for sleep to come. I must have drifted off; because the next thing I remember was my mother yelling my name from my kitchen.

I glanced over at my nightstand, my phone reading 6:46AM. I rolled out of bed and stumbled to my doorway where my mother was standing in the kitchen with her hands on her hips. She was already dressed for work in an army green pants suit that fit like a glove, high heeled spiked shoes and hair pulled into a neat low bun. She was the face of professionalism. And she looked madder than a pitbull on a short leash.

"Mom." I said flatly. Not like I *wasn't* expecting this.

"Alexa." She said drawn out with a sigh. "Well, obviously I know what happened at work yesterday. And I know that you were fired. Do you have any idea what it's like to get a phone call from Roger apologizing that he had to let you go; and under those circumstances?" She moved around the kitchen, judging and taking in every corner of my space with a disapproving look. It was like she was working the room in a courthouse but it was me that she was judging; picking apart.

I crossed my arms over my chest and worked on steadying my breaths. I wanted to scream out that it wasn't my fault. But how could I not take any of the blame? "Mom, I don't really know what to say about all of this. I don't apologize for my relationship with Angel; only regret that the mess I caused with Randy resulted in all of this." I shrugged my shoulders. I knew nothing I said would be good enough of an explanation.

"I'm giving you until the end of the week to find a place of your own." My mom shot out as she turned to face me.

I barely reacted, only raised my eyebrows in acknowledgement. "Fine." It was time to get out from under my mother, stand on my own two feet and not keep apologizing for living my life. It was obvious we were very different people with very different motives. While I was on her bad side, it dawned on me that now was as good a time as any to press about my father.

"I want to know about my father. You can't keep this from me forever." Her face turned from shock to stone in a matter of seconds. She schooled her emotions and held her lips tightly.

"No. There's nothing to tell."

"Mom, I'm not stupid. I found the pictures. I know about the hotel, the concert tickets. *He* was someone. I need to know. You own me that much."

Her anger erupted before me. She swung her arms in frustration and huffed out a low growl. "You had no right to go into my private files!" She yelled. Her shrill voice echoed in my ears and bounced off the walls.

I lost it on her, I slapped my palm down on the cold marble countertop then stepped close to my mother's face. "I have never asked you for anything. I obeyed your every wish growing up. I was a good kid. I never asked for your time because you had no time to give to me. Give me this! I want to know who he is. Why can't I know?" I spoke through my teeth, my anger rising to match hers. I clenched my fists at my side and stood tall. We stared at each other; willing each other to break contact. I didn't back down.

Her bottom lip quivered slightly as she took a calming breath and whispered, "He didn't want us. He left me the second he found out I was pregnant." She backed up away from me. My mom slowly made her way to the door; leaving me with my mouth open and confused. That was all she was going to tell me? "One week. You have one week to be gone." She spoke quietly over her shoulder. Then she was gone with a slam of the door; leaving me empty and alone in my kitchen.

Chapter 18

Alexa

I showered and changed into jeans and a tank top. I had a renewed determination to get the hell out of my house. While I was in the shower, I thought about all the small towns that I loved hanging out in; I always thought it would be really cool to live above a small shop or restaurant and be able to walk to everything. I decided I'd hit up South Street, it was close to where Sarah lived and had the best shops and boutiques. I had some money in savings but I figured before I started my house hunting; I'll stop at the bank. My mom had told me when I graduated high school I had a trust in my name that I would have access to after the age of 25. Money was never a problem for me; so there was no need to ever touch it. In fact, I almost forgot I even had a trust. Maybe some of that money will come in handy to rent a new place and carry me until I found a new job.

There was a bank on the corner of South Street and Maple. So I parked in the public parking lot and figured I would walk up and down the street looking for For Rent signs. And if that didn't work; I could always try the online classifieds and rentals. I stopped in Desert Valley Bank and waited for a bank teller to become available.

A man with graying hair came up to me asking if I needed help, "Good morning. Is there something I could help you with?" He guided me to his desk and offered me a coffee, which I was very thankful for. I was still tired and I sure had circles under my eyes.

"Yes, actually. I do my banking here and I understand that I have a trust fund that is now available to me. I was wondering if I could find out about that and see about taking some money out for renting an apartment." I asked with my hands laced over my crossed legs.

"Yes, of course. Your name?" He sat poised at his computer.

"Alexa Ramirez."

"Alexa Ramirez." He repeated as he typed it into his computer. "Are you the daughter of Sonya Ramirez?" He asked with a raised eyebrow.

"The one and only." I replied with a smirk.

"Oh, it's so nice to meet you. I've helped your mother on occasion. She's very sweet." He said with a big smile. I smiled back, reading his name tag on his neatly pressed shirt. Bill Evans. "Thanks Mr. Evans."

"Oh, please, call me Bill. I just need a driver's license for confirmation and social security number."

I gave him my credentials and waited as he printed out a statement of my trust account.

Handing me the printed paper, "Ok, here's what your trust is looking like. You're over 25 so you have complete access to it and can take money out of it."

My eyes bugged so far out of my head and nearly choked on my coffee that I was still swallowing. Two point five million dollars.

'Ms. Ramirez? Are you ok? Is this not what you were expecting." Bill asked with a slight giggle.

"Ummm. No. Ummm. I was never told how much was in it." I just stared at the paper. Oh. My. God.

"Should I give you a few minutes?" He asked; leaning back into his chair.

"Um, is there any way you could tell me where the money came from? If someone was depositing money into this account?" I asked, still staring at the paper, shaking my head.

"Well, I can't disclose where and how the money was deposited. It does look like it transferred banks about twenty five years ago or so from a bank in Mexico. I can try and get in touch with them, but I'm pretty certain they won't give me the originator's name for the account. Let me make a phone call while you look that over." Bill rose from his seat and left me alone at the desk, with the paper firmly held between my fingers.

Mexico? The money came from Mexico. What the hell. Was this my father's parting gift? I sat there for what felt like twenty minutes reading the details of the bank statement over and over again. The document contained details of the trust's purpose; listed no beneficiaries other than 'Alexa Ramirez' and managed by the trustee, Desert Valley Bank.

Bill sat back down with more papers in his hands. "Here, these are some facts and information sheets about trust fund accounts to read up on. I'd love to be able to help guide you in any way to avoid any taxable situations. Or I can refer you to a financial advisor outside of this bank. Oh, and I did have a bit of luck with the bank in Mexico."

I interrupted looking up at Bill, "Does my mother know how much is in this account?"

"Nope. She does not have access in any kind to the account; so we would never disclose that to her. If she knows; then she would have likely found out from the person who created it." Bill said as he examined my face.

"So, my mom didn't open this trust fund for me?" I asked, but it was more of a statement.

"No, she did not. The bank in Mexico named a man. Antonio Castillo. Their laws are a little more loose than the U.S's but they did not have any contact information for him." He scribbled down the name and handed me the paper.

"Antonio Castillo?" I said his name in a whisper. "Ok. Well. Jeez, I don't even know what to say. Um, I'll take the name of the financial advisor; that'll be a start. I'm looking for apartments today; so I may need to write a check from my personal account."

"Ok. Here's my card and the info you need. You have any questions, Alexa, just call me. I'll be more than happy to help you out." He stood and we shook hands. I left the bank still staring down at the paper that read. $2,500,000.00 next to my name. The man's name ran in a loop through my head. I walked in a daze towards the line of shops down South Street.

The sound of motorcycles snapped me out of my day-dream and I almost didn't want to look up and take a peek at the riders. It wasn't Angel. Or Roman or Taylor or anyone else I would recognize from the Los Demonios Locos; but they wore their cut. The big letter spelled out on their vest along with the skull with roses for eyes. They passed me in a rumble of speeding tires and when I looked around to see how far I was since I left the bank; I noticed an adorable little boho boutique with a big For Rent sign on the adjacent door that led to the upstairs apartment. I quickly got out my phone and dialed the number.

After chatting quickly with the landlord; she agreed to meet me in a half hour to show me the space. I wandered through the boutique. They had beautiful boho inspired tops with soft lace details and summer dresses with paisley patterns. I talked briefly with the sales girl who seemed really sweet and eager to make a sale; when I explained that I was interested in renting the apartment above the store. She actually knew the landlord; she owned the store as well and told me she was an older woman that had recently gotten divorced and opened up her dream clothing shop with her divorce settlement money.

The landlord and shop owner arrived. She was great. Shirley Hadley was a middle aged woman with red hair and a kind face. She shook my hand excitedly and led me upstairs. The space was open and bright. A small kitchen spanned the one side of the floor plan with plenty of room for couches and kitchen table in the main area. There was one bedroom, kind of on the small side but had great closet space and one bathroom. The bathroom had a beautiful claw foot tub and plenty of storage with a built in vanity and shelves. Shirley explained that when she first left her husband; she rented and remodeled this apartment and when her divorce was finalized; the same day, she bought the shop below and started her brand new life. I loved Shirley right off the bat. She had great energy and was filled with positivity.

Without thinking twice; I told her "I'll take it!" There was just something about this place that felt so right and I didn't even want to look at another place. We went over the details of rent and so on; there was parking out back for my car. Thank god I didn't have to park on the street everyday. I gave her all my information and she said I could move in right away. Shirley left after giving me a big hug; clapping her hands, she said she was excited to be a part of my new journey and handed me the keys right there. She said she'd email me the contracts and so forth and I handed her a check for the first and last rent and security deposit.

As soon as I got back to my car; I texted Sarah and let her know I was moving out! On the way home; I stopped and bought a trunk load of boxes and bubble wrap and could not wait to get home and pack. Sarah texted back telling me that she'd be over after work to help. In the meantime I called a few local moving companies and got quotes for moving my furniture.

I thought that the day I had to move out of my home; I'd be upset. But I was anything but! I was excited for my life to finally start. Maybe this was the kick in the ass to get me going with what *I* wanted to do.

The next few days went by so fast. I packed all day and Sarah came over at night and we ate on the floor while we packed and laughed at some of the crazy things I held onto over the years. Old tee shirts from private school, photo books with prom and graduation. Ticket stubs and old phones I had held onto. The moving trucks were coming tomorrow to move out the furniture and I had slowly moved over the contents of my closet and kitchen during the day.

While Sarah and I sat cross legged between the towers of boxes and packaging material I decided to tell her about the trust fund. I didn't tell her at first because I could hardly believe it myself. Also, I was determined to hunt down this, Antonio Castillo; so I had put in a few phone calls to private investigators in Mexico. You could imagine how difficult it was to find one that would take my case. It was like a needle in a haystack.

"So, I have some news to tell you." I said with a scrunched

up nose.

Sarah was mid bite into her fork full of salad when her eyes shot up to mine. "Oh god, do I even want to know?" She mumbled.

"You do. So I went to the bank the other day because my mom had told me a while ago that I had a trust fund there."

"Okay, I'm listening." She eyed me skeptically.

"Well. It's for 2.5 million dollars."

Sarah choked on her salad and pieces of cucumber fell out of her mouth. "What? Oh my god! You're lying."

"I'm not." I laughed. I handed her some napkins to clean up her mess, and dug out the papers from my back pocket.

"Oh my god, Alexa. This is insane!" Sarah held the trust fund statement in her hands, eyes scanning over the details of the account. "Damn, your mom really set you up with this."

"Um, my mom didn't set up this trust." I answered with a raised eyebrow. Sarah's eyes snapped to mine as she cocked her head.

"No. Are you saying this is from your *father*?" Sarah often read my mind, this time she was spot on.

"Well, at least I *think* it's him. The bank was able to tell me that it originated from a bank in Mexico by a man named Antonio Castillo. But they couldn't give any contact information."

"Really? That's insane. This is insane." She said wide eyed; shaking the piece of paper. We both laughed. "Did you tell your mom? Do you think she knows?" I got up and shuffled some boxes around while Sarah rapidly fired questions at me.

"I don't know if she knows how much it was for; she's not on the account, so she's never had access. I'm definitely not going to tell her. After the way she acted the other day; I think it's best if we just talk when we absolutely have to."

"Ugh, that's just sad. I can't believe your mom won't talk to you about your dad. It must have been really bad, ya know? I mean, to deliberately hide your kid's father from her?" Sarah helped clean up after our dinner and hopped up on the counter while I washed our dishes.

I turned to her with a smirk and wiggled my eyebrows at her. "Well, I'm going to find him. I hired a private investigator. He's a retired cop that used to live around here but moved to Mexico. I gave him all the information I had on him; scanned the pictures I had and hopefully he'll come up with something!"

"Really? That's pretty awesome. I really hope you find your answers, Alexa. You deserve it." We talked for a bit as we packed up the last of the kitchen into boxes. The moving trucks won't be here until noon tomorrow and then I'll be officially in my own place by tomorrow night. "Hey, let's go out on Friday to celebrate! There's that bar that just opened down on South Street and Grand. I think it's called The Mile. It looks pretty cool from the outside, it's supposed to be like a bar and restaurant on the main floor with a loungey vibe, dance space upstairs. It's been a shitty month; let's just go and destress."

I hesitated to share her enthusiasm for going out. I was excited about my new place but I still wanted to wallow in my heart ache over Angel. "Oh, um, I don't know. I'm not really in the mingling mood." I groaned.

Sarah hopped off the counter and put both her hands on my shoulders. "Listen, I feel like shit too. But I think if we just go out and try to have a good time; we'll see that we can put all of this behind us and start a new chapter. Believe me, I'm not ready to go sleeping with some other guy. For fuck's sake, I've only ever slept with Josh. But it won't hurt to have a little fun." Sarah looked me in the eyes with her big bright smile and I couldn't say no.

"Fine. Okay. I guess you're right." I conceded.

Sarah clapped her hands and did a little dance. "Woohoo! Okay, I gotta get going, I have an early meeting but call me if you need my help tomorrow night. I'm sure you'll have your hands full with settling in. I can't wait to see your new place." She grabbed her bag and kissed me hard on my forehead. "Oh! And I'm pretty sure we can walk to The Mile from your place! So I'll come over and we can get ready together."

"Okay! Sounds like a plan." I said with a forced smile that

Sarah shook head about. After she left; I laughed to myself. Sarah was such a great friend. I'll humor her and try my best to have a good time. In the meantime; I wanted to get some rest so that I'll be ready for the moving truck tomorrow.

Angel

Not another run. Fuck. I was sick of going down into the tunnels to babysit the prospects. The Prez was impressed with the way we handled the Serpent's mule and decided that Roman and I are essential to weeding out the competition. There's been a lot of backlash from killing one of their members; but Prez and VP said they had things under control. Taylor had gotten some intel that a few Serpent's had rented out an old farm house on the outskirts of town to keep an eye on us. So we've spent a few nights scoping them out and following them to a tunnel system they were using to get to our Mexican distributors. Tonight we were going to follow them, and cut them off. If this final warning didn't work; I know the two clubs would go into battle. And I wasn't looking forward to that.

Roman and I left the clubhouse around 1AM to head off the Serpents. Two other trucks followed, filled with Los Demonios; but they were there for backup while we went down into the tunnels. We wanted to make sure this wasn't going to be an ambush. Like clockwork, we navigated the tunnels where the Serpent's were prone to showing back up after making the trade off with the Mexicans. We waited with guns in our hands.

"This is fucked, I can feel it." I whispered to Roman where he was crouched down in the tunnel.

"Shut up man. It'll be fine." Roman barked back. He was just as sick of doing tunnel runs as I was. The air quality sucked and the tunnels smelled like stale urine. Sweat dripped off of our heads and landed in the dirt. I barely could stand fully in most of the tunnels and my back was killing me from ducking down. Two hours passed before we heard the shuffling of feet. There was a strange moaning sound and it sounded like someone was being dragged.

Before the Serpents came into view, Roman knocked out some of the lights that lined the tunnel; leaving us in darkness and adding to the element of surprise. The two guys were practically on top of us before they realized we had guns to their heads. They were young; prospects by the patch on their cut and looked exhausted. They were pulling a heavy wagon behind them that was packed high and covered with a big canvas tarp.

There was plenty of pleading and begging on their parts for us to not kill them. This was their first run-in with Los Demonios but they all had heard what we did to their last mule. We dropped the guys down on their knees with guns to both of their foreheads. Tears ran down the one guy's face while the other simply closed his eyes, accepting his fate. Roman and I looked at each other; wordless but we knew we couldn't kill these guys in cold blood. They were submitting to us. We weren't cold blooded killers; but we would defend ourselves and our club. In true MC fashion, we couldn't just let them off easy so instead we decided to take the fingers of both mens' right hand. This will teach them not to touch what doesn't belong to them and they would be able to go back to the Serpent's clubhouse and show them our warning. The rest will be up to Prez and his officers.

After the screaming and bloodshed; the Serpent's wrapped up their hands in their shirts and we made them pull the wagon the rest of the way to the entrance of the tunnel; where our trucks were waiting. Our brothers were waiting nearby and once the Serpents were on the road driving away from us; they followed them to ensure they wouldn't double back.

Roman and I were left to load their drugs into the compartment built into the bed of Roman's F150. When we lifted the canvas cover, curled up between the heavily wrapped packs of heroin; a small boy was hiding with a baby in his arms.

Roman stepped back, "What the fuck." We both looked at each other and back at the boy. I put my hand on my hips as

I peered down at the boy and baby as if they were aliens. The boy must have only been around three years old and the baby, as small as a newborn. "I knew this was going to be fucked up, man. I fucking knew it." The boy started to cry when he looked up at us with big brown eyes. The baby in his arms started to wiggle and squirm. The boy automatically shushed and rocked the baby in his arms. I knelt down so I wouldn't scare the child any more than we had.

"Hola. My llamo Angel. Quien es? *Hello. My name is Angel. Who are you?*"

The boy looked between me and Roman, his lips quivering as he sniffled. "Soy Carlos. Y mi hermano es Miguel. *I'm Carlos. And my brother is Michael.*" His whole body was shaking and he looked hot and sweaty. Roman backed away to grab a bottle of water for him.

"No tienes que tener miedo de nosotros. ¿Dónde están tus padres? *You don't have to be afraid of us. Where are your parents?*" I asked as I handed the boy the water. He was hesitant; but he slowly sat up and took the bottle carefully from my hand. The baby settled back down; he pulled the baby to his chest.

"No lo se. Me dijeron que tenía que ir con los Serpientes y no volver. *I don't know. I was told I needed to go with the Serpents and never come back.*" The boy drank slowly as Roman and I looked between each other. We backed away so we could talk and the boy just watched us with tears growing in his eyes.

"What the fuck are we going to do?" Roman whispered. "I gotta call Prez."

"Fuck if I know. It's not like we can just return them from where they came from." I leaned on the tailgate of the truck while Roman got Prez on the phone.

"Prez, we got a problem......Yea, we took care of the competition..... There was a surprise in the package. .... No....... Um, there's a kid, and a baby in the transport......Yea..... Prez, I can't do that. .... I...... No, but. ....." I was only hearing Roman's side of the conversation but it didn't sound good. There was a long beat of silence from Roman. "No, Prez, I'll handle it.... I've got an idea.....We'll check in in a few hours." Roman hung up and kicked the dirt as he walked back to me.

"What did he say. And don't tell me that we're killing a couple of kids; because I draw the fucking line at killing kids." I crossed my arms over my chest and stood tall; bracing myself for what Roman was about to tell me.

"He wanted us to leave them in the desert." Roman started to load the product into the truck. "But we're not doing that. Come on; let's get everything loaded."

"Ro, what are we doing with the kids?" I yelled at him. I must have startled the baby because he started to cry and the boy rocked him and spoke softly to him.

"I have a plan, but you're not gonna like it." Roman laughed. "I'll tell you once we're on the road." It took a few minutes to get everything secure and the kids in the back seat.

Roman drove and I looked in the back seat at the boy who looked scared but trusting that we weren't going to harm them. "Okay, so what's the big plan?" I said as I narrowed my eyes at Roman who had a big ol smirk on his face.

"We're gonna take them to Alexa." He said casually.

I closed my eyes and just shook my head. "No. No way I'm involving her. At this point she may even call the cops on us." I said sternly.

"Bro, she won't call the cops. This is what she does, right? Take in children. Angel, she won't turn them away. It's the only choice we've got here." Roman was right. We couldn't just drop these kids off at a shelter without getting a million questions about where they came from. Butterflies swarmed my stomach at the thought of seeing Alexa. And I had to admit I was terrified to see her reaction to all of this. But Roman was right; these kids only had us right now. And we needed to put them somewhere safe. The baby started to cry as we pulled onto the highway that led back into town.

"Stop at the store and pick up some diapers and formula before we get to Alexa's or this kids gonna scream bloody murder soon." I barked at Roman. The crying grew more frantic and high pitched.

"No te preocupes. Vamos a traerle leche y pañales a tu hermano bebe. Tenemos un lugar seguro para los dos. Nos encargaremos de ti. *Don't worry. We'll get your baby brother some milk and diapers on the way. We have a safe place for you both. We'll take care of you.*" I explained to the young boy who visibly relaxed after hearing we were going to help them.

Roman stopped at the store and went in to buy supplies while I stayed in the truck with the kids. He came back out a few minutes later with two packs of diapers, a huge can of formula, loads of junk food and some gatorade. He smiled at me as he piled the bags into the backseat. Roman was tough when he needed to be; but inside he was a softy with a big heart. We drove out to Alexa's house; hoping the code she gave me to get into the development still worked.

As he punched the code in and the gates opened; Roman asked me, "You ready for this bro. I mean, it'll be fine. She won't be able to turn you away." Roman elbowed me as we pulled into her driveway. The lights were on in the guest house but the main house remained dark.

I took the baby in my arms and helped the boy down from the truck. He stared at the huge house with bewilderment as he stayed close to my side. He shuffled his feet behind me as we made our way to the side door and rang the doorbell. The baby cried softly and I pulled him to my chest as the boy gripped the back of my jeans. He was so scared; his small fingers trembled around my belt loops.

I scrubbed a hand over my face and ran my fingers through my hair. I must look and smell like a disaster. Definitely not the way I wanted to see Alexa again. But she was these kids' only hope. Roman worked on the bags of stuff he bought at the store and updated Prez as he paced her driveway when I heard footsteps coming down the stairs towards the door. I didn't even realize it was 5 oclock in the morning. We've pulled all nighters so often that my days were nights and nights were days. Alexa opened the door slowly, her face peeking out the side of the door.

Her eyes widened as she took me in with the sleeping baby in my arms.

"Angel." She gasped. Her hair was pulled into a messy bun and she wore a tight black tank top and silky green shorts. Her voice was sexy and raspy from sleeping and I tried my best to not pull her into my arms when she opened the door to stand in front of us. Her eyes darted to the small boy hiding behind my back and Roman was coming around to join us.

"What is this? What the hell is going on?" She whispered; still in shock.

"We need your help." Alexa studied my face as I spoke, softly biting her bottom lip. I tried not to scan her body; her nipples pebbling in the cool morning air. She pulled back the blanket from the baby, realizing that we were in one hell of a predicament.

"Come in." She said quietly as she led the four of us upstairs. The place was filled with boxes as I scanned around and Alexa took the baby from my arms.

Roman came in and dumped the bags on the counter top. "You going somewhere?" He blurted out.

"Um, I'm moving. Um, can someone tell me what the hell is going on here." She spoke so quietly as to not scare the boy who still hid behind my legs. She knelt down with the baby in her arms to see the boy and offered him her hand. He took it slowly and her face filled with kindness and love as she smiled at him.

"We ran into sort of a problem. Club business. But we hope you can help us out." Roman went on to explain a shortened version of how we acquired the children. She nodded but stayed silent. She refused to look me in the eyes and I was too focused on her beautiful face to speak. She handed Roman the baby as she sifted through the bags Roman brought in and made a bottle for the baby and laid out fresh diapers. The boy stayed quiet as Alexa handed him a banana and gatorade and she led him out to the island to sit while she moved around. Alexa was a natural with children. Watching her move silently as she cared for them made my chest ache; and I shifted the weight on my feet trying to push her out of my mind.

She handed Roman the bottle and showed him how to feed the baby. "Okay. Well, I gotta call Sarah. I need her to bring them to the shelter." Alexa explained after a long beat of silence.

"I don't want to involve anyone else. Can *you* bring the kids there?" I asked as her eyes finally met mine. Her honey brown eyes threatened to make me take her in my arms but her reply hit me like a knife to the gut.

"I don't work at the shelter anymore. I was fired." She said coldly. She grabbed her cell phone and walked into her bedroom to call Sarah.

Roman and I shuffled around. We helped ourselves to some snacks that he bought and cleaned up after the boy when she came out of her room; dressed in jeans and a sweatshirt.

"She's meeting us in the shelter parking lot in twenty minutes." She silently picked up the now sleeping baby and took the boy by his hand and led them downstairs back to our truck.

I watched her as she carefully got into the backseat of the truck with the baby tucked into her and the boy nestled in tight. She looked like an angel. Her eyes stayed on the children and avoided any talking or eye contact with me or Roman.

I heard her whispering to the boy. "No va a pasar nada. Mi amiga Sarah te va a ayudar y a mantenerte a salvo. *It 's going to be okay. My friend Sarah is going to help you and keep you safe.*" She rested her head lightly on top of the boy's head as we pulled into the parking lot. Sarah was already there. She stood next to her Jeep with a disappointed look on her face. Roman was the first out of the truck and strode up to Sarah like it was a day at the picnic.

"Hey, thanks for doing this." He smiled at her.

She breezed past him without a word to help Alexa down from the truck and took the baby from her. "I'll take them in." Sarah said quietly as she ruffled the boy's hair that now stood next to her.

"Roman, give Sarah the bags. She'll have to take them in by herself." Alexa instructed.

Sarah gave Alexa a kiss on the cheek and they shared a glance; but otherwise were quiet.

"I'll call you later, Al." Sarah called over her shoulder as she walked the boy and baby into the shelter's back entrance.

"We should go. Before someone sees us out here." Alexa instructed quietly.

We drove back to Alexa's house in silence. The air in the truck was so thick with tension but even Roman knew to keep his mouth shut. Alexa was doing us a huge favor and I didn't want to pressure her into talking to me if she didn't want to. I stared at Alexa's reflection from the side view mirror. She kept her head low, staring at her feet as we pulled into her driveway. As soon as Roman put the truck in park, Alexa was out of the truck and moving quickly to her door. I looked at Roman who raised his eyebrows at me and nodded in Alexa's direction; so I bolted out of the truck and raced after her.

"Alexa, wait. Can I talk to you?" I yelled after her. She was already turning the knob on the door before she stopped and turned on her toes.

The look on her face stopped me in my tracks as I got to where she was standing. "Angel. You treated me like a whore. You got me fired and *now* you want to talk to me?" She stood tall with her hands on her hips and took a big step towards me, getting in my face.

I was defeated. I looked at the ground and my hands fell to my sides. "I'm so sorry, Alexa. For everything." When I picked up my head, her eyes were already filled with angry tears. Her lips turned into a frown and her eyebrows knitted down. This was all wrong. There was no way to make this right.

"You did the right thing by bringing the children here. Thank you for that. Now, if there's nothing else; I need to go." She turned her body away from me.

"Alexa. I never wanted to hurt you." And before I got anything else out; she slammed the door in my face.

Chapter 19

Alexa

My doorbell rang at 9PM on the dot. Sarah bursted through the door when I buzzed her in and threw down her bags and gave me a huge hug. We talked briefly after the Roman/Angel ordeal and we both decided the whole thing was better left unspoken. The kids were safe; the shelter didn't ask any questions and they were keeping them together. It was up to the system to either find them a home or try and look for their parents in Mexico.

"Ok. First show me around then we'll get ready. Let's pour some pre-party drinks though." Sarah bounced up and down as she pulled a bottle of champagne from one of her bags. She popped the cork and I searched for glasses. I had most of my kitchen and bathroom essentials unpacked and organized. The movers came and it was pretty flawless. I only took the couches, my bedroom set and spin bike for the big stuff. The rest were boxes and bags. I half thought my mom would show up as I was leaving. But she never did. Not a phone call or email; nothing.

I showed Sarah around; she loved the bathroom and closets. The main seating area had an exposed brick wall that had built in wood shelves and big picture windows that overlooked the street below.

"Wow, this place is fantastic. I'm so happy for you, Al!" Sarah spun around, sipping her champagne. I was showered already; I just needed some makeup and to get dressed. I had no idea what to wear.

"Yea, I really love it. Shirley is the landlord and owns the shop below us; she's already been here to bring me pizza and bottle of wine when I moved in." I drank down my champagne;

letting the bubbles go right to my head. I needed tonight to just let go. I was so stressed out with everything that's been going on; I just want to forget if only for one night.

"Alright, I brought black jeans with a nude tank top body-suit. It shows just enough side boob to be sexy without being completely classless." Sarah giggled as she laid out her clothes. "What are you wearing?"

"Um. I have a cute black leather mini skirt that I've never worn before. I forgot I even had it but I found it when I was packing. And I have a white crop top tee and wedge booties?" I scratched my head. "Or.....I can wear jeans and a tight black cami?"

"NO. Leather skirt; all the way!" Sarah yelled excitedly. "Damn girl, you're gonna look hot!"

I couldn't help but laugh. We were like two teenagers going out for the first time. I poured us both a second glass of champagne and we worked on our makeup. I went for simple winged eyeliner and no eye shadow with a glossy lip; I left my hair half up, half down and waved it to get a beachy, sexy look. Sarah had a smokey eye with red lipstick and she put her hair up in two little buns on top of her head. She looked sexy and cute.

"Alright. You ready?" Sarah yelled from the kitchen. I came out from the bathroom and did a little spin for Sarah. She whistled and catcalled while I laughed and drained my glass.

"Oh my god. You're too much." We laughed together as we grabbed our purses and headed out to the bar.

We were just a block away when my stomach was dancing with butterflies. My palms were sweaty and I tried not to look nervous. Sarah looked over at me with a big smile on her face and laced her fingers with mine.

"Ok. We're gonna have fun. Stick together. And just try to relax." She squeezed my hand as we stepped in line to get in. There was a bouncer at the door checking ID's; it was already 11PM by the time we got there and there was a short line already waiting to get in. As we stood in line the low rumble of motorcycles reached my ears. A few bikes were already parked in the side lot across the street; but I forced myself to not even look at them. The motorcycles turned into the parking lot with a rev of their engines and Sarah and I gave each other death glares and I wrinkled my nose at her.

"Stop. Don't think about it. This night is about you and me. If you get creeped out or anything; we can go. I think some of the guys from the gym are here; I overheard them talking about coming tonight. So maybe we can find them and I'll introduce you." Sarah pulled me into the doorway as we handed our ID's to the bouncer. Without a second glance, he let us in and we walked up the stairs to the lounge/dance area.

The lounge upstairs was decently packed. Bodies swayed on the dance floor and there were booths lining the room filled with chatting groups. Sarah and I made our way to the bar. The bartender was adorable. Dark hair with that messy sexy look, blue eyes and dimples for days. He flashed Sarah a smile but his eyes stayed glued to me when he asked us what we would like. Sarah asked for two beers and put some money down on the bar.

"First time here?" His deep husky voice asked.

"Um, yea." I gave him a shy smile and turned to see Sarah smiling all goofy at me. I gave her a quick elbow when the bartender turned to reach for our beers.

"I'm Sam. Let me know if you need anything else, ok?" Sam, the bartender gave me a quick wink and moved on down the bar.

"Damn girl, he's hot." Sarah said playfully as she sipped on her beer. She knew I wasn't a drinker; but she also knew I'd feel better sipping on something. It gave me something to do with my hands; especially when I was feeling nervous. Sarah hopped up on the bar stool next to her and I stood by her; our backs against the bar so we could people-watch.

The space was classy and open. It had dark walls with camel colored booths. The lights were dimmed but light enough to see clearly. Everyone's face had a soft glow but you could easily hide in the corners for privacy. The music was sexy and upbeat; with the bass vibrating up through my toes and it made the butterflies in my belly disappear. I scanned the crowd, noticing a huddle of men in the far corner booth. I couldn't quite make out their faces from where I was standing; but their leather vests were clear as day. Los Demonios Locos. Several girls in spiked high heels lingered around the table, flipping their hair and sticking out their tits towards the guys. Sarah followed my gaze and I could hear her gasp quietly.

"I'm not even going to say it." I said mostly to myself.

"Say what?" Sarah asked; eyes still searching the group.

"Say that I wonder if Angel is over there somewhere." I took a deep sip of my beer and cracked my neck left and right to shake off that feeling.

"We could leave. Anytime you feel not right, okay?" Sarah turned to me, placing her hand on my arm.

"No, it's fine. I don't see him. I'm just going to ignore it. Come on, let's go dance or something." I pulled Sarah off the barstool and walked over to the other side of the dancefloor away from the DLs. Sarah was insanely beautiful; she had that beach barbie vibe mixed with sex kitten. Men were flocking to her as we danced; but she stayed close to me and ignored everyone around us. I finished my beer and placed the bottle on an open table near us. The champagne from earlier and now an entire beer made my head feel light and my body slightly tingle. I was such a lightweight; but tonight I was going to enjoy the buzz.

Sarah spotted some of the guys she knew from the gym and we made our way over to say hi. They were really nice and super flirty. One guy even twirled me around before pulling me into his chest and asked me to dance. His arms were thick and corded and his stomach flat and firm. But it felt all wrong to me. He didn't have that smell. He was overloaded with cologne and aftershave. So I casually laughed him off and excused myself to use the bathroom. Sarah gave me a nod as she was already in flirt mode with a swoony blonde guy that was hanging all over her.

I was pleasantly surprised with the bathrooms. They were clean and spacious. I didn't really have to go; but I washed my hands and glanced at myself in the full length mirror. My leather skirt fit tight over my thighs and made my butt look firm and perky. My stomach peaked out from my crop tight just enough and I loved my black booties. I swiped on some more lip gloss and made my way out of the bathroom. Just as I was through the door; I felt a strong hand grab my bicep and pull back. The force of the pull had me stumble back into a hard chest as I whipped my head around to see who grabbed me.

"Alexa." His voice was soft and needy. My body tensed and relaxed in seconds as I melted into his chest for a brief moment before I pushed back.

"What are you doing? You scared me." I said; my arm still firmly held in his grasp.

Angel pulled me closer, his eyes dark and hungry as his gaze swept over my body. He licked his lips and softened his grip on me only to touch the side of my face so softly.

"Can we talk?" He asked. His delicious smell of musk and man and a hint of leather washed over me, making me squeeze my thighs together.

"I...I have nothing to say." I said weakly.

"I can't sit here and watch men fall all over you. Touching you. When it should be *me* touching you." He dipped his head towards me, slightly brushing his lips against mine.

Somehow I pulled back, "Then don't, Angel. I need to go." I stepped back, ready to turn my back to Angel and walk away when he grabbed my arm again. But this time he pulled back so hard and spun me into his chest, I had to brace myself on him with both hands. My body hit his and he held me there as he walked us backwards slowly into the shadows of the darkened hallway.

"Angel" I said in a whisper as he took my mouth. His lips moved over mine softly and slowly. His body was so warm and firm against mine and I could feel myself start to melt. I knew he felt it too because he deepened our kiss, sliding his tongue into mine. The music from the dancefloor seemed to quiet in my mind and all I could hear was our breathing. My heart beat so fiercely in my chest and I couldn't help my hands from exploring

Angel's chest and back. I dipped my hands under his cut, raking my nails down his back as he pushed his hard length into my stomach.

"I missed you." Angel breathed into my mouth. He moved his hands around my waist, pulling me harder into him, then slowly sliding one hand down my ass as his fingertips glided up my bare thigh.

I felt goosebumps all over my body as Angel's rough fingertips traveled up underneath my skirt. I broke our kiss long enough to glance around at our surroundings. Somehow Angel backed us up into the darkest corner in the long hallway; away from prying eyes. I gasped as his fingers traced the line of my panties.

"Open your legs for me." He demanded.

"Angel. Stop. We can't." I begged, but it was useless. My words held no conviction; my body responded to him anyway.

"You're soaked for me, Alexa." I felt him smile against my neck as he dipped a finger into my warm, wet core.

I panted as I tipped my head back, feeling Angel finger me harder and faster. It wasn't going to take much to make me come. I was just thankful that the music was loud enough that you couldn't hear how wet I was as he rubbed and pumped me. He kissed and licked up and down my neck and I held on to the sides of his vest as I felt my body start to shake and shiver.

"That's it baby, come for me. I've missed this body." Angel whispered in my ear. He rubbed my wet clit and I came, my legs slightly losing strength as he held me upright.

I was trying to regain my composure as Angel lifted his fingers to his mouth and sucked on the fingers that were just inside of me. Shit. What did I just do? Reality came crashing down around me as I put a hand up on his chest giving me some distance. He reached for me and frowned at my hesitance.

"Baby." He begged, his arm reaching for me.

"Angel, this can't happen. You said…. I'm not…." I stumbled and stuttered looking for the right thing to say but was coming up empty. Just as Angel went to reach for me again,

Sarah appeared at my side, putting a hand on my shoulder.

"Alexa. Jesus." She said wide eyed as she looked between me and Angel. I feel like what we had just done was written all over my face.

"I was waiting for you. The guys got a booth for us and some drinks." She said as she started to pull me away. "Angel." She added flatly.

"Sarah." Angel responded.

"I've gotta go." I said to Angel. His eyes searched mine but before he could say anything else I turned and walked away with Sarah.

We walked back over to where the gym guys were waiting for us. I felt like I was floating. My head swam with what just happened and my heart ached for Angel.

"Um, would you like to tell me what the hell just happened?" Sarah whisper-yelled at me.

"Nothing." I said, shaking my head.

"Nothing my ass. You're all flushed and your lips are puffy and smeared with lip gloss." Sarah raised her eyebrows, a smirk growing on her face.

"Oh my god, Sarah. I don't even know." I put my face in my hands and giggled.

"Jesus. Okay. Well, Roman is here too. As soon as I saw him, I knew Angel was probably here as well." Sarah and I sat down in the booth with the guys. There were four of them; all cute and muscley but I could barely look at them. My mind and body was on Angel, who was walking across the dancefloor towards his brother.

Roman stood with his thick arms over his chest as he watched Sarah, nodding to her when she glanced over to look at him. Roman had a little smirk on his face and his eyes roamed her body. Angel walked up to him, and he looked uneasy. I watched as he ran his hands through his hair and took two shots in a row that were waiting for him on the table. I could see Roman pat him on the back and laugh.

When I looked back at Sarah, she was making a sexy smirk

at Roman nonchalantly. I smacked her hand, making her turn back to me; she was blushing.

"And what was that all about?" I teased.

"What?" Sarah took a shot from the guys and downed it without pulling a face.

"Oh my god, you're into Roman?" I said with my mouth hanging open.

"Noooooo. Jeeez. You're insane." Sarah avoided looking at me. "He's hot and all, but I'll leave the bad boy stuff up to you." She winked at me. She was well on her way to getting drunk.

We laughed and danced with the gym guys but the whole time I could feel Angel's eyes on me. He watched me from afar; even when I was dancing with a guy; he kept his distance. I could see out of the corner of my eye that he was taking shot after shot. The group of Los Demonios were inundated with girls and biker groupies, but Angel just sat and watched me. It was after 2AM when I finally had to sit down at the bar and rest my aching feet. Sarah was delightfully drunk and ready to go home. The gym guys were sloppy drunk and most of them found girls to hang all over. Sarah wasn't into the one night stand thing; so she thankfully pawned off the guys to willing girls. Right before we were about to say our goodbyes, Roman came up to us with Angel stumbling behind him.

"Hey ladies." Roman said with a bright smile. You couldn't help but smile back at him, he just had that wit and charm.

"Hey Roman." Sarah perked up.

"Hey." I said quietly.

"So, this guy (pointing to Angel) can't get on his bike tonight. Do you think you can give him a ride back to our place?" Roman asked as Angel braced himself on his brother.

"Oh, I didn't drive." I shook my head as Sarah interrupted.

"Yea, she lives right down the street. We walked." She said with a big smile and cocked her head at me."

Angel perked up as his drunken smile met mine. "Oh yea?"

"Yea. Um, I guess you can crash at my place. If you can walk a few blocks." I suggested.

"Hey, I'm not sleeping at your place with you two!" Sarah complained as she smirked at me.

"I can take you home. *I* don't drink when I ride." Roman stepped up. He had eyes for Sarah all right.

"Oh. Yea. That would be ok. Alexa, you good with that?" Sarah hopped up off the barstool and stood next to Roman. She was drunk and giddy and I couldn't help but laugh at her.

Angel smiled at me and I gave in. "Yea. It's fine. Call me tomorrow. And Roman, be careful." I kissed and hugged Sarah and gave Roman a death glare. He squeezed my chin with his fingertips and gave me a wink.

We all walked out of the bar together; Roman and Sarah heading towards his bike parked across the street. Sarah looked back at me to give me a shrug and a lopsided smile. Angel stayed quiet next to me. His eyes were still dark and hungry. He had a little sway that told me that he was feeling all those shots he took tonight.

"I'm this way. You ok to walk? Or should I flag down a taxi?" I asked as I started walking down the street.

"I'm ok." Angel sipped on a bottle of water as he quietly walked next to me. It was a beautiful night; the sky was so clear you could see the stars. The warm breeze flowed down the street, cooling my face. Angel downed the rest of the bottle and tossed it in the trash bin. He almost seemed nervous to speak to me. I guess I was sending him mixed signals.

We were a block away when Roman and Sarah passed us on the bike, revving his engine and Sarah looked nestled into his back. When we got to my door, Angel's hand landed on mine before I turned the key.

"I can get a taxi home if you don't want me here." He said honestly. His eyes looked sad and tired; his lips soft and pulled down at the edges.

I continued to turn the key and open my door, "No, it's ok. I guess we need to talk about tonight." I said without looking up at him. "Not that I think you're sober enough to have that sort of conversation." I added.

We headed up the stairs and into my apartment. I left a few lights on knowing we would be home late. Angel entered my space and it didn't feel weird. When we were at my mom's guest house/my place; Angel always seemed out of sorts. Like something wasn't right. But here; in my new place, the vibe was warm and cozy and he seemed to just fit in.

"I'm not really that drunk. I think the walk here sobered me up." Angel took his vest off and placed it on the kitchen chair. "I like your place. Suits you better." His eyes glanced over his surroundings.

"Maybe we should just get some sleep, Angel. We can talk in the morning." I moved away from him, getting each other fresh bottles of cold water. "You can sleep on the couch; there's a blanket in the corner." I added quietly.

"Okay, thanks." Angel stood in the middle of the room. He licked his lips and nodded his head as I turned and walked into my room. As I got into a loose tee shirt to sleep in, I could hear Angel taking his boots off and the sound of his belt buckle hitting the ground. I'm sure the last thing he wanted to do was sleep in his jeans again. I crawled into bed but I wasn't the least bit tired. I was so amped up from tonight and now having Angel just in the next room. I was mad with him; obsessed with him; hell, I wanted him. But I couldn't forget the things he said to me and the things I watched him do to Tim. I felt like nothing was making sense anymore. There was this natural pull to him but I wasn't sure if he was just using me. Something in his eyes spoke to my soul and I felt deep in my heart that we belonged together.

Listening to him toss and turn on the couch, I couldn't take it anymore. I wanted his hands on me again. I wanted to look in his eyes and know that he needed me and I was his again. I crawled out of my bed and tiptoed towards the couch. It was dark aside from the glowing lights from the kitchen. When I approached him; he didn't move. He was sitting up with the blanket tossed over his lap. His eyes were on me, devouring me. I was so wet; I ached for his touch again.

I stood in between his knees, my hands down by my sides.

"Angel." I breathed out, needy and desperate. In a split second his hands were around my waist pulling me down on top of him. I straddled his thick thighs and pressed down on his hard cock. Angel's hands were in my hair and his lips took mine in a desperate kiss. We kissed so frantically and hard as I grinded down on him, finding friction for my throbbing center. He moaned into my mouth as I worked up and down on him. He pulled my shirt up over my head in one quick motion and his mouth was on my hard nipples the next.

Angel

I took her hard nipple into my mouth while palming her other breast. She was soft and supple and I was hungry for her. I could smell the sweet scent that pooled between her legs and it made my mouth water. I pushed my hips into her as she straddled and grinded on me. Her hands roamed down my bare chest and teased the tip of my dick. I was so hard and aching, I was leaking already. She played with the wet tip as I grabbed and kneaded her ass.

"I want you." She moaned.

"I want *you*, Alexa. All of you." I stood with her in my arms and her legs wrapped around my waist. I walked us into her bedroom and I laid her down. Her room was brighter and I could see her face; she had fresh tears in her eyes and her lip quivered. I kissed and sucked that bottom lip and stroked her hair.

"I'll never hurt you again, Alexa. I need you. And I want you to be mine." Tears slid down the sides of her face and dampened the blankets beneath us. I ran my thumb, drying her tears away as she nodded and closed her eyes.

"How could I trust you?" She whispered.

"I'll prove myself to you." I kissed down her chest and her stomach as I reached for her hands and pulled her off the bed so she was standing in front of me.

"What are you doing?" Alexa said as she shook her head at me in question . I could tell her head was filled with doubt and worry. In one slow movement, I knelt down on both knees in front of her. I held my arms at my sides as I looked up to her beautiful face. Her eyes were like sweet honey and hair wild with soft waves. Her body glowed in the moonlight; the curve of her hips and muscles of her strong legs. Her breasts were full and round and she didn't shy away from standing before me in only a black lace thong.

"This is me, Alexa. This is the man I am. But I give myself to you. All of me, my heart and my body. My soul is yours." She blinked back tears and she peered down at me; her hands now clasped together by her lips.

"I may not believe in many things. The MC has taught me respect, loyalty and devotion. I submit to you. I'm on my knees as the ultimate sacrifice of power. It's your choice if you'll have me." I searched her face as her eyes softened and her lips turned slightly up at the corners. She reached for me slowly, taking my face in her hands.

"I want it, Angel. I want all of it." More tears dripped down her face and she smiled and giggled as I rose up, taking her with me and laid her back on to the bed with my body on top of hers. I couldn't stop kissing those beautiful lips as my hands grabbed for the back of her knees, bringing her center up to meet mine.

"I need you, Angel. I need you inside of me." She pleaded as she pulled my hair slightly and arched her back off the bed.

Those words were all I needed to hear. I ripped her panties off of her in one strong yank. She was unbelievably wet, dripping for me. I didn't waste another second and I plunged into her. My cock was so hard, I stretched and filled her. I started slow; bringing my cock almost out of her and then plunging back in again. She grasped the sheets beside her and moaned my name over and over. It was the best sound in the world.

"Angel, you feel so good. I'm going to come already." She yelled and wiggled underneath me. But I held her knees tight and pulled her legs around my back so I could sink into her deeper. Her pussy started to squeeze me and pulse and I knew I was going to lose it.

"Oh my god, Alexa. Fuck, this pussy." I growled as I pumped faster and faster in and out of her. I pulled her up to me so we were both sitting up and held her by the waist as we both came together. I came so hard, my hot come filling her as she shook and shivered all over. Sweat covered our bodies and she went limp in my arms. Spent. I laid us both down onto her bed and pulled her into my chest, kissing her lips, her cheeks and head. After a few minutes, I felt her steady soft breathing and I drifted off to sleep still inside of her.

Chapter 20

Alexa

I woke up to the vibrating sound of my cell phone dancing across my nightstand. I was laying on Angel's chest with my legs intertwined in his. We were still naked with a blanket pulled up to our waists. Angel stirred slightly as my phone stopped vibrating. I didn't want to move. I wanted to stay in this moment forever. But I couldn't help slide my hand down Angel's chest down to his stomach just to where the tip of his hard cock was. I let my fingertips dance softly down his shaft as he started to breathe heavier; his hand coming up to meet mine. Angel wrapped his hand around mine and together we stroked him. I lifted my eyes to his face and he was staring down at our hands with a sweet smile on his face; lightly biting his bottom lip.

"Does that feel good?" I asked in my sleepy voice.

"Everything you do feels good." He answered. I moved to straddle him, letting my hair dangle around our heads as I bent down to kiss his lips. I unapologetically rubbed myself on his length. I was wet and sore but so needy. Angel tossed an extra pillow behind his head so he could watch us.

"Pick your knees up. Put me inside of you." He instructed.

My eyes met his right before I sank down on his throbbing cock. "We need a condom." I stopped. Oh shit. "Angel." I said with a gasp.

"What?" He sat up with his eyebrows pinched together.

"We didn't use a condom last night. You came inside of me." I was slightly panicking. I'm not on birth control. I had made a doctor's appointment the week before Angel broke it off with me to get on the pill; but I cancelled the exam.

He put his hands on either side of my face. He was calm and sweet. "Shhh.. It's going to be ok. It was just once. What are the chances?" He spoke so softly, gently.

Internally I was counting the days until I was due for my period. Realizing I had just finished it the other day; I assumed that everything was going to be ok. "Okay. I'm sure it's ok. But we need to use a condom until I can get on the pill, okay?"

"Whatever you want." Angel pushed my hips down so that I could sink down onto his hard, waiting cock. And nothing else mattered in that moment. Sex with Angel was pure bliss. He was sweet but rough, caring but forceful; and I loved when he talked dirty to me.

I rode him slow. Using all the strength in my legs; I picked up on him and slid down his shaft; making him moan and claw at my ankles. "Condom, Angel. Do you have one?" I asked with a smirk.

He quickly flipped me over onto my back and scrambled out to the living room to grab his jeans. He came back with a condom and quickly sheathed himself. He stroked himself slowly as he looked hungerly at my sex. I was spread out on the bed for him.

"Play with yourself." He stroked as he came up to kneel between my legs. "Let me watch you." I hesitated but kept my eyes on his beautiful cock. "Alexa. Rub that pretty little pussy." Angel growled and I obeyed.

"Oh Angel." I moaned as I rubbed my fingertips along my wetness. I started to feel little tremors in my core and I was dying for Angel to be back inside of me.

"That's it baby. You want me? You gonna come for me again? I want to see your face as you come all over my cock." He slipped back inside and pumped me hard. Our fingers laced and he watched my face in awe as my orgasm ripped through my body; sending goosebumps and shivers throughout me. He kept thrusting inside of me; and tiny ripples of pleasure kept pulsing through me. When he came, he collapsed on me, kissing my lips and holding me.

We stayed in our little cocoon for a while. I think I drifted in and out of sleep. My phone was vibrating like crazy so I finally gave in and grabbed it off the nightstand. A missed call from the private investigator and voice mail and two text messages from Sarah:

Sarah: Morning sunshine… how was last night?

Sarah: I woke up alone and hung over…. Shocker.. I'm guessing you didn't?? Call me later.

I rolled back over and Angel wrapped me in his arms again. I breathed into his neck as he played with my messy hair.

"I guess we should talk about all this, right?" He asked curiously.

I pushed back to look at his face. "Yea. We should definitely talk. I'm going to go make some coffee, okay?" I answered quietly as I untangled myself from him and walked into the bathroom. I brushed my teeth, washed my face and put on a robe. When I came out, Angel was already in the kitchen, dressed in his jeans and no shirt. The sight alone was mouthwatering. He was working on the coffee pot and searching the cabinets for mugs. I leaned on the door jam admiring him in my space and the butterflies were back. But this time, they were excited, happy butterflies.

I made my way over to him and took out the milk and sugar. We worked silently in the kitchen together. When the coffee was ready; he poured us both full mugs.

"Sit, Alexa. I want to go first." Angel eyed me, I could tell his mind was working on overdrive and he was measuring his words. I sat on the couch with my mug pulled into my chest. I was nervous and scared to get our past all out on the table. Angel sat on the coffee table in front of me, with his elbows on his knees. I couldn't help but admire the smooth muscles of his arms and the ripple in his abs as he leaned over.

He went to speak but I stopped him abruptly. "Wait, Angel. Um, first. I just need to know this before it drives me insane." His eyes looked serious and dark again. "Last night, um, we didn't use anything. Um, did you…" I was so afraid of his answer I could barely finish my sentence. Thankfully Angel took over my line of questioning.

"No, Alexa. I didn't even look at a single girl since you. And I'm clean. I've never gone bare with anyone." I let out a huge sigh of relief and felt my shoulders relax.

"Ok. Thank you. Sorry, I just needed to know." I took a small sip of my steaming coffee. Coffee relaxed me. The sweet, strong taste soothed my nervous system.

"Alexa, when I met you; I felt like everything clicked into place. I've had a tough life and I've made choices I'm not proud of but you're the one thing that made absolute sense. I would never turn my back on my MC; but for you; I'd risk everything to show you that I could be the man you deserve. So when your mom came to me..."

"Wait, what?" I snapped my eyes up to Angel. "My mom?!" I growled through my teeth. I got up and paced the length of the living room. A million thoughts ran through my head. How could she go behind my back? Why would she interject herself in my relationship? How could she do this to me? I turned back ready to fire off questions when I walked right into Angel's chest.

"Baby, calm down. I'll tell you what happened. I should have stood up to your mom but she involved the MC and Roman. I had no choice but to walk away from you; push you away." Angel explained what happened when my mom showed up at the Los Demonios Locos clubhouse; the things she said to him, threatened him. I sat on the edge of the couch just shaking my head. "She made me feel that you deserve way more than I could ever offer you. She was a big reminder of where I came from and where I belonged." Angel's eyes were sad, tormented again.

I went to him, nestled into his lap. "Oh Angel. I am so sorry. I should have known she would do something like this. No one besides me, gets to decide how I'm going to live my life." I kissed him hard on his lips and his arms came around me. I never felt safer than when I was with Angel.

We talked some more and I told Angel all about my lunch with my mom and how she told me I had to move out. He listened in silence; never judging or commenting on how evil my mother could be. He was just supportive, apologetic.

Angel

"I feel terrible that I caused you to lose your job." I held her in my arms as we spoke. I've never had such an open and honest conversation with someone. I felt like she could tell me anything, she really trusted me. "Ugh, and that guy. Jesus, I'm an asshole." I rubbed my face and shook my head at the memory.

"Yea. Not one of your most wonderful moments." Alexa teased. "But I understand why it happened. When I stormed into the clubhouse that day; I saw red. I wanted to kick those girls right in their faces." She laughed at herself.

"But I don't regret getting fired. I mean, I loved helping all those children but I always felt like my hands were tied. The government and community only helped so much. And my mother always made me feel like I needed to do more to be like her. Picture perfect. Never go against what people expect of me; never go against the rules." I watched as Alexa spoke animatedly. I loved watching her. The way she used her hands to emphasize her words, how her body naturally swayed and the muscles in her legs twitched as she rocked from one side to the other. She had the kindest, warmest hearts and I was in complete awe of her.

She was digging through a box in the corner of the room. "I think my mom is purposely hiding things from me." She handed me two copied pictures. The first pictured a woman and man; the woman looked like a skinner version of Alexa with slightly darker hair standing with a Mexican looking man. The other was just the woman; I assumed it was Alexa's mom. They had the same bright, eager eyes and they held themselves the same way. When I looked up at Alexa; she was biting her bottom lip and she looked hopeful and excited.

"I think this is my dad. I found the pictures locked up in my mom's office. I asked her about it but she went ballistic on me. That's pretty much when she told me that I needed to move out." I studied the pictures; there wasn't too much in the background but there was a farmhouse with some people standing around.

"She wouldn't tell you who your father is?" I was annoyed at her mom's lack of veracity.

Alexa shook her head and I handed her back the pictures. "No. She basically told me that he walked out on her the second he found out she was pregnant with me. I guess that's why she and I were never close. I think she has been holding that against me my whole life." Alexa studied the pictures.

"Oh! Jesus! I completely forgot!" She jumped up and ran into the bedroom. "I hired a private investigator" She called out from the other room. "I think he called early this morning." Alexa scrambled back out with her phone in her hand. "Yes! He left a message." She hit the voicemail button and turned her speaker on so I could hear.

"Hi Alexa. This is Robert Alverez. I dug up some information on Antonio Castillo I think you'll want to hear. Give me a call and we can discuss."

"Oh my god. I'm nervous." Alexa held onto her stomach as she listened to the message one more time.

"I'm here for you. You deserve to know where you came from Alexa. Do you want me to call him back for you?" I asked as I held her face in my hand. Times like this, Alexa felt small and fragile in my hands; but she was anything but. She was a powerhouse and didn't even know it. She was a strong and a beautifully smart woman.

"No, I'll call. I'm just going to shower first and get dressed." She let out a relieving sigh; like she had been holding her breath listening to the voicemail.

"Okay, I'll join you." I said darkly as I wiggled my eyebrows at her and got her to laugh.

I took her again in the shower. I couldn't help myself as I watched her soap and lather her sexy body. I pressed her front up against the cool tiles and lifted her leg as I thrusted into her. I pulled out this time and she watched as I fisted myself and came in white hot spurts onto the shower floor.

Alexa threw on a pair of tight fitting white jeans and a navy blue tank top. While she was getting dressed and got ready, I walked down to the bar's parking lot and brought my bike up to the sidewalk in front of her apartment. When I came back up-stairs, she sat cross legged on top of her bed staring down at her phone; biting her fingernail.

"You ok?" I laughed as she sat nervously.

"Ugh, yea. I'm scared to hear if he says he couldn't find anything. And even more scared if he tracked him down. Does that make any sense?" She fidgeted.

"Makes sense to me." I sat down next to her and held her hand. "Come on. Dial the number. Who knows if he'll even an-swer right now." Alexa squeezed my hand as she hit the speaker button when the phone dialed the private investigator.

"Hello."

"Hi. Mr. Alvarez? This is Alexa Ramirez; I got your voice-mail this morning."

"Oh yes, how are you Alexa?" He responded. He sounded professional yet cordial.

"Nervous actually. I'm hoping you have some news for me?" She squeezed her eyes shut waiting for his reply.

"Actually yes. So I had my digital specialist blow up the pictures so we can find some hints as to the location and try to get an idea where the pictures took place. We got lucky with a reflection in the men's sunglasses. We found that there were several men standing around your dad that wore a leather vest. Much like the ones you'd find on a motorcycle club member. Are you familiar with what I'm talking about?"

Alexa looked over at me, her eyes were as big as saucers. "Yes. I know of them."

"Okay, well it seems like the vests read El Diablo's. They're one of the biggest MCs in Mexico. Now your dad isn't wearing the vest; so we can't jump to the conclusion that he was or is one of them. But that's a good starting point. El Diablo's don't really come onto US soil; so my best bet is that this was in Mexico. I'm still working on tracking down an address or accounts associated with his name; but I'm coming up empty."

"Mmmhmmm." Alexa was taking in all the information as I stood and I paced her bedroom. I knew the MC, El Diablos, well. We have had many business transactions with them. If you had to picture the baddest and most aggressive MC in your mind; you'd be picturing them. They were ruthless, well organized and owned most of the cops and government in Mexico. Nobody messed with them.

"Okay, so I'll keep working on it. I'll see about finding a contact to talk to El Diablos. I'm an ex-cop; so I'm not sure they'd feel good about me poking around. I'll do my best though and give you a call in, say, a week." The private investigator offered. No way was he going to walk into El Diablo's clubhouse and walk out alive.

"Okay, thank you so much. This is great. I really appreciate all of this." Alexa finished the call and jumped up on her bed and bounced up and down.

"Oh my god, Angel." She looked at me in disbelief.

"Okay, before you get your hopes up. Let me tell you, I know the Diablos." I looked at her stern and serious.

"You do?" She stopped dancing on her bed and jumped down to stand in front of me.

"Yea. Alexa, they make Los Demonios Locos look like pussy cats. Not that I'm talking down about my own MC. But they're bad, Alexa. Fucking dangerous." I reached into my pocket and tapped out a message to Taylor. He handles most of the encrypted messages to and from the different MCs that we worked with.

"Angel. Do you think you can find him?" Alexa whispered.

"I'm texting Taylor to see what he could find out. Give me a day or two, okay." I finished my message and sent it off to Taylor, copying Roman as well.

Me: Taylor.. Need a contact with E.Ds.. off the books. We'll talk more at the club tonight.

Taylor: Bro, Prez will kill u for messing with the EDs without his permission; but hey, it's your funeral. I'll get you a guy.

Me: thanks

"Jesus Angel. I can't believe it. Do you think my dad is an El Diablo? I mean, why would he be standing around with them?" Alexa asked. She had so much nervous energy; she wouldn't sit still. She worked on unpacking some books and frames as we talked.

"Well, I can't picture some run of the mill guy hanging out with El Diablos for shits and giggles. We'll figure this out. Listen, I'm starving; you wanna walk down to the deli and grab some lunch with me?" I asked as I spun her into my arms.

"Oooo, yes. Sounds good to me." Alexa smiled so bright, her face lit up with affection and happiness. I never wanted to see her without a smile again.

Later that night, when I had to finally leave Alexa for a club meeting, I was hoping to meet up with Taylor and Roman outside of the club. I had stopped home to change when I realized it didn't look like Roman had been home at all.

Taylor was already waiting for me; away from prying ears. "Yo man. Sorry I didn't come to the bar last night; fucking family drama at home." Taylor explained.

"It's all good man. Place was crawling with club bunnies and bad music." I joked. Taylor was the last person to want to touch a club bunny. Girls constantly threw themselves at him but he just wasn't interested. Taylor had a thing for older women.

"Okay, so I got in touch with a dude named, ready for this? Killer. Original, right?" Taylor chuckled. "I helped him out back in the day with some police records. Anyway, he said he'd help you out with whatever, on the down low." Taylor spoke quietly, and handed me a piece of paper with 'Killer's' contact information.

"Killer, huh. Great." I huffed.

"So, what's this for anyway?" Taylor cocked his head at me. He was a trustworthy guy. We've had each other's back for the past few years. I knew he wouldn't go blabbing to Prez that I had put in a favor to the El Diablos.

"I'm back with Alexa. She needs help finding her dad. She hired a P.I. and he thinks her old man may be a part of El Diablo's crew." I spit it out plain and simple for him.

"No way man, good for you." Taylor patted me on the back. "So are you just gonna spit in Prez's face when he finds out you went against his orders to stay away from her?" he joked but he was completely serious.

"Fuck, man, I know. It's complicated. Let's just keep this between you and me until I can figure this shit out." I spotted Roman parking his bike with a big ol grin on his face. What the hell was up with him?

"All good man. Let me know if you need anything else. I'mma go in and get a beer." Taylor nodded to Roman and headed into the clubhouse.

Roman strode up to me with a stupid smile and a bounce in his step. I slapped the back of his head when he got up to where I was standing.

"The fuck?" He moaned and burst out laughing. That's Roman; everything was a fucking joke. He rubbed the back of his head, raising his eyebrows at me, "you have a good night with Alexa?"

"Shut up. Let's go inside and get this shit over with." I slung my arm around Roman's shoulders and we went into the clubhouse for our meeting. "I'll tell you later."

Alexa

Sarah: Well? Stop leaving me in suspense!
Me: I have no idea what you're talking about.
Sarah: Don't make me come over there and tickle it out of you!
Me: No tickles…. My body is too sore for that.
Sarah: You dirty little girl, you!
Me: Ha! Ugh… Sarah… he's amazing. WTF
Sarah: I hope you got some answers out of him; not just sex!
Me: I'm going on a run… I'll stop by in a bit.

Sarah: okie dokie....

Sarah's little bungalow was just about two miles down the road. The sun was starting to set and Angel had just left me to go to a club meeting. He promised he'd come right back to me after it was over and we were going to watch a movie and order in. I was on cloud nine. Having Angel back in my life was exactly what felt right. All I needed now was to figure out a job. I've been out of work for over a week and already felt antsy. I promised myself I would hit the classifieds this week and send out some feelers.

Running felt good. I was sore in all the best places but my legs felt strong and my head, clear. I passed the downtown shops in no time and the street opened up to small cottages and bungalows that were landscaped beautifully. I slowed down as I got to Sarah's. She was sitting on her porch waiting for me with a glass of wine in her hand and a bottle of water for me by her side.

"Hey" I panted.

"Hey, yourself. Good run?" Sarah asked.

"Yea. Short but good." I took the water she offered and stretched out my legs on her front porch steps. "Nice night." I commented.

"Mhmmmm" She glared at me with that knowing gleam in her eye.

I laughed at her 'all knowing' glare. "Shut up, oh my god." We laughed together and I sat opposite her in her little bistro set that was on her porch.

"Well, last night had an interesting outcome." Sarah teased.

"You could say that." I added as I sipped. "We talked. Angel and I. We laid everything out on the table." I said into the darkening evening.

"Okay. Good." Sarah nodded.

I turned to her, "Did you know my mom stormed into the Los Demonios Locos clubhouse and threatened him?"

"Stop it. No." Sarah choked on her sip of wine.

"Um, yea. Can you believe that? I'm still in shock, I think." I filled her in on the rest of the gossip of my mom and Angel. And the phone call with the private investigator. She was excited that I had a lead on my dad. But she was worried that I'd be getting involved with a scary Mexican motorcycle club.

"Angel coming back to your place after the meeting tonight?" Sarah asked.

"Yea. We're going to watch movies and order in. Wait, how did you know they had a meeting tonight?" I asked as I furrowed my brows at her.

"Ummmm" She guzzled the last few sips of her wine.

"Sarah." I said in a warning voice.

"No, it's just... Roman told me." Sarah waved me off, trying to change the subject.

"Wait, wait, wait. He took you home last night. He just dropped you off, right?" I leaned in so Sarah couldn't avoid my glare.

"Well, he came in for a drink." My jaw dropped. "Oh my god, Al. It wasn't like that. You know me. We just talked. He's sweet. And so funny." She had a silly smile on her face.

"Mhhmm. Gotcha. Yea. I think Roman's great."

"Anyway. Well, I'm really happy for you. I know Angel makes you happy. I really hope things work out for you and him." Sarah said sweetly.

"Thanks Sarah. Now, I just gotta figure out what to do with my mom. I haven't even heard from her since she stormed into my house and kicked me out. Annnd, find a job."

"Well, I'll let you know if I hear anything about job openings. But you gotta find something you love. Life's too short to do something just out of obligation." Sarah explained as she poured herself another half glass of wine.

"Obligation?" I asked.

"Yea. I mean, don't take offense, please. You know I have your best interest but I just think your mom pushed you into the Social Worker position because she thought that would keep you 'politically correct'. I know you loved working with the kids but the job sucked. Too much ass kissing and not enough action for these poor kids. I know you could really make a difference outside of the Shelter." Sarah offered. She was so encouraging but always gave it to me straight.

"Hmm. Maybe you're on to something. I do have a nice fat trust fund to help out, right?" I wiggled my eyebrows at her and she laughed. "Maybe I can start something up on my own? I'll have to give it some thought." I got up, drained my water bottle and gave her a big hug.

"Alright, I'm gonna head back. I need a soak in that tub if Angel's gonna come back tonight." I teased. "Love ya."

"Ewwww. But yea, get it, girl! Have fun. Love you too." Sarah called as I made my way out of her driveway.

Chapter 21

Angel

The meeting ended and I didn't feel like sticking around. The guys usually drank beer and watched whatever sports were on, on the big screen and sat around bullshitting. I had someplace to be. I was trying to duck out unnoticed but as soon as I got to my bike, I heard Prez yell my name.

"Hey, Angel. Hold up a sec." Rey yelled.

I straddled my bike as he walked towards me. "Rey, man, everything ok?" I asked him.

"Yea; just wanna check in with you. You tired? You've been pretty quiet lately." Rey stood with his arms crossed over his thick chest. You never got into personal details with Rey. Hell, he didn't want to hear every guys' sob story.

"Yea, I'm good Prez. Just laying low, ya know. Those tunnel runs just about did me in." I laughed it off.

"Yeah. You did a good job down there, Angel. I'm proud. You know, your brother, Roman is gonna be promoted and I was just wondering where your head was at. If you want to step up with him?" Rey searched my face for the truth. Honestly, I didn't want to step up with Roman. I was more than happy staying in the background. Things with Alexa weren't even off the ground yet and I really was looking forward to spending more time with her.

"If you want me there, I'm there. You know that Rey." We spent a few beats staring at each other. I think deep down he knew I wasn't meant for his world. But he wasn't going to just let me bow out.

"Yea, we'll see. Why don't you think about it a bit. I'll pick on some of the prospects to do surveillance out in the desert. Looks like The Serpents are heeding our warning. We got you to thank for that." We shook hands and without another word, Rey headed back into the clubhouse. It erupted with music and the club bunnies were already flocking to the building. I was more than happy to be out of there and headed towards Alexa's.

I stopped at the store to pick up a box of condoms on my way to Alexa's. All I could think about was burying myself inside her again. It was a short ride to her apartment; and I was trying my best to push everything Prez was saying out of my mind. I spent too many years living for someone else and doing everything that I was told. For the first time in a long time; I wanted to do something for myself. Be something to someone that was worthwhile. Work on my future instead of just focusing on the now. Alexa was my future. I felt things for her that I only thought were capable in tv shows and movies. When I looked at her; my world stopped and everything else could go to hell. I wanted to be the man that she needed me to be. A lot of what her mom said truly bothered me still. Alexa comes from a wealthy, prestigious family; what did I even have to offer her?

When she buzzed me into her apartment, the mouth-watering scent of coconuts and lemons permeated the air. She was fresh out of the shower, with her hair still damp and she was curled up on the couch with tiny cotton shorts on and a Led Zepplin crop top. If I could come home to this sight everyday; I'd die a happy man. She bounced over to me and put her arms around my neck.

"Mmmmm, how is it possible that I missed you already?" She kissed me softly with a big smile on her face. Her face was glowing and skin was soft and makeup free.

"I'm sorry I had to leave you. But I'm all yours now. Prez is giving me a much needed break." I picked her up and moved us back to the couch.

"Oh. You didn't tell him we were back together, right? I don't want you getting in trouble over me." Alexa fussed.

"I didn't say anything. *That*, I'll have to figure out. I think as long as your mom doesn't go storming in there again; or locking me or Roman up; we'll be fine." I sighed and ran my hands through my hair.

"I'm so sorry, Angel. We'll figure it out. But for now... what are you in the mood for?" She asked, sitting on her knees next to me.

I laughed at her, she seemed so much more at ease. "You. I'll take all of you." I said darkly.

"Mmmm, well, that could be arranged. But I was talking about food. Are you in the mood for Chinese food? And there's that new scary movie on tonight, ugh what's it called. Oh, um The Asylum!"

"Funny, I wouldn't peg you for the scary movie type. But yes, I'll eat anything. I'm not picky."

"What, do I look like the RomCom type? Thanks but no thanks." Alexa laughed as she grabbed the menu off the counter.

We spent the night picking on Chinese food and Alexa stayed cuddled up next to me during the movie. I loved that she wasn't super girly and was able to handle a slice 'em and dice 'em type of movie. That and her love of fast cars made my dick swell. The movie was just about over and as soon as the credits rolled; I picked Alexa up over my shoulder and took her to the bedroom. She squealed and giggled but didn't fight me. I threw her down on her bed, giving her my best 'serious, scary face'. I playfully crawled slowly towards her as she giggled and squirmed out of my grasp.

"Are you afraid of me, Alexa?" I said in a deep, threatening voice. She laughed some more and shook her head. I caught her by the ankle and pulled her towards the end of the bed. She twisted and turned and laughed so hard, it made me laugh as I dove into her neck, kissing and giving her soft bites on the bottom of her chin. I finally lifted her tee shirt off of her, pulling down her bra to suck on her sweet nipples. She calmed and stilled under me and I felt her back arch off the mattress.

"Angel." She moaned and she tried to wiggle out from under me.

"Mmm.. where do you think you're going?" I pulled her back down so I could yank her shorts off.

"Angel. I want... mmmmmmmm" She tried to speak but I was already rubbing her wet clit through her underwear. She was soaked and swollen. Her eyes met mine and she trapped my hand between her strong legs.

"Open for me." I demanded.

She slowly shook her head 'no' and pushed me back so that she could stand facing me. She licked her lips seductively and suddenly I was so hard it hurt. My hard on pressed painfully in my jeans as her hands traveled down my stomach and started to unbuckle my belt and jeans.

"I want this." She said quietly. I studied her face as I left my hands down by my side.

"What do you want, baby?" She trailed her fingers down my cock as my jeans fell to the floor. She dipped a finger into the waistline of my boxers and pulled slowly down. I felt my cock jump as she bit that plump bottom lip and she moaned quietly when she freed me. She stroked me slowly and raised her face to meet my eyes.

"Tell me what you want. Do you want to suck my cock, Alexa?" I was leaking with pre cum, I wanted inside that beautiful mouth. Silently, Alexa sank down to her knees, taking me in her mouth. Her lips softly caressed the head and she licked and sucked sweet kisses down my length. "Fuck, Alexa." I could barely hold on while she sucked and stroked me. I watched her and she kept her honey brown eyes on me as I moaned and wrapped her hair around my hand so that I could move my hips to thrust in and out of her mouth.

She softly moaned and the vibration went straight to my balls. "Oh my god, Alexa. Fuck. You want me to come down your throat, baby?" She didn't stop as I sunk my cock down her throat and she took all of me, swallowing and smiling. I pulled her up and kissed her lips and spun her around with her hands on the mattress and her ass in my hands.

"I'm going to eat this beautiful pussy. And then I'm going

to sink so deep inside you and make you come all over my cock." I spread her wide and licked and sucked on her swollen lips until she was quivering and I could feel her cunt squeeze my fingers that I pumped into her.

"Angel, please. I want you." She looked over her shoulder at me with that beautiful smirk and need in her eyes. I grabbed a condom and sank so deep inside of her, stretching her and filling her up before I came out and pumped her hard, until I had her screaming my name.

Alexa

I laid on Angel's chest, tracing his tattoos with my fingertips while Angel lightly played with my hair. I was sleepy and deliciously sore; my whole body hummed with satisfaction. The room was quiet and filled with the sexy scent of Angel and me. Angel's phone dinged with an incoming message and he groaned at the sound.

"I can grab it for you; I gotta use the bathroom anyway." I yawned.

"Thanks." I dug the phone out of his jeans pocket and tossed it over to him. I closed the door to the bathroom and couldn't help to notice my puffy pink lips and my wild sex hair. I giggled to myself and ran my fingers through my hair and used the bathroom. I could barely keep my eyes open as I stumbled back to bed and got under the covers.

"Everything okay?" I asked as I nestled into Angel's arms.

"Yea, the contact Taylor got me, got back to me. Said he doesn't want to talk over the phone. He'd rather I come down to meet up with him."

"Oh? Is that bad?" Angel had warned me how brutal these guys were; I didn't want him taking a risk for me.

"It's fine. I've actually been down there before. It's a few hours' ride from here though." He explained. Angel sat up a little so he could look down at my face. "You should come with me."

"Yea?" I blinked at him. "Is it... dangerous?" I asked curiously.

"Los Demonios have a good relationship with El Diablos. They would never hurt you as long as they knew you were mine. And besides, I get to have you on my bike again." He traced the curve of my lips and there was no way I could resist spending more time with Angel.

"Okay." I smiled up at him. He kissed me softly and then we both settled into a deep sleep.

The next morning I woke up to the smell of bacon and eggs frying in the kitchen. I stretched and yawned as I flipped the covers off my naked body. Angel looked like a god as he stood in my kitchen with a spatula in one hand and coffee in the other. He peered over his shoulder when he heard me come in. I was dressed in his tee shirt and put my hair up in a messy bun. I loved that he felt comfortable here. I still had some unpacking to do, there were boxes stacked neatly in the corners of the room.

"Good morning." I said sleepily as I poured myself some coffee and downed a glass of water.

"Good morning." Angel responded as he pressed a firm kiss to my lips. "I figured you'd be hungry. I hope you don't mind me using your kitchen."

"Of course not. I will never argue about you making me breakfast. You are making *me* some, right?" I teased. He plated up two dishes with eggs and bacon and I cut up some bananas to go on the sides. I put the news on as we ate quietly and stole glances at each other with silly love sick smiles.

"You want to head out around 3 today?" Angel asked as he finished his last bite.

"Oh. We're going today? I mean sure. My schedule's clear." I teased.

"Yea. Killer wants to meet up at a bar down the street from their clubhouse. Taylor and Roman are going to come too. I was hoping it was just us; but it'll just be safer to show up with a few of us." Angel leaned over the kitchen table.

"Killer? His name is Killer?" I asked with a raised eyebrow.

Angel laughed at my face. "Ha, yea. Taylor said he's fine.

He's an old timer. Been with El Diablo's for probably 30 years. Taylor helped him out awhile back. It's the new guys you have to worry about. Always scheming and fucking around. Not the long time members; they don't mess around. They shoot straight and they're loyal as hell to their Prez.

"Okay, whatever you think. So Roman and Taylor know we're together then?" I asked, still sipping my hot coffee.

"I mean, yea. They know. But it's not like I kiss and tell, Alexa. That shit is mine. I don't share you with anyone." Angel leaned back and crossed his arms over his chest.

"Got it. Okay. Well, good… I'm nervous as hell.. But hey, it's a learning experience, right? Should I bring the pictures with us?"

"Probably a good idea. It'll be fine. The hardest part will be the long ride. I'll tell the guys we'll meet up here around 3." Angel got up and cleaned his plate.

We lounged around all day, Angel helped me unbox some of my stuff. And he watched me as I hung a few pictures and framed photographs I took with me from my mom's place. I loved my desert photography. It was soft and calming along with the sunsets and expansive valleys. I showered and wanted to be ready before the guys got here. I was so nervous. On one hand; I got to ride with Angel and get a glimpse into his world; on the other, I saw what it was like to deal with a scary as shit MC. But I kept repeating to myself that I'll finally be getting the answers I've been looking for. I'm praying this guy, Killer, knows my dad and can tell me where to find him. I was in the bathroom braiding my hair when I heard the rumble of bikes in the parking lot behind my building. Moments later, heavy boots climbed the stairs to my apartment. Angel let them in and I can hear them talking to one another.

I came out of my room, still barefoot, in jeans and a black, tight fitting, long sleeve body suit that dipped low in the back. The three men stopped talking and stared at me.

"Um, hey guys." I said as I gave a small wave. Taylor gave me a small smile and head nod and Roman walked up to me and gave me a big hug.

"What's up baby girl. You ready for that ass to be sore as hell?" Roman said as he pulled away from me.

"Uh, excuse me?" I wrinkled my nose at him.

Angel slapped him on the back. "He means from the bike. You're not used to riding long distances." Angel pushed him again and Roman laughed him off. "And don't call her that." Angel warned in a deep grumble.

"Ease up bro. One big happy family, right?" Roman shrugged.

"Baby, you have boots? And you'll need a jacket. The desert gets cold at night." Angel said sweetly.

"Oh, yea. Boots I got. And I'll grab a jacket." I winked at him.

"Alright, we'll stop off at the route 30 turn off, Alexa will probably need to stretch her legs by then. We're meeting Killer at Chico's, right outside of the clubhouse." The men nodded to each other and I took my cue to put my boots on and grab a jacket. I had a black bomber jacket that was lined with soft Sherpa. That was sure to keep me warm.

Angel kissed me as we made our way out of my apartment and down to the bikes. The sound of all three bikes firing up excited me. I felt my cheeks blush as my adrenaline spiked and the butterflies fluttered in my belly. Angel made sure I was comfortable before we pulled out onto the road.

"Alright, just tap me if you need to stop. Lean with me and hold on." I gave him a thumbs up and wrapped my arms around him.

We stopped quickly at the halfway point; I got off and stretched my legs. My butt was slightly numb and the guys took turns walking into the desert to pee. The sky was just starting to turn pink and orange by the time we made it to the bar. The ride took a bit longer than two hours. We all got off the bikes, you can tell the guys were on high alert. Scanning their surrounds, there were plenty of bikes parked out front; the bar was a dusty old desert bar in the middle of nowhere. Trucks parked in random spots around the building and a couple of old men sitting on benches smoking and talking by the front door.

"Stay right by my side, Alexa. You don't walk around without one of us; not even to use the bathroom, alright." Angel said seriously.

We strode up to the bar and once inside; I could see why he wouldn't want me to wander off. There were men everywhere with women half haphazardly dressed, draping themselves over tables and straddling them. I tried to school my face and not stare at anyone in particular. The guys nodded and shook hands with the men that sported the El Diablo cuts. The mutual respect was unexpected but welcomed.

We ordered a few drinks as a man with a long, graying beard strolled up to us. He must be in his late fifties but looked older with the signs of being out in the hot sun aging his face. He was tall and broad, wore black jeans with an El Diablo cut on. His boots were dusty and dirty and had tattoos up and down his arms. As he extended a hand out to Taylor, I noticed the tattoo 'Killer' on his inner forearm with a naked woman with devil horns underneath it. Taylor took his hand and made the introductions.

"Killer, my man. You looking good. This is Roman and Angel." They shook hands and nodded at each other. "And this is Angel's girl, Alexa." Taylor stood back so that I could shake his hand. Killer shook my hand with a firm grip and let it linger longer than normal. His eyes raked over my body and his lips tipped up in a smirk. I felt my cheeks blush and my body tensed. This guy scared the shit out of me but I didn't want to appear disrespectful. Angel put a soft but possessive hand on my shoulder and Killer broke contact with me.

Looking at my face now, he squinted his eyes and nodded. "Yea, you're Toni's daughter, all right." Killer stated. My eyebrows jumped in reply and I gave an excited glance at Angel over my shoulder.

"We're gonna go grab some food and beer." Taylor's heavy hand landed on Angel's back and Angel nodded at Roman and

Taylor as they made their way to a booth. It was obvious the guys were comfortable here; no sign of danger or unease.

"Let's go for a walk. These walls have ears and I'd like to speak with you about your father." Killer shuffled out to the door, pulling a pack of cigarettes out of his pocket. I looked at Angel for approval and laced his fingers with mine.

"I'll come with you. He may be old, but it's not like he wouldn't hit on you." Angel winked at me. We left the darkened bar and met up with Killer who was over by his bike.

"Wow, man. This is a beautiful machine." Angel backed up so that he could admire the shiny bike.

"Yea, man. It's a 1987 Softail. My first true love." Killer laughed. It was all black with some custom pinstriping and lettering on the gas tank. The chrome was spotless.

"So, you didn't come all this way to talk about bikes. Ask me what you want to know, beautiful." Killer glanced down at me; his eyes squinting in the setting sun's rays.

"Um, so. .. I was just wondering if you know him, Antonio Castillo? Um, if he's still here in Mexico?" I asked him. I was so nervous I didn't even realize I was twirling the end of my long braid.

"Yea, you could say that I knew him. He was an old timer like me. We patched in about the same time. Seems like a lifetime ago." Killer sat on his bike as he spoke. He spoke like a seasoned veteran and I was hanging on every word. "Toni and I go way back. Partying, riding. We got into plenty of trouble together. When he was around your age; he moved up pretty quickly in El Diablos. Became the Prez's right hand. Toni was real good with money. He was next in line to be our treasurer. You see, back then, there was a lot of push and pull from the government. El Diablos were taking over and a lot of us got locked up or ambushed during some of our *activities*. This was before El Diablos owned the police. Toni got in deep. He was sent out along with a bunch of us to work on a deal between us and another local MC. We were trying to combine our efforts to regain territory the police had seized. Anyway; Toni and a few guys got cut off on the highway. Word was a few cops took it upon themselves to run our brothers off the road. There was a shoot out and your dad was one of the ones that were killed. The cops left him on the side of the road. Me and a few guys had to drive out there to pick up the bodies. Brought them home and buried them."

The silence hung between us thicker than the dust that was being kicked up by the trucks in the parking lot. I looked down at the ground as I felt Angel's hands come onto the tops of my shoulders. He pressed his front into my back. I reached up to his hand and shook off the feeling of failure.

"So he's dead." I deadpanned.

"Yea, beautiful. He is. Died almost 25 years ago." Killer said matter of factly.

"So, did he ever mention my mom? What happened? Did you know her? I asked, rubbing my forehead with an oncoming headache.

"We didn't bring our old ladies into any of our business. Most of the guys left their personal lives private. You're lucky you're here with this guy or you wouldn't be hearing this story at all. But I do remember him hanging around a girl though. It was so long ago; I really don't remember." Killer got up and stepped on the butt of his cigarette.

"Well, thank you. I really appreciate you telling me all this." I stepped back. I couldn't help but feel completely disappointed. I didn't think this guy was going to deliver my dad on a silver platter and we'd play family. But I wasn't prepared to hear that he was dead.

"I'm sorry, beautiful. Listen, there's a waitress in there. Name is Marisol. She's been around here forever. Why don't we go ask if she remembers anything. Other than that, that's all the information I have for you. I'm sorry." Killer took my hand. He looked into my eyes in a sincere way; not a creepy way. Angel didn't move, neither of us feeling uneasy by Killer touching me. "You're the daughter of an El Diablo. If you ever need anything; you know we would have your back. Although I can see that this guy is taking great care of you. You'll always have a home here."

He patted my cheek with his other hand and we shared a smile.

"Thank you." I said in a shaky breath.

"I'll go find her. You come in when you're ready. Get a beer, relax before you head back out tonight." Killer said over his shoulder as he walked back into the bar.

As soon as the bar door swung closed behind him; I spun around and put my head into Angel's chest and let out a giant sigh. He wrapped his arms around me and neither spoke for a few minutes. When I looked back up at him; he had a small smile on his face and kissed me ever so gently.

"You ok? I know that's probably not what you wanted to hear." Angel asked into my hair as he pulled me close.

"Yea. I'm okay. Just disappointed I guess." We looked at each other; still wrapped in each other's arms.

"Well, let's go see if Killer found that woman to talk to. Are you hungry? We should eat before we get back on the road." Angel took my hand and led me back into the bar.

We found Roman and Taylor in the booth, having already eaten. There was a soccer game on the tv and the bar was packed with El Diablos now. A young waitress strolled over to us, eyeing Angel from head to toe. Angel barely acknowledged her aside from asking for a burger and a Corona. She licked her lips as she wrote down his order then snarled at me when I asked her for a burger and bottled water. She turned on her toes and wiggled her ass as she walked away from us. Neither of the guys paid her any attention.

As we waited for our food, I was quiet. My head was swimming and the noise from the cheering soccer fans echoed in my ears. Angel looked over at me, putting his hand on top of mine just like he did the very first time I laid eyes on him and he winked at me. I gave him a small smile back.

"What are the chances this place has a ladies room?" I whispered at Angel.

"I'll take her." A woman in tight jeans and an equally tight button up shirt walked up to the table taking my hand in hers. Her monogram on her shirt read Marisol. She was an older woman, with kind, aged eyes and her hair was pinned up in a french twist. For a woman probably in her sixties, she had an amazing body and held herself with respect.

"I'm Marisol. Killer told me that you would like to speak with me." She explained with a heavy spanish accent.

"Oh, yes. Thank you." I glanced over at Angel to make sure it would be okay and that I would be safe with her. He nodded.

"We'll be right here, baby." He said more to Marisol than to me. His face was stern and serious again. I grabbed my bag and allowed myself to be led to the bathroom by the woman.

We walked into the back of the house, passing a few offices and closed doors. "You don't want to use the bathrooms out there. They're disgusting. I use the owner's private one. We can talk there. We walked into the bathroom and she was right. It was clean. There was a separate toilet room where I excused myself to while she freshened up her lipstick in the mirror outside.

"So, you're Toni's daughter? Killer told me that you came looking for him. Shame what happened to him."

"Um, yea. Definitely not what I was expecting." I flushed and pulled my jeans up and came to join her by the sink. I washed my hands as she studied my face and body.

"I knew your mom. Sonya, right." Marisol spoke quietly.

"Yea. That's right." I spun around to her to give her my full attention.

"I can see her in your eyes. But mostly you look like Toni. Toni and Sonya were so in love. She would come down to visit him almost every weekend. Toni begged her to stay here in Mexico; but she always refused. She was busy with school, I guess. Smart girl, she was. He even made her his old lady after he found out she got pregnant. Had the ceremony down at the old farmhouse." I pulled out the picture of my mom in the white dress alongside my dad. Marisol took in her fingers, a sad smile appearing on her face.

"Yup. They were definitely in love. Toni thought that making her an old lady would mean more to Sonya. But she just kept leaving him to go back home. She was stubborn. Your dad was no better though. He was in deep with El Diablos and ran to the clubhouse every chance he got. He was well respected here. Could have been big. A while after he was killed and buried; Sonya came looking for him. I remember the day she burst through the bar's doors. She had a round belly and tears in her eyes. A couple of the guys had to tell her that Toni had been killed. She was mad, threw a barstool across the room and stormed out of here. We never saw her again." Marisol lit up a cigarette. The smoke filled the small space and made my eyes water.

"So he knew about me?" I asked.

"Oh yea, Sonya had a little belly at the ceremony she was trying to hide. But we all knew Toni wouldn't settle down unless he was forced to." Marisol said with a shrug.

"Well thanks. I'm glad I came here and met you. I appreciate it." I gave Marisol a small sad smile and she gave me a hug in return.

Not long after we ate and the guys talked to a few El Diablos; we were back on the bikes headed home. Angel knew I was upset; I barely spoke the rest of the night. We got back into town around midnight; Taylor and Roman breaking off to go their separate ways. Angel parked his bike in my lot and we went upstairs to my apartment. I was tired, dirty and my butt was so sore. Roman was right.

We both stumbled into my bedroom; Angel wordlessly stripped me of my boots and jacket. And then moved on to my jeans, top, bra and underwear. He turned the shower on and warm steam filled the bathroom. I helped him out of his clothes as well, then we both just stood under the hot water; letting the road grim drip off of us. Angel lathered up my body; using careful attention to my most sensitive areas. Then we took turns, I ran my soapy hands up his chest and down his arms; his hips and thighs, then slid down his hardening cock; rubbing the head between my fingers. We kissed slowly as if the day had drained us of all our energy. Pressing my back against the cool tiles,

Angel lifted both my legs and slipped inside of me. He slowly worked in and out of me, taking his time and kissing me deeply. This felt different. Intimate. As if he sensed that I was frail and vulnerable from the long day and the news of my father. He took me slow and deep. We panted and moaned, I closed my eyes as I felt my core start to tighten and pulse. Angel growled into my ear as he pulled out of me and came all over my stomach and legs. He washed me down again and held me until I felt like a puddle in his arms. We were both exhausted. So I toweled off and crawled into bed. Angel made sure the front door was locked and set his phone on the kitchen counter to charge before he joined me.

When I woke up in the morning; I felt better. I felt the huge weight that had been sitting on my chest for so many years start to lift and I could finally put this chapter behind me. Thinking of my dad; doing the right thing and being with my mom when she got pregnant made me smile and obviously he cared enough to set me up with that trust fund. I hadn't told Angel about the money yet. I wasn't hiding it. I just didn't know how to tell him that I had 2.5 million dollars sitting in the bank for me. I got up and slipped out of bed while Angel slept on his belly with his thick arms under the pillow. I pulled on some workout leggings and a sports bra. I wanted to sweat out everything from yesterday. I sat on my spin bike; my butt was sore but it felt good to pop in some headphones and center myself.

The next few weeks went by in a wonderful blur. Angel spent most of his time at my apartment and only really left me to attend club meetings or to get clean clothes. I had applied to a few township jobs I found online; but wasn't having a lot of luck. Unfortunately I think my tarnished reputation was coming back to bite me on the ass. Sarah was busy working and stopped by for dinner on the nights Angel was gone. It was great to spend time with her. She was enjoying the extra time to herself and hitting the gym a lot more now that she was single. Angel and I went on walks up and down South Street and shopped for knick knacks for my new place. We went to the movies and did 'couple' stuff. But my favorite thing was to take off on the bike around sunset and drive out to the desert if only to just drive right back. We often stopped off at the deserted camp area where Angel took me on my first motorcycle ride with him. We made out and talked and stared up at the stars together. One night, Angel had asked me what I wanted for my future. I told him that I saw myself with a family of my own and that I never wanted to stop helping people. I was starting to throw around the idea of starting up my own non-profit to serve the community and aid the migrant children that were entering the country.

I asked Angel the same question; he shrugged his shoulders in reply but then finally conceded that he wanted a family of his own one day; where he would always be able to provide for and protect his family. As he spoke, tears ran down my cheeks. I felt so sorry that he had a sad upbringing; that he lost his mother when he was six and that he was burdened with raising his little brother. Angel kissed my tears away and held me close.

On a morning that I slept in a little, Angel got up to make breakfast for me. He knew I loved it and couldn't wait for my first coffee of the day. But I woke up feeling a little dizzy; so I sat at the edge of the bed until it passed. I think all those night rides on the motorcycle were toying with my equilibrium. I threw on some clothes and walked out to the kitchen. Angel was already eating and left my plate in the microwave to keep warm.

"Hey. Tired? You never sleep in." Angel asked as he sipped his coffee.

"Ha, yea. I think not having a job is making me lazy. I could have slept all day." I said as I yawned and stretched.

"I was going to ask you about that. You know, if you need money. I could help out. I don't want you to think I'm freeloading here." Angel stood to give me a good morning kiss.

"Actually, Angel. I've been meaning to talk to you about that." I said as I grabbed my breakfast and sat down with him.

"Oh. I, um, I don't have to stay here every night. You should have told me it was too much." Angel stuttered out with his eyebrows furrowed.

"Oh gosh, no. Not that. I love having you here. It's the

money thing I wanted to talk to you about." I pushed my plate to the center of the table. I hated talking about money and I didn't have much of an appetite anymore.

Angel sat back in his chair and crossed his arms over his chest; looking too serious for 8 o'clock in the morning. "So, I didn't know exactly how to tell you this. Um, the way I found out my father's name wasn't my mom or the private investigator."

"Okay. So how?" Angel cocked his head to me.

"A few years ago, my mom had mentioned that I had a trust fund down at the bank. I think she mentioned it because I was trying to go for my master's degree and was figuring out money. Anyway, I never thought much of it because I got caught up with work and I didn't have the time to focus on more school. So after my mom threatened to toss me out; I went down to the bank and found out the trust was set up by a man named Antonio Castillo and it originated in Mexico. From there, I hired a private investigator and so on."

"Alright. Makes sense why you wanted to track him down all of a sudden." Angel added as he leaned forward on the table.

"Yea. Um, now I'm trying not to jump to conclusions here. But after Killer told us that my dad was good with money and was about to become the treasurer of El Diablos and such; I can't help but wonder. Angel; the trust is for 2.5 *million* dollars."

Angel blew out a breath and sat back looking shocked. "Holy shit."

"Yea." I agreed. "I mean, you don't think..." I hesitated.

"I know what you're gonna say. You think your dad stole the money from El Diablos and stuck it in a trust fund for you?" Angel finished my sentence.

"I just don't know. I've had this sinking feeling in my stomach since we went down there. I mean if it's drug money... I mean, is it weird that I use that money for my future?" I shook my head, completely confused on how to feel about my dad. "There's two sides to every story. What if my dad wasn't killed by the cops, but his own brothers?" I held my stomach, the idea of it making me nauseous.

"Okay. Well we can't jump to conclusions. I know you probably don't want to hear this; but maybe you should ask your mom. It's possible Toni talked to your mom about El Diablos or what he was doing." Angel pulled my chair so that our knees touched and held both of my hands.

"Ugh. You're right. Maybe I'll email her. I won't feel better about it until I know." Angel kissed the top of my head and then got up to clean his plate.

"So you're a millionaire." He said playfully and laughed.

"Funny, right. I honestly don't want to touch the money until I absolutely have to." I stood up to toss my uneaten breakfast out.

"Not hungry, baby?" Angel glanced at me.

"Nah."

Chapter 23

Angel

I got a phone call from Roman that he got into it with a few Serpents that were eating at the bar across town. But I didn't know how bad it was until I saw him. I left Alexa at her place; she was working on her resume and had an interview later on. I pulled up at my house to see Taylor's bike parked in the driveway and Sarah's jeep. What the hell was she doing here? I burst through the front door and Roman was doubled over on the couch, clutching his side. Sarah was on her knees in front of him, holding a towel that was soaked in blood.

"What happened." I growled out, scaring Sarah enough that she jerked away from Roman. Taylor was on the phone with what sounded like Prez.

Roman picked up his pale face and tried to laugh. "Assholes fucking stabbed me." He groaned as he spoke and Sarah moved back to him to apply more pressure on his wound.

I stomped into the kitchen where Taylor was pacing back and forth talking quickly on the phone. He held out a finger to me and I impatiently waited.

Taylor ended the call and tossed his phone on the kitchen counter. "Prez is sending a doctor over. Fucking Serpents." Taylor ran his hand through his blond hair.

"Can someone fucking tell me what happened. Why is she here?" I pointed to Sarah.

"Thanks Angel." Sarah yelled. "Roman called me to come pick him up. When I got there, he was slumped over his bike bleeding." Sarah's face was red and sweaty. "When is the doctor coming? Shouldn't we just take him to the hospital?" She was panicking and I felt terrible for yelling at her.

"We got a doctor coming, should be here in a minute." Taylor grabbed more towels and helped lay Roman down on the couch so we could get his shirt off. Sarah stood back and watched as we ripped away his shirt and tried to clean the area.

"Roman, bro, what happened?" I searched his face. He was pale but I knew he'd be fine because he was smiling and trying to joke around.

"I don't know man. I was leaving the bar, I just grabbed something to eat when these two guys followed me out. They pulled a knife on me and I told them to shove it up their asses. That's when shit hit the fan." Roman coughed and groaned. "There was no way I could get back on my bike and ride; so I called Sarah."

Sarah paced the small house and finally washed the blood off her hands when the doctor came in. We always had a doctor on our payroll for times like this. Hospitals asked too many questions and drew too much attention. Roman was stitched up in no time and given some heavy pain medication and a shot of antibiotics. He passed out after Taylor and I helped him get in his bed.

"Sorry I was a dick, Sarah. Thanks for picking him up." I apologized to her. She looked really upset.

"It's fine. He didn't even tell me what happened; I just saw all the blood and freaked out." Sarah held her arms over her chest. "If you want, I can stay with him for a bit. Make sure he doesn't bleed through his bandages."

"Thanks, Sarah" She gave me a hug and I went out to talk to Taylor who was helping himself to a bowl of cereal.

"Think Sarah will let us borrow her jeep so you can bring Roman's bike back." Taylor said with a mouthful of food.

"Here." Sarah poked her head out of the bedroom; tossed her keys to me, I guess she overheard us.

"Finish up and let's go. They better not have fucked with his bike."

I dropped off Roman's bike off at the house, grabbed some

clean clothes and Taylor and I went back to the clubhouse to talk to Prez. Taylor had already told him what was up. But I wanted to find out where we stood with the problem of the Serpents on our territory.

"How's Roman." Prez asked as we opened the door to his office.

"He'll live. Few stitches." I answered.

"Taylor, let me talk to Angel for a second." Prez nodded towards the door, asking Taylor to step out.

"How's everything going Angel. Enjoying the break?" Prez's eyes were dark and settled on my face. I doubt he knew I was back with Alexa. But something was lingering in the air between us.

"Yea. It's been good. You know if you need me, I'm there." I reassured Rey.

Rey came to sit on the desk in front of me. He braced his hands behind him, crossing his legs at the ankles. "Listen Angel. A little birdie told me that you've been spotted with Ramirez's daughter again. And before you go and deny it or ask who said something; that's not important. You know we got guys all over this town. Fuck, even I saw her on the back of your bike the other night."

I kept my eyes emotionless. I wasn't going to interrupt or fight the inevitable.

"Listen. We've talked before about your future with the club. If you want it; you're in. You'll be moving up with Roman and eventually taking rank as an officer. But if that's not what you want; I need to know. You've done us all proud and have been loyal. I don't deny you that. But if you want to hand in your vest. You tell me now." Rey's eyes bore into my soul and I couldn't look away. What he was offering was something most brothers dreaded to hear. Most of us were lifers. If we had a chance to step away; we'd most likely do it because we were forced or killed.

I bit my lip as I stood to eye level with Rey. "Can you give me some time? I want to talk to Roman about it first."

"Yea, I get that. That's fine. One week, Angel." Rey got up

and I was dismissed.

Alexa

I was supposed to be sending out resumes and I had spent the last hour on the phone with a potential job offer. But I just couldn't stop thinking about what Angel and I were talking about. I decided to send my mom an email after all. Bite the bullet.

Mom,

As you probably noticed, I moved out a while ago. Found my own place that I love and I'm really happy here. I wanted to say that I'm sorry that I've disappointed you in some way. If living my life and falling in love were our downfall; then I guess I'm sorry for that too.

I did a lot of soul searching and actually decided to track down my father. Hired a private investigator and everything. Antonio Castillo. He was a member of El Diablos in Mexico.
Angel took me down there to talk with them. I thought I'd be able to find my way to him.

And yea. I'm back with Angel. He makes me happy and we belong together.

El Diablos told me how Antonio was killed by the Mexican cops. How he made you his old lady. How you tried to hide your pregnant belly in front of the Diablos. And when you came down to Chico's bar with a large belly; they told you Antonio was killed. I'm sure there's more to the story. But that's not something you've ever offered me. For some reason you were repulsed by my father and refused to tell me where I came from. So you see; I had no choice but to dig for the information for myself. If you ever change your mind; I'll be all ears. If you ever want to repair our relationship, I'm here for that too.

Talk soon, I hope,
Alexa

Angel came back to the apartment just as I hit send on

my email. Angel looked like he was deep in thought and moved through the apartment quietly.

"Hey. Everything ok?" I asked as I moved towards him

"Roman was stabbed. I'm sorry, I just have a lot on my mind." Angel came to stand in front of me with his arms hanging at his sides. He looked tired and agitated and I couldn't help but put my arms around him and just hold him.

"Is he okay?" I asked as tears slid down my face. Angel breathed in my hair and held me tighter.

"Yea, he'll be fine." He said as he wiped my tears away. "Baby, it's ok. We got him a doctor and he'll be just fine." He laughed softly.

"Sorry. I don't know why that made me so upset. Everyone loves Roman. Who would do that to him?"

"Serpents. We have had some problems with them." Angel answered. He was being vague but I didn't want to push him to explain club business. I felt my stomach flip flop and I pushed away from him. I hadn't noticed the blood smeared on his shirt until now.

"Angel, you have blood on your shirt." I blinked up at him.

"Oh shit. Sorry. I grabbed some clothes before I left. Come shower with me and we'll order something for dinner."

We showered and I threw on some sweat pants and tank top without a bra. Angel loved when I went braless. We ordered from the deli down the street that delivered so we wouldn't have to leave our little cocoon that we've made here. I got chicken soup; my stomach still doesn't feel right. I think all the stress of not having a job and me emailing my mom has finally gotten to me.

Angel called Roman after we ate to check and see how he was feeling. "How's he doing?" I asked as I cuddled up on the couch.

"Um, fine. Sarah answered his phone. She was over there when Roman called me to meet him at our house." Angel said with a small smirk.

"What? Sarah? My Sarah?" I said as I slapped my hand

down on the couch in disbelief.

"Yea. I know. It was kind of weird. Roman called *her* to pick him up when it happened. He couldn't ride his bike back in the condition he was." Angel shook his head.

"Sarah?" I said again to myself.

The food came and we ate. Angel was still pretty quiet even though his brother said he was ok and he was already sitting up and Sarah made him eat something.

"Whatcha thinking? I can tell somethings on your mind." I asked as I laid my legs across Angel's lap on the couch.

"I'm thinking about leaving Los Demonios." He said flatly.

I sat up quickly. "What? Why? Because Roman got hurt?"

"No. I mean bad shit happens but it's more than that. Prez sat me down today and gave me an out. That doesn't usually happen in an MC. Either you're kicked out or killed. There's not too many guys that'll hang up their cut."

"So why would *you*?" I searched his face. This conversation made my stomach try to reject the chicken soup I just ate.

"My hearts just not in it. I told you how this all came to be and I never wanted to disappoint my brother. But I just think I want something else for my life." Angel's eyes stared off into my quiet apartment.

"You know I understand that. What do you want? What's one thing you would do if you weren't a Los Demonios Locos?" I sat up and straddled his lap. I braced my hands on either side of his face and gave him my best supportive girlfriend face.

"It's been a long time since I've thought of what I wanted to do. But if I had to pick right now; it would be to own a motorcycle shop. Motorcycles are all I know. And I'm good at it." Angel answered as he absentmindedly traced the outline of my hardened nipples. He made a shiver run down my spine and it made him smile.

"Enough heavy talk. I want these nipples in my mouth." Angel breathed as he pulled my shirt up and I arched into his mouth. We spent the night pleasuring each other instead in front of the tv and I was completely fine with that. We both needed the stress release and Angel's hands all over me drove me crazy.

Unfortunately, my mind wasn't exhausted enough to sleep soundly. I tossed and turned and woke up Angel several times. Finally, he pulled me tight into his arms and asked me if I was feeling ok. I was hot and restless and every time I closed my eyes; I had nightmares. Nightmares about being on the back of Angel's bike and I'd fallen off but he kept riding; not realizing I was bleeding and bruised on the road. Or the newest one was where I would come home to my apartment and Roman was standing in the middle of the room with Angel's vest in his hand and he would tell me how Angel was killed while taking care of MC business. That one had me bolting out of bed and trying to calm myself and my tears while sitting on the floor in the bathroom. I didn't want my insecurities to scare Angel. We had such an amazing thing going; I didn't want to pressure him to leave the DLs; that choice was his and his alone.

Around 6AM, I finally gave up on sleep and crept out of the room to work out. I had moved my spin bike out into the living area for that reason. Angel was still asleep and I needed the time to clear my head and try to get some energy back. My workout was great; I was a little more tired than usual but I'll blame that on my stupid nightmares and not getting enough sleep. Angel was still asleep; so I powered up my computer and checked my emails. I had applied to two more positions; they were an hour's commute from here. But I wasn't having any luck with local charities, shelters or even municipal positions. I probably had my mother to thank for that. I glanced through my list of unread emails and I noticed a reply from my mother. My stomach sank and before I clicked on it to open it; I made myself a cup of coffee and ate a banana.

Okay; here goes nothing. I clicked on the email and focused my eyes on the long message.

Alexa,

Allow me first to address your notion of understanding who your father was. Yes, Antonio Castillo is your father and yes he was

a member of El Diablos. But there are two sides to every story. I probably should have told you this and saved you a trip into Mexico but
here it is:

I met your father while at a concert me and some girlfriends
attended. He was charming and exciting. We fell in love very quickly
and I made it a point to drive down to Mexico almost every weekend
to be with him. He made it quite clear that El Diablo's came first
in our relationship; but I was young and in love, so I overlooked it.
Not much time passed and I became pregnant with you. Antonio was
ecstatic; and I begged him to leave El Diablos to start a life with me
in the States. I was in law school by then and didn't want to throw
my school career down the tubes. Antonio thought that if he made
me his "Old Lady" aka: illegal motorcycle club marriage; I would give
in and stay with him in Mexico. We started fighting; a lot. And he
started becoming very important to the MC. Leaving me to fend for
myself. So many times I would go down to Mexico to be with him and
he would be off tending to some crazy club bullshit. So, the next time
I saw him; I gave him an ultimatum. Come to the States and be with
me and help raise the baby with me or we would be finished. Three
months went by with nothing. So, the last time I set foot in Mexico
was to face him in person and pray that he picked 'us'. But he was
already dead; his brothers said that he was ambushed by cops out in
the desert.

So, Alexa. You can see why I cannot support your relationship
with Angel. He has proven to be just like every other motorcycle club
thug, committing crimes and acting like an animal. He will only hurt
you or leave you in the end. You have no future with someone like
that. Angel will be your downfall; and I will not be there to witness it.
Your father ruined my life while he continued to live his; so much so
that he was killed for it. I'd hate to see the same thing for you.

I love you Alexa. I know our relationship hasn't been the best.
I'm sorry I wasn't a good mother to you. But I hope you understand
that all I wanted for you was the best and to be successful.

I hope that one day; when you've moved past all of this- we
could sit down and talk.

-Mom

I sat with my head in my hands for a while. The words on the screen blurring until I finally had to blink back the tears that threatened to fall. I slammed my hand on the table refusing to cry over my mom's words. It was crazy that she was comparing my relationship to her own. But the ache in my chest made me feel like maybe she had a point. I got up, marched into the bathroom, stripping down to take a shower. I refused to become a bitter woman like my mother was now. I needed a plan and I decided another trip down to the bank would help give me clarity.

Chapter 24

Alexa

I quietly got dressed and left Angel a note on the kitchen counter that I needed to go to the bank and that I'll be back soon. I clicked the door quietly behind me and jogged down the stairs with renewed ambition. I had tossed around the idea of starting a non-profit for children in need but while I was in the shower; I had an epiphany that I needed to start a non-profit organization to support *education* for migrant children. It dawned on me that all the children that were taken into the state's shelter barely spoke english. These children would eventually be filtered through the system and be adopted or fostered out to homes across the nation. So what better than to help provide a way to give these kids a fighting chance by teaching them english and basic skills before they are shipped off to schools that may not even have an English Learning System. I knew plenty of teachers that would volunteer their time.

I headed towards the bank. I needed to get all my ducks in a row if I was going to present a business plan to the city and apply for grants. It wasn't going to be easy; but I've met a lot of really great people in the field that would jump at the opportunity to expand community service to migrant children.

I spent an hour sitting with a financial advisor at the bank asking questions and listening to all of his advice and I couldn't wait to get started. I texted Angel that I was on my way back home and decided to stop at the store and grab the ingredients to make a home cooked meal. My grandmother taught me how to make amazing enchiladas and I wanted to make them for Angel tonight.

When I got back to the apartment, Angel was just getting out of the shower. He smelled like my coconut shampoo and my mouth watered as beads of water dripped down his bare chest.

"Where'd you go this early in the morning?" He asked as he ran a towel across his wet hair.

"Bank. I think I have the perfect idea." I said as I unloaded the groceries into the refrigerator. I explained my idea and rattled off the things I would need to get done to propose a business plan to the city. I was hoping Sarah would help me too; she had a great head for business and had plenty of contacts. Angel loved my idea; said I'd be the best person for the job. He put his arms around me and kissed my lips.

"Wanna go for a ride today? It's beautiful out." Angel asked.

"Sure. To tell you the truth; I think I'm getting a little bit of cabin fever. I've never not had a job and I feel lazy." I groaned as I piled the vegetables onto the counter. "Tonight, I'm going to make my grandmother's enchiladas."

"Sounds good; as long as I get *you* for dessert." Angel teased.

I changed into sneakers and pulled on a light weight sweater as Angel was pulling on his boots out in the living room.

"So, I heard back from my mom." I called out from the bedroom.

There was silence and then Angel appeared in my doorway with arms crossed over his chest.

"Is this what sparked the urge to get up and go down to the bank?" Angel leaned onto the jam; waiting for me to elaborate.

"Well, she certainly has a bitchy way of motivating someone. I mean, I'll let you read the email. But it's more of the same crap she's been spewing. Although, she did tell me that she had given Antonio an ultimatum when they found out she was pregnant with me. And I guess he chose the club over my mother. I think that's why she's so bitter and honestly; I think she regrets getting pregnant and has been holding it against me all my life." Angel came to sit next to me on the bed. I was trying really hard to not let my mother's email eat away at me, but saying it out loud hurt. There was so much resentment in her words and I think she thought my relationship would fail because hers did.

"You're your own person, Alexa. I think your mother is forgetting that. Sure, she wants the best for you; but she's forgotten what it's like to be young and in love." Angel's face reddened. A little smile crossed my lips when he said the last part. "I mean, you know, to be happy; with someone." He stuttered.

"Mmmmhmmm. No you're right. About everything." I looked up at him slowly; hoping he'd understand my hidden meaning. I was falling so very hard in love with Angel. And I was hoping he felt the same about me. He bent to kiss me ever so softly and pulled my hands so that I was standing.

"Come on. There's somewhere I've been wanting to go and I want you to be there with me." Angel said cryptically. "Ready."

"Sure. Oh, don't you want to read the email?" Angel was dragging me through the apartment towards the front door as I pointed behind me at my laptop.

"Nope. It's not important. What you feel and what you think are important." He deadpanned before he opened the door to leave.

"Okay. You're right." I nodded and after those few words; the stress of my mother and the biting words of her email washed right out of my mind.

We got on his bike and the rumble between my legs sent goosebumps all over my body. I don't think I'll ever get over how exciting it was to ride on the back of his bike. He helped strap on my helmet and as he pulled out of the parking lot; I couldn't help but in complete awe of this man. He looked insanely hot on a bike, his eyes shielded with dark sunglasses, his rugged jeans and boots, his strong arms and hands controlling the dangerous machine and the best part was when we rode together; he always had a hand on my knee that was squeezed into his side. It was like he was claiming me for everyone to see; and I fucking loved it.

The ride wasn't long; we took local roads to get to the opposite side of town. I knew he lived on the West side; maybe he was taking me to his house? When we pulled up to a faded brick building and pulled over to the side of the road, I had an idea of where we were. We got off the bike, wordless. Angel couldn't take his eyes off the building. There was something in his eyes; a glimmer of happiness and sadness. The building looked like a small warehouse but as we rounded the side; an old faded sign read: Mack's Machine Shop.

I laced my fingers in Angel's hands as we got closer. The building looked abandoned, the glass windows were boarded up and graffiti littered the garage doors.

"This is it? Isn't it?" I asked in a quiet voice. Angel just nodded. We stood back to admire the broken down building; Angel kicked the broken glass that was on the ground.

"I haven't been past this place since I was taken out of it in handcuffs. I've done everything to avoid coming down this road for over a decade." Angel was quiet, pensive.

"No one's ever opened it back up?" I studied the area, the surrounding buildings seemed to be in good standing. It was a decent blue collared neighborhood, small shops lined one side of the street with some larger buildings on either side of the shop.

"Police tore it apart and after Mack was found dead; the city took ownership."

"Oh. So you know that Mack was killed?" I looked up at him, the sun shining in my eyes.

"Yea. I know." He said with a knowing smirk. The smirk told me he knew exactly who killed him and how. No doubt Los Demonios wasn't about to let Mack get away with everything that happened.

"Thanks for coming here with me. I thought coming here would bother me more. My whole life changed right here in this parking lot. But I have a lot to be thankful for too. I can't sit here and regret my life, Alexa. It made me the man I am today. And it saved Roman and I from a life that could have ended up very differently. I don't regret my life as a Los Demonios; I have a family in them. And I have you." Angel pulled me into his chest and kissed my cheek so softly. His lips travelled down my neck and his arms tightened as his mouth grazed my ear. "And I'm in love with you." He said ever so softly, making my entire body weak.

When I glanced up at his face, he looked at me nervously but I couldn't help but smile; taking both of his hands in mine and whispering back, "I'm in love with you too, Angel." He kissed me good and long as I felt his heart beating fast and hard in his chest. My own heart matching his. He put his arm around my shoulders as we both took a long look at the building; silently thanking it for bringing us together; in a weird and wild journey sort of way.

"Think anyone will ever buy this place?" I asked.

"I don't know. I'm sure there's a shit ton of red tape; but this place could be pretty amazing." Angel's eyes squinted as I could see a million thoughts run through his mind.

We walked back to the bike hand in hand and he gave me one last kiss before strapping on my helmet.

"Um, I live a few minutes away. Do you want to go check up on Roman?" Angel asked, scratching his head. He looked nervous about me seeing his place. He had to know that I'd be the last person to judge him.

"Sure." I replied with a big smile. We got on the bike and headed out; Angel taking a final glance at Mack's as we drove away.

Angel

We pulled up at the small faded yellow house Roman and I called home. The chain link fence now housed tall weeds and the gutter on the front of the house was falling down. I used to pay the kid down the street to mow the lawn but it looks like he hasn't been here in a few weeks. Roman's F150 was parked in the driveway so we parked behind it and got off the bike. Alexa took a long look at the house and her surroundings. The neighborhood was full of houses in multiple stages of neglect but it was quiet; and the neighborhood kids minded their own business.

Alexa took her helmet off and flashed me that smile of hers. I couldn't help but feel embarrassed about where we lived; but Alexa didn't even wrinkle her nose about it. We walked into the side door that led to the kitchen. Roman was sitting at the table cleaning his gun.

"Hey man." Roman nodded at me as he threw a towel over the gun pieces spread out over the table; realizing Alexa was coming into the house behind me. Alexa eyed the gun parts but she didn't even flinch. She just walked over to Roman and gave him a soft hug.

"Hey Roman. How are you feeling?" Alexa asked as she pulled out a chair to sit next to him.

"Sore but I'm ok." Roman leaned back into his chair with a groan. "I guess I should feel lucky that this was the first time I got stabbed and walked away from it." Roman laughed off.

"Well, I'm glad you're ok." Alexa beamed.

"What are you guys doing around here?" Roman asked, standing up to grab Alexa a bottle of water from the fridge. I was flipping through the mail that was strewn about the counter top and weeded out all the flyers and bills.

"Um, Angel brought me to see Mack's." Alexa answered honestly.

"Yea, bro? You avoid that place like the plague. She's pretty beaten down, right? Shame. It's such a good spot for a bike shop." Roman held his side as he spoke. He was in more pain than he led on.

"Roman, you're bleeding man." I pointed at Roman's shirt that showed his bandages were bleeding through to his shirt. As Alexa's eyes travelled down Roman stomach where the blood was; Alexa gagged and slapped her hand on her mouth. I moved to her quickly. Her face was pale and instantly sweaty and I helped move her to the bathroom where she closed the door on my face.

"Baby, are you ok?" I asked as I heard Alexa throw up in the toilet.

"Ugh, yea. I'm sorry. I guess I'm not very good with blood."

Alexa mumbled out as she threw up one more time. "I just need a minute."

Roman came to stand next to me, he raised a curious eyebrow and then moved to the bedroom for a clean shirt. I helped him change his bandages, his wound healing but looked swollen and sore.

"She ok?" Roman whispered to me. I nodded with a shrug in response. We moved out to the front room to give Alexa some privacy.

"Roman, you taking it easy? That wound should be healed by now." I sat on the couch as Roman neatened up the magazines that covered the coffee table.

"I'm sick of sitting here talking to the damn walls; I had someone over last night." Roman smirked.

"Shit. Well tell her to take it easy on you." I laughed at Roman's antics. He couldn't go a week without pussy.

"Nah bro, she likes if fucking rough." Roman laughed just as Alexa came out of the bathroom. She looked flushed but I was happy to see some color in her face.

"Oh my god, I'm so sorry." Alexa blushed and held her stomach.

"It's fine. Maybe we should get you home though. You still look a little pale." I got up and moved across the room towards her. "Besides, Roman just promised me to take it easy tonight." I shot him daggers and a raised eyebrow. He put up his hands in surrender.

"I'd come and give you a hug goodbye baby girl, but I don't want you to throw up again." Roman teased Alexa. She laughed and told him it was fine and settled for a wave.

We got back to the apartment and Alexa looked much better. I'm sure the fresh air helped ease her stomach. Alexa was excited to start cooking; she was making me her grandmother's recipe tonight for enchiladas. I sat at the kitchen counter watching her move around the kitchen. She was a great cook and I couldn't lie that watching her ass as she hummed and danced around while slicing up vegetables was fucking hot as hell. She peeled off her sweater, leaving her wearing tight blue jeans and a lace tank top. She piled her hair on top of her head, exposing that beautiful neck and her tits looked round and perky. It was hard for me not to come up behind her and fuck her against the kitchen sink.

Alexa turned to me, holding up a slice of red pepper and munching on a green slice of pepper with the other. You could tell she was working through a thought by the far out look in her eyes. I squinted my eyes at her waiting for her to speak.

"What's going on in the beautiful head of yours?" I laughed as I stole the red pepper from her fingertips.

"Hey." She snapped away from her daydream, giggling. "What if you could *buy* Mack's?" She asked as she popped a hand on her hip.

"Buy Mack's? I don't know Alexa. That building's been shut down and locked up for a decade. I wouldn't even know how to go about figuring that out." I leaned back in my chair.

"Well. I could help you. You said that the city took possession of it. Well, cities don't really like to hold onto vacant buildings because legally they have to maintain it in some way or keep it secured. What if we petition the city for the building to get auctioned off? It happens all the time. Buildings will go for auction but typically already have a buyer. It makes all that red tape disappear." Alexa spoke so quickly; it was making my head spin. I came to stand with her, placing my hands on her hips. I thought about what she was saying as I reached behind her to steal another slice of red pepper and popped it in my mouth.

"Hey! That's for dinner." She laughed as she playfully swatted at my chest.

"That's a good thought but, Alexa, I don't have that kind of money." I kissed her again, her lips tasting like sweet candy.

"Hmmm. Would you be ok with me looking into it, at least? Just find out what the deal is with the building." Alexa peeked up at me with those honey brown eyes.

"I'm not going to stop you." I quipped.

We spent the rest of the night making dinner together and

eating. The food was amazing and after we finished; I pushed the dirty dishes aside and took Alexa right on the kitchen table. I spread her out so that I could suck on her wet pussy as she moaned and giggled; sending utensils and a dish flying to the floor. Not giving two shits about the disaster in the kitchen, I picked up Alexa and brought her to the bedroom. I lowered her body onto the bed; stripping off my shirt and pushing my jeans down around my knees.

"Get on your hands and knees." I growled out. I was already stroking my hard cock and she complied with a whimper.

I pulled out a condom from the bedside table and sunk into her slowly. I made it painfully slow for her as she panted and tried to back her ass up onto me.

"Angel." She begged. I moved in and out of her with my hands rubbing and squeezing her ass. I licked the tips of my fingers and reached around to rub her needy clit. As soon as I touched her; she moaned and closed her eyes. She was so wet and tight; her pussy squeezing me.

"Come baby. Squeeze my cock with that beautiful pussy." Her body quivered under mine; she loved to hear me talk dirty to her; her body responded to every word.

She came so hard, her pussy so tight; I couldn't help but pound into her; my balls squeezing with my own orgasm. I collapsed on to her back; both sweaty and panting hard. After our breathing and heartbeats came back down to normal, I got up; taking care of the condom and threw on a pair of gym shorts.

"Why don't you go shower; and I'll clean up our mess in the kitchen." I leaned over to kiss Alexa's puffy lips.

"I won't fight you on that." Alexa smiled into my mouth. She got up from the bed and I gave her ass a light swat as she moved into the bathroom.

We passed out somewhere around midnight; talking and telling stories from our childhood until Alexa passed out on my chest. A strange noise in the middle of the night had me sitting straight up in bed. I reached out to Alexa's side of the bed and she was gone. I glanced over at the clock, it was 5 AM and it was still dark out. I got up, realizing I was hearing crying, and found Alexa locked into the bathroom.

"Alexa." I knocked on the door. I heard her groan and the flush of the toilet. "Are you ok?"

"I don't know." Her voice was shaking.

"Let me in." I demanded, twisting the doorknob in my hand.

"No, Angel. I'm ok. I don't want you to see me like this." She wretched again and I can hear the contents of her stomach emptying into the toilet bowl. "Oh my god. I think I gave us food poisoning." I stepped back, trying to figure out how to get into the bathroom.

"Alexa. Open up. I don't care that you're puking." I banged on the door now.

I heard the toilet flush and she slowly opened the door, her hand still over her mouth. Her face was pale and sweat dripped down her forehead.

"It's got to be food poisoning." She said, shaking her head.

"Baby, I'm fine. I ate everything you ate." I wet a washcloth with cold water. I wrung it out and put it to her forehead. She leaned on the sink looking into the mirror with me behind her. She let me hold her weight as she brushed her teeth.

"Baby. You don't think you might be pregnant? Do you?" I asked quietly as I kissed the side of her head. Her eyes snapped to mine and I can see she was panicking and thinking it over. I spun her carefully to look at me and held her in my arms. "When's the last time you had your period?" I searched her face as she mentally counted in her mind.

"But, but we've been careful." She shook her head; but not completely letting go of my theory. "Angel, oh my god. I, um, I need a calendar. Where's my phone?" She wiggled away from me and scrambled out to the bedroom. I watched as she brought up the calendar on her phone and counted days. She sat on the bed, fear and shock washed over her face. "Angel, I'm late. Like two weeks late." Big fat tears started welling up in her eyes and spilled over as I came to kneel beside her. I tried my best to wipe away her falling tears as her whole body trembled.

"Shhhhhh. Baby, it's going to be ok." I'll go down to the store and go get a test. Then we'll figure this out, okay. Don't panic. I love you; everything is going to be alright." I rocked her in my arms as my own thoughts raced. "Here, get into bed and rest. I'll run down to the corner; they're open 24 hours. I'll be right back, okay?" I pulled the covers up and kissed her lips. She held onto my hand, her eyes meeting mine. She looked so worried. "It's going to be ok." I smiled at her as I grabbed a sweatshirt and ran out the door.

By the time I walked back into the apartment, Alexa was already up and pacing the length of the living room. She had pulled on an oversized sweatshirt and her blue cotton shorts. Her hair wild with sexy waves. Her eyes were red and she looked like she was going to throw up again. I put the test down on the counter and filled up a large glass of water for her. I was quiet. I didn't want to say the wrong thing or freak her out any more than she was; so I just waited for her to be ready. Alexa walked over to the glass and took several small sips.

"Angel, what if.." Alexa's big honey brown eyes looked up to mine. I put my hand under her chin and spoke to her calmly.

"It will be ok, Alexa. I love you. We do this together, okay." I reassured her. She kissed me and took the test, tearing open the side and sliding the thin plastic test onto her palm.

She took a deep, cleansing breath and nodded.

"I'll be right here." I said as I stood in the kitchen; leaning on the countertop.

"Okay." Her voice was shaking and she walked quietly to the bathroom. A minute later she came out and placed the test on the counter in front of us and came to stand in front of me. I wrapped my arms around her and we just breathed for a few minutes.

"Angel, we've never even talked about this stuff. I mean, what if I am pregnant. I don't even know if you want a baby with me." Tears rolled down her cheeks again as I interrupted her with kisses that helped relax her racing mind.

"Baby, if you're pregnant. I'm all in. I know this wasn't planned but I love you and we'll make this work." I held her close but my heart was racing and I was trying to hide my emotions. On one hand I was scared out of my mind; but on the other I was excited. "You ready to look." I said with a big smile.

She blew out a big breath and her shoulders relaxed. "You look. I'm too scared, I can't stop shaking." Her hands trembled on my chest. I moved around her and looked down at the test. Two lines. Bright pink and I couldn't help but have the biggest smile on my face as I turned to face her.

"What? What does it say?" She rushed out. Her eyes trying to peer over at the test. I moved to her and scooped her up in my arms, burying my head into her neck and warmth.

"You're pregnant, baby. We're gonna have a baby." I pulled back to look at her face. She bit her quivering bottom lip with a small smile growing on her face and I knew I had tears in my eyes.

"Holy shit." She finally said as I kissed her hard and worked my way down her neck and chest. "Oh my god, I can't stop shaking." She laughed out loud as I spun her around her kitchen.

Chapter 25

Alexa

A week later and I still could not believe that I was pregnant. I called the doctor's to change my appointment from a normal exam to an OBGYN exam and that's when it all started to sink in. We wanted to tell Sarah and Roman in person, so Angel and I decided to ask them over for dinner next Friday night. Angel's been amazing. He stopped at the store to pick me up crackers and soup, prenatal vitamins and ginger candies for my morning sickness. Today was the first day that I didn't wake up puking. He won't let me ride on his bike with him but he enjoys taking my car when we go out.

I'm still having trouble sleeping at night. So while Angel's asleep, I've been sneaking out of bed and cozying on the couch with my computer on my lap. I've been doing tons of research about starting a non profit and even have a potential building that I'm working on purchasing; with the help of my new financial advisor. The building is small but could at least house three or four classrooms. It's only a block away from the Migrant Shelter that I used to work at so that'll be super helpful if I can get Roger to agree to extend his community outreach to include schooling for these kids. I sent him an email outlining my business plan as well as a lengthy apology about everything that happened. I'm hoping that he sees what I'm trying to do for these children is as important as I believe it is and agrees to working together. Sarah is already on board and has reached out to some teachers and volunteers that we've worked with in the past. As long as I can get approved for the grant and building permits; it looks like everything can start happening in the next six months.

The baby is due in the beginning of June. So as much as I don't want to rush into anything; I can't wait to throw myself back into work. Angel has been super supportive and helping with the potential building plans. Two days ago, I called down to the city trying to get some information on the motorcycle shop building. The clerk was kind enough to explain that the building was recently reevaluated, deeming it outside of city limits. That was a great benefit to us. City buildings always had more red tape and guidelines. The fact that the township owned it made me positive that I could petition it to be auctioned off.

Angel had a meeting today at the clubhouse. Last night he told me that he had a long talk with Roman just the other day. Without telling Roman I was pregnant; Angel rehashed his conversation with the President about Angel hanging up his cut. Before leaving that night to meet up with his brother; Angel told me that he was 90% decided on leaving Los Demonios. He assured me it had nothing to do with the baby and that he has wanted this for himself since before he even met me. The baby and I just were a wake up call to regain his life and start doing something for himself. I was nervous about how Roman would take the news; but Angel came back feeling good about the conversation but he was a little worried how the MC would feel about him cutting loose.

Roman was barely surprised by the news. Angel was never into club life like Roman was. The two brothers have always been close; always had each other's backs and Roman understood that Angel just wanted different things for himself. Tonight was the table meeting where Angel would announce that he was going to hang up his vest. I'm sure the news won't go over well, I just hope they don't give Angel a hard time, thinking I pushed him into this.

I was laying on the bed, trying to take a nap when Angel came in to kiss me goodbye. I looked up at him with his faded baggy jeans on, boots, black long sleeve shirt and Los Demonios Locos cut. His eyes looked serious and thoughtful. Damn he looked so good. He bent down to kiss me and softly rub a hand over my lower stomach. He made this a habit everytime we parted ways.

"Sleep, you look exhausted. I should be back in a few hours." He whispered into my lips. He pulled the blanket up over my shoulder and I whispered back, 'good luck'.

I slept for an hour. I found that naps took the edge off my morning sickness and feeling of complete exhaustion during the day. I hope in a few weeks I'll start feeling better and getting back into a normal routine. I was already out of bed and making a snack for myself when I heard Angel's bike pull into the back lot. Moments later he was coming up the stairs and into the kitchen. I sat on top of the counter; anxious to hear how the meeting went. As he came in front of me, without his vest on, I cried silent tears.

He came to stand between my legs and brushed the tears away, hushing me and wrapping his strong arms around me.

"Shhh, it's okay baby." He said as he nestled in my neck and hair.

"How'd it go?" I asked as I hiccuped.

He pushed back and grabbed a beer from the fridge. He leaned on the counter opposite me, knowing the smell of beer made me gag.

"It was ok. Not as bad as I thought it would go. The guys were surprised but they understood. Roman stood at my side the whole time. As I hung up my cut, they promoted him to officer. We drank some beers and talked for a while. Those guys will always be my family, regardless." He explained quietly.

"I'm happy everything is ok. Are you okay?" I asked cautiously. I was scared to death that Angel would blame me for him stepping down. That he would come to regret the decision and leave us. After all, it wasn't just me that I was worried about anymore.

"Alexa. I'm fine. This was a long time coming. I only want to look forward to our future." He set his beer down and crossed to me, putting his hands on my knees. "You have nothing to worry about. I want this." He gestured to him and I. "And this" He rubbed my little belly.

"Come on. I want to make love to you." He pulled me slowly down and off the kitchen counter. And I silently followed him to the bedroom.

Angel

Roman and Sarah were coming over for dinner tonight and Alexa was just getting her appetite back; so I helped her make some steaks and a few sides. I could tell that she was nervous but excited to tell everyone that we were having a baby and I watched her dance around the kitchen with the same admiration and felt my dick harden at the sight. She was wearing a strappy summer dress that hugged her swollen breasts but hung loosely over her stomach. Her hair was down with loose waves and she looked like she was glowing.

Roman showed up first, then Sarah a few minutes later. We all exchanged hugs and Roman made himself at home on the couch with a beer. Sarah sat on the arm of the couch chatting with Roman as we put the food out.

"Angel, good to see you're all domesticated and shit." Roman laughed at me from the living room. I shot him a look and shook my head.

"Alex, this place really looks great, I love the pictures against the brick wall." Sarah complimented.

"Thanks! I can't believe you haven't been here in a few weeks! Work that crazy?" Alexa and Sarah caught up on work drama and Roman came to grab another beer from the fridge.

"How's it going man? Miss seeing you at the club. And at the house. You even living there anymore?" Roman teased as he slapped me on the back. I saw that Alexa was blushing already; looking like she was going to burst at the seams if we didn't tell them our secret soon.

"Sorry. Yea. Alexa is a hell of a lot cleaner to live with. And she puts out." I joked as Alexa shot me a funny look. "Ha, sorry.

But yea I guess it might be pointless to move all my stuff in here though." I looked up between Sarah and Roman who looked confused.

"Yea, we're going to move into a bigger place. I found a small house just a few blocks over that has two bedrooms and a cute little yard." Alexa added. Sarah stood to join the conversation.

"That's great. Is your lease up already though?" Sarah asked, pouring herself a glass of wine.

"Well no. But, we'll need a bigger place soon anyway." Alexa's face reddened and I couldn't help but have a huge smile on my face. Sarah's mouth dropped open and her eyes lit up with excitement.

"What?" Roman looked between the three of us. "What the fuck am I missing here." Roman said, annoyed.

I came to stand behind Alexa and wrapped my arms around her waist, my fingertips rubbing small circles over her tiny baby bump.

"You gotta be shitting me." Roman spit out.

"Oh my god!" Sarah jumped up and clapped her hands. "You're pregnant?" She yelled with a huge smile on her face.

Alexa's eyes filled with tears again and she nodded her head yes over and over. I squeezed her to me but let go when Sarah jumped over to give us both hugs and kisses. Roman stood there still in shock but a small smile played on his mouth. We walked over to each other, nodded and smiled while we hugged and he slapped my back.

"Congratulations, man." Roman said softly as we hugged. When I pulled away, we both were choked up but coughed and tried to be manly about it. Roman walked over to Alexa, giving her a kiss on the cheek and a soft hug.

We all sat down to dinner, Roman was mostly quiet and we listened to the girls chat excitedly. Sarah was asking all sorts of questions about how Alexa was feeling and about the new house. I couldn't help but watch Alexa speak. She seemed really happy and relieved that Sarah took the news well. Alexa always guarded her feelings; her mom was pretty harsh with her grow-ing up and I think Alexa always expected a fight.

"Okay, so a June baby! Oh my gosh this is so exciting Al! And a new house!" Sarah sat back as we all finished up our meal. Roman raised his eyebrows at me, taking this all in. I'm not sure how he felt about his big brother stepping up and moving on with a baby on the way; but I know deep down he's really happy for us.

"Mmhmm, we close on the house next week. There's some repairs and I want to get it painted before we move in; but it's so cute. I can't wait for you to see it." Alexa gushed.

"Oh! I didn't realize you bought it; miss money bags. Guess being a millionaire helps out." Sarah teased. "I'm just glad you're still within walking distance!"

"Millionaire?" Roman asked under his breath as he exam-ined my face.

Alexa heard him and quickly cleared that up. "Um, yea. My father, he left me a trust fund for 2.5 million. At first I didn't even want to touch the money but when we found out I was pregnant; it just felt right to invest in our future." Alexa gave a small smile.

"Mmmmhmm" Roman said skeptically. The girls got up to clean up the kitchen and Roman and I walked over to the liv-ing room. The apartment was small so we kept our voices low. Roman eyed me and shook his head. Like he had something on his mind.

"What." I asked point blank.

"Nothing." Roman forced a laugh. "Just convenient, that's all."

"What are you getting at?" I gritted my teeth. Roman and I hardly argued but I could tell that we were about to butt heads.

"No, I mean. It's just convenient that you leave the club around the same time you find out she's knocked up. That's all." Roman's eyes were serious for a change. I stepped into his space.

"It's not what it seems. I love her. And I decided to hang up my cut way before we found out she was having my baby.

Roman, for fuck's sake, you know I wasn't into the club the way you are." I growled. The girls were oblivious to our heated conversation.

"Okay, okay. Back down there romeo. I just wanted to hear what you'd say. I know the club wasn't your lifelong dream. You don't have to convince me of that. I'm proud of you." Roman put his hand on my shoulder. "And I'm happy for you. Now you just have to figure out how you're gonna support this girl and your baby." Roman shook me back to reality. It weighed heavily on my mind how I was going to support my family. But I would do anything for Alexa. I would never bail on my family the way our father did to me and Roman.

Alexa

Yesterday was the baby's first ultrasound. Angel held my hand the entire time and we kissed and laughed when we saw that little flutter of a heartbeat in my belly. Angel couldn't be more happy and sweet. He brought me flowers the other day and we soaked in the tub with romantic bubbles and music playing. I had a little something up my sleeve as well and couldn't wait for the confirmation email so that I could tell him.

Last week was so busy. I got approval from the town that I could rent out that building for the school and Roger actually agreed to partnering with me so that we could rotate children in and out for classroom sessions. Everything was falling into place. I worked on hiring a contractor to start with the internal building and renovation and Angel was amazingly helpful. He came with me to help plan out the area with the architect and met with the town's planning board. Angel was encouraging and insightful and I couldn't wait to tell him what I had in store for *him*. I just prayed he didn't get mad at me or reject the idea. Angel was looking for a job at a few mechanic shops but wasn't having a ton of luck. A lot of those places made you start at the bottom and work up. But Angel was a wiz with bikes. He knew them in and out and was really passionate. That's why I secretly worked with the township to persuade them to auction off Mack's building; to me. I worked with an amazing financial advisor that helped me invest the money smartly; I paid for our new house so we didn't have a mortgage and the rent for the school building was being subsidized by grants and government fundings.

When we had dinner with Sarah and Roman, Sarah pulled me aside and asked if I had told my mother that I was pregnant. I'd be lying if I said it didn't bother me that I couldn't tell her the happy news. I had no idea how she'd take it. She took everything like crap and didn't handle my situation very well to begin with, with Angel. I wasn't set on cutting her completely out of my life so I threw her a life line and emailed her to see if we could meet up to talk. She replied a day later agreeing and we set a time and place. My mom had eyes and ears all over this town and I'm sure Roger confided in her that I was setting up the non-profit. So hopefully she was proud of the success I was making for myself and would be able to accept that Angel and I are together and having a baby.

I finally got the email I was waiting for. The town was auctioning off Mack's building at a 'private' public hearing and gave me the date and time to show up. It was tomorrow and I wanted to surprise Angel; so I texted Roman to help me out.

Me: Hey Roman- got a little thing I'm working on.. Need your help.

Roman: Okaayyy.. Sounds shady.

Me: Very funny. Can you get your brother to Mack's tomorrow at 11 AM -sharp-?

Roman: Yea, I guess I can make that happen. Whatcha got up your sleeve?

Me: You'll see. Keep it quiet... see ya tomorrow.

I got to Mack's right on time and met with the auctioneer and township committee person. We exchanged formalities and made small talk while waiting for Angel and Roman to arrive. The Auctioneer knew what I had planned the whole time and was just happy to see this building go to good use. The rumble of bikes made my belly tingle and goosebumps ran down my spine. Roman and Angel got off the bikes and Angel curiously and cautiously walked up to stand next to me.

"What's going on, sweets?" Angel kissed me quickly and eyed the two other men. Before I could answer, the auctioneer announced that the bidding had now officially started for 1001 Elm Street, Block 205. Roman stood in the background, waiting to see how all of this was going to play out.

"I bid 300,000 dollars." I stepped forward, the auctioneer grinning from ear to ear. We were alone at the bidding; the meeting set so quickly, I'm sure no one else knew the building was up for auction today.

"Sold. To the beautiful lady in front of me." The township man gladly took my check that I had ready and already made out. And we shook hands. I glanced back at Angel's confused face as he was scratching his head.

I walked back over to him, nervously biting my lip. "Are you mad?" I asked as I squeezed my eyes shut and put my hands over my face.

Angel pulled my hands down from my face, revealing a soft smile across his beautiful lips. "Baby, what are you doing?" he whispered.

"I bought the building?" I still cringed. I couldn't figure out if he was happy or mad. Maybe both?

"You're insane. I can't let you do this. I, uh, I, I don't even know what to say." Angel looked as if I could blow him over with a soft breeze.

"Well... I mean, if you don't want it. We could sell it, but..." I searched the ground trying to think of a quick recovery when Angel smashed his lips into mine. We kissed and laughed as he picked me up and spun me around.

"So does this mean you're happy?" I giggled into his neck.

"Oh my god, Alexa. I don't even know what to say." Angel put me down and we just both stared at the building. "This place. Jesus. It probably needs a ton of work, but..oh my god. I just.. I don't have words." Angel scrubbed a hand over his face as Roman came to join us. He slapped Angel on his back and gave me an approving nod.

The auctioneer thanked us and handed the keys to me; and I in turn handed the keys to Angel. He took them, wordlessly, still shaking his head in disbelief.

Angel looked at me solemnly and took my face in his hands. "Baby, this is your money. You shouldn't be doing this for me."

"No Angel. It's for us. For our future. I'm getting my dream and I want you to get yours. You deserve this." I pulled his hand down to feel the growing baby in my belly. "We deserve this." Angel pulled me in tight, the tears streaming down my face and he just held me.

"Thank you. Thank you so much."

"Don't thank me yet." I said as Angel pulled away slightly.

"What do you mean?" Angel looked at me skeptically.

"Um, well. I made plans to have dinner with my mom tonight. And I want you to come." I had almost forgotten Roman was standing there witnessing this whole crazy thing when he piped up.

"Oh fuck, man. Good luck with that." Roman joked as he ruffled Angel's messy hair.

"Thanks Roman. How very supportive of you." I joked and gave him a dirty look.

Angel blew out a breath. "Well, it's the least I could do being that you bought me a building today?" Angel smiled that cute smirky smile and I knew everything was going to be just fine.

Chapter 26

Angel

We drove into the city in Alexa's Dodge Charger to meet her mother for dinner. God I loved this car. The seats pulled you right in and the black leather wrapped you into the cockpit. I'm just praying that Alexa will decide to keep this car and get a different one for when the baby comes. I'll have to make sure I talk to her about that. But for now; she's fidgeting and antsy in the seat next to me as I pull up to the restaurant, La Luna. She tried on ten different outfits in hopes to hide her little belly so that she'd have a chance to ease her mother into the idea of 1: me being there with her and 2: we're having a baby; before Sonya noticed Alexa was pregnant. She settled on a paisley wrap dress that camouflaged her stomach with the ruffles of material. She had her hair up, showing off that beautiful neck and she looked amazing.

We pulled up to the valet and the kid helped Alexa out of the car, discreetly raking over her body as I came around the car tossing the key into his hand. I couldn't help but smirk at the valet as his eyes followed Alexa towards the front door, checking her ass out. He gave me a nervous head bob when he noticed I was watching him. I still felt naked without my cut. I spent over a decade putting it on every morning. Today I wore jeans and my regular boots and a black button down shirt with the sleeves rolled up a bit. Even without my cut; people still got out of my way. I guess I've been so used to intimidating people with the way I looked and dressed; I carried that with me even without the leather vest.

Alexa took my hand, hers was shaking already and she

was eerily quiet. Before we got to the host podium, I bent down to kiss her softly and gave her a wink. She smiled nervously at me as her eyes scanned the restaurant for her mother.

"Ramirez, party of, well it's going to be three of us." Alexa's voice was shaking and she had her hand on her small round belly.

"Oh. Ms. Ramirez is expecting you; and yes, I believe we have the reservation down for 3." The hostess said with an extra big smile. "Right this way."

"Oh my god, I'm so nervous; I think I might puke." Alexa whispered as we made our way to the back of the restaurant.

"It's going to be ok. Just stay calm and everything will turn out ok." I assured her, right before we approached Sonya.

Sonya was facing us as we got up to the table. The look of disgust and hatred soured her thin face. Her fake plump lips were pressed into a hard line and her eyes, which were once honey brown like Alexa's, were dark and fixed on me. She made no move to get up or greet her daughter as she cocked her head when I pulled out the chair for Alexa.

"Mom." Alexa sounded hopeful.

"What is he doing here." Sonya said quietly. Her face was dark and fixated on mine.

"Angel is here with me. Is this going to be a problem?" Alexa was growing a set of balls right before my eyes. Gone were her nerves and now she was laser focused on her mother's scowl.

"I'm not going to entertain this little relationship. I came here to talk to you." Sonya's eyes finally met her daughter's. We weren't even sitting yet and I wanted to bolt already. But I knew how much this meant to Alexa. Sonya should at least hear it from us that she was going to become a grandmother. And I wanted Sonya to know that I was 100% behind her daughter.

"Fine. Sit." Sonya barked out.

I sat next to Alexa at the small round table and sat back in my chair. I didn't want to interrupt their little stare down but it was really starting to piss me off.

"You made the reservation for 3. I assumed you already

knew Angel would be with me." Alexa asked as the waiter came over with our waters and menus.

Sonya ignored the waiter and her daughter as she leaned into the table with her arms crossed over her chest. Her voice was low and threatening, even I had to lean forward to hear her. The table Sonya picked was way in the back of the restaurant; away from prying ears and eyes but I'm sure she was pissed off that we were starting to cause a scene with our body language alone.

"Alexa. I can't believe you would do this. You bring *him* here when you say you want to talk things out? I can't be seen with this, this *criminal*."

Alexa sat back in her seat; Sonya's words hit her like a stray bullet. I was fucking pissed off but I was working really hard at not flying off the handle. No one spoke to my girl like this. I was clenching my jaw so hard; I thought I may break my teeth as I fisted my hands on my lap.

Alexa blinked a few times and took a deep breath. "I cannot believe you. You can't even do this for *me*? You can't set aside your precious reputation to hear me out?" Alexa was getting madder now, her body stiffened and her voice was louder than it probably should be. I placed a hand on her shoulder, hoping I'd get her to calm back down but it was no use. She started to rise up out of her seat as she leaned over with both hands on the table.

"You may be my mother. But I have never been more disappointed in you than I am today." The angry hot tears started to fall from her eyes as she spoke. "And that's saying something." Sonya looked appalled and shocked at her daughter's words.

"I thought that you would come here with an open mind. But, I was wrong. You'll never see past your own history. You'll never understand that Angel loves me and I love him. I'm not you, mom. And he's not Antonio." A sob escaped from her throat and she grabbed her bag off the back of the chair and stormed out of the building.

It all happened so quickly, that she was away from the

table before I could catch up to her. I got up from the table and threw my napkin down. I gave Sonya one last glance. Her mouth still hanging open in shock, her face red from embarrassment. I turned to leave as I met her eyes and saw tears starting to fill them.

"Oh my god." She whispered to herself. "I've lost her, haven't I?" She said to herself but it stopped me in my tracks. I sat down in the chair next to her and leaned in close.

"I know you don't like me. But I can't apologize for my life or my history. You know, I didn't have a mother to look out for *me*. When I had no one, Los Demonios became my family and no matter how much I screwed up in the beginning; they *never* turned their back on me. I love Alexa. She's changed my life and made me become a better man. A man that will take care of her forever and the baby that's growing inside her belly." Sonya looked up at me with her eyes wide and sad. Realization crossed her face and she hung her head as the tears fell on the napkin across her lap.

Alexa's mom watched me as I slowly rose from the table, pushed my chair in and walked away. I walked straight out to the valet stand looking for Alexa; but she was nowhere to be found. I saw the valet kid fiddling in the corner with his phone and stormed up to him.

"Hey. You see my girlfriend come back out?" I barked out. He looked terrified as he scrambled to his feet.

"Uh yea. She didn't want to wait for me to get the car so she grabbed the keys and took off." He stuttered out as he pointed in the direction of the back parking garage.

Alexa

I'm so stupid to think she'd be any different. I thought she would have an open mind. For fuck's sake; just hear me out! I couldn't get out of the restaurant any faster. I was either going to lose it on her and cause a horrible scene or I was going to throw up. My emotions were all over the place and I just needed air. I stomped up to the pimply faced kid that valeted the cars. I didn't feel like waiting for him to get off his ass so I grabbed the keys and headed to the parking garage. It wasn't until I rounded the building that I realized that Angel wasn't behind me. But I was too mad and too far gone to turn back and look for him. I'm sure he'll realize where I went. I wasn't about to sit in that stuffy restaurant and beg my mother to be a good human being.

I clicked the lock button of the key fob trying to find my car. The damn parking garage was four floors and with my luck, the Charger was at the top. I clicked and clicked until I heard a far off honk. Bingo. I walked up the ramp of the first floor just as I heard my name being called. But it wasn't Angel's voice. I stopped and looked around until I saw a man coming towards me.

"Alexa. Hey. Funny running into you." It was Randy. God damn it. Can I just escape this hell without dealing with another asshole?

"Randy. Hey" I replied very unenthusiastically. He was on the second floor near where I think my 'honk' came from. I shimmied between cars to get closer as my car was finally coming into view. Randy was standing right next to it.

"You ok. Where are you going? I was coming to see you." Randy moved closer to me and something in my gut told me this felt off.

"Your mother invited me to dinner. So sweet that she wants to make sure we're getting along." His words stopped me in my tracks as Randy stood in front of me. So she *did* make the reservation for three. But she invited Randy. What the hell is wrong with her.

"Randy, now's not a great time. I'm, I'm not feeling great." I tried to duck under his arm that was resting on the hood of my car. But he grabbed my wrist and pulled me into him.

"Fuck, Randy. Let me go." I seethed and tried to pull away from him. But this time he wasn't letting me go.

"Now, now, Alexa. I think we should at least *try* and get along." Randy had this weird smirk on his face and his eyes narrowed at me. He was hurting my wrists and backed me up so I was wedged between my car and the one parked next to it.

"Randy, I swear to god, if you don't let go of me." I tried so hard to squirm away but he leaned his body onto mine; I had no room to kick out or hit him. I felt his erection poking at my stomach as he pushed me up against the car. I was so scared, I didn't even think I could scream. My voice was stuck in my throat and I felt my whole body shake.

"Fiesty little girl. I've always liked that about you. Shame we never got together. You would have liked the things I could do to you." Randy's mouth was on my neck and I could feel him rub himself on me.

"Hmmm. Got nothing to say now, Alexa? This *feel* good to you?" he said darkly as he spun me around, pinning the back of my neck between the car and his firm arm. With his other hand he traveled up underneath my dress and I felt his hands start to pull away at my underwear.

"Randy, no, please." I sobbed out only to feel him push me harder into the side of the car. My chest was so constricted; I felt like I could barely breathe.

"You know no one gets away with making me look like a fool. Not even you. You treated me like shit, Alexa. All I wanted was a fucking date." As his harsh grumbling words came out of his mouth, I felt my underwear being torn away from me. I couldn't see through my flowing tears and I felt like I was going to pass out.

But in a split second, the pressure was gone. I fell limply to the ground and Randy was no longer touching me. When my world came back into focus, the sound of breaking bones and grunting filled my ears. Angel was on top of Randy, holding his shirt in one hand and punching the hell out of him with the other. The sickening smack of knuckles meeting Randy's face made me cringe as I got to my feet and started screaming for help.

Angel let go of Randy, both men were covered in splattered blood and Randy was barely conscious. Angel pulled me into his arms and nervously looked me over, feeling my chest and stomach with his bloodied hands.

"I'm ok. I'm ok" I said hurriedly over and over. The sound of fast-paced clicking heels had us looking down the way to see my mom running towards us. Her hand was over her mouth and she was crying hysterically.

"Fucking hell Alexa. Oh my god. Are you ok?" Angel pulled my shaking body into his and just held me.

"Oh my god. This is all my fault. Oh my god." My mother was sobbing as she got to where we were standing. More sounds of people yelling and the distant sound of sirens started to ring in my ears.

I couldn't bring myself to lift my head out of Angel's chest. And he wasn't about to let go of me. Flashing lights soon lit up the entire floor of the parking garage as the police came to a halt in front of us.

My mom started barking orders, telling the police to arrest Randy for attempted rape. It wasn't until I heard the word 'rape' that I looked down realizing my torn underwear was sitting in the middle of the parking lot and my dress was ripped. My neck was sore from where Randy held me down but I couldn't stop crying as Angel just rubbed my little belly and asked me over and over if I was ok.

Chapter 27

3 months later...

Angel

I woke up to the sound of muffled music and heavy breathing. Before I even rolled over to see what time it was; I knew it was Alexa on her spin bike. She was almost 7 months pregnant and feeling great. Her energy was insane and we had so much going on. Tomorrow is the opening of the non-profit school and Alexa has been working night and day to make sure it goes off without a hitch. We moved into our new home last month and while I worked on plans to renovate the garage Alexa bought us, she spent most nights setting up the nursery. I was ready for her to slow down a bit. But she was headstrong and wanted to make sure she had everything ready before the baby got here. She promised me things would be a lot calmer after the baby arrived; but I knew that would be anything but true.

Alexa had a great idea about getting the members of Los Demonios to volunteer some of their time to help with the school building renovations. She made it a community project and was helping shed some light on local charities and outreach. Los Demonios may have their dark side but they were as much a part of the community as the rest.

Roman and I spent a lot of time in the bike shop, which I renamed Second Chances Motorcycle Shop. He helped me plan out the bays and order tools and machinery I needed to start up. Surprisingly, a lot of equipment was still in the building. Lifts and hand tools; some outdated, but I could replace them as business picked up.

Alexa still hasn't spoken to her mother. And Sonya hasn't made an effort to reach out. Sometimes, things just don't work themselves out. I hope that one day, Sonya decides to make Alexa and her grandchild a priority. And maybe she'll even accept me. But for now, Alexa and I have enough happiness to focus on. I'm so proud of her and she continues to amaze me everyday.

I've been working on something huge; and I can't wait until tomorrow. I tap out a text before Alexa finishes her workout.

Me: Ro, we all set for tomorrow at 9 AM?

Roman: We'll be there.

Me: Still good to pick up Alexa at 8:45AM?

Sarah: Yup! Cannot wait to see her face!

Just as I get out of bed and start to pull my shorts up, Alexa comes into the bedroom, sexy, sweaty and looking fucking amazing.

"You sure that baby can handle those workouts?" I tease her. She comes waltzing over while swiping her sweaty forehead with a towel.

"Doctor said, as long as I feel good, I can keep up with my spin classes." Alexa had a big smile on her face. She was all belly and her legs were just as amazing. She wore little bike shorts with a sports bra with her smooth round belly on display for me.

"Come over here." I pulled her in between my legs, leaving my shorts around my ankles. My dick throbbed for her and she licked her lips glancing down at my erection.

"Mmmm, Angel. I'm all sweaty." She moaned but continued to straddle my lap. My hard cock rubbing on her overly sensitive clit.

"I don't care. I need to bury myself in this wet pussy." I moaned as I played with her full, swollen breasts. I let my other hand drift down to the top of her needy clit and rubbed her lightly. Alexa was so sensitive now, I barely had to look at her and she was coming for me.

"Fuck, Angel. You know I can't handle that." She moaned into my lips and she started to rock up and down the length of my cock.

"Stand up and take these clothes off." She got up without a fight and peeled her shorts and sports bra off, leaving her beautifully naked in front of me. I loved smoothing my hands over her belly and watching her squirm and shake as I started to play with her.

She was more comfortable with riding me these days and hell if I was going to complain about it. I loved it when she straddled me and would slowly sink down on to me until her ass hit my thighs. Alexa used her strong legs to pick up on me so slowly that I was begging for her every time. This time was no different. She braced her arms on my knees behind her and leaned back so I could watch her. I lightly rubbed my thumb over her clit; she was so wet and tight. She pounded on me harder and I helped support her by holding her hips. I moved with her and thrusted my hips up into her until she was panting and quivering.

"That's it baby, fuck me harder until you come." I moaned out trying to hold onto my own release until she came.

"Oh Angel, I'm coming, oh." Her pussy squeezed me so tight that I came with her, sending my hot come deep inside of her.

We laid on the bed together, kissing and cuddling. We had a walk through at the school building in an hour so I knew we would need to get up soon.

"I wish we could stay like this all day. Ugh there's so much to do before tomorrow." Alexa got up and moved to the bathroom. The shower steamed up instantly and I joined her. The rest of the day was odds and ends for the opening. Alexa was so nervous; she couldn't sit still. She thought I was being weird when she mentioned how quiet I was being; but in all actuality, I couldn't be more excited for tomorrow. The opening was at 10 AM but I had everyone meeting me there at 9 for a little surprise. Yesterday I called her mother. Of course she didn't answer but I left her a message anyway. Telling her about the opening and asking to be a part of her special day. I couldn't help but try and mend their relationship. Having family around you is important and I know even though the two were never super close; Alexa has finally accepted her mother for who she is and her actions.

We never do talk about the day Randy attacked her. For weeks after he tried to rape her; she just stayed buried in my arms and didn't want any contact with anyone. It wasn't until Sarah and Roman threw us a Housewarming party that Alexa finally started putting the past behind her. Having the right kind of people around you to support you was way more important than holding onto the past.

Alexa

It is finally opening day for the school and I cannot be more excited. I woke up and Angel made love to me and then surprised me with a delicious breakfast. He knows how much I love breakfast, and the man can cook! I was still trying to figure out what my new body looked best in, so of course I had to try on several different outfits. I felt like my belly was growing every hour but I was really happy that I felt great and the baby was healthy. I settled on a long, sage green lace maxi dress with sweet little flutter sleeves. My boobs were slightly spilling over the top but when I showed Angel, his reply was to kiss them and pull my body into his growing erection.

"Baby, you look beautiful." Angel breathed into my neck and hair. Sarah was picking me up so that we could swing by the township building for some last minute signatures before the opening. Angel said he'd meet us there and was just about to get into the shower.

"Oh gosh, I'm so excited. And nervous. And I have to pee, again." I danced around our beautiful kitchen. He laughed as I spun back around and made a beeline to the bathroom. When I got out Sarah was already in the kitchen talking to Angel, both of their faces smiling excitedly.

"Hey. Holy crap, Al, you look amazing." Sarah gushed as she rushed over to hug me and rub my belly.

"How's my little niece or nephew in there?" Sarah spoke to

my belly. She was so excited to become an Aunt. She showed up with a new baby present every other day. Sarah convinced Roger, her boss, to split her time between the Migrant Shelter and the school. I made her a partner in the non-profit and I couldn't ask for a better business partner.

"Ugh, he or she's been kicking away today. I guess the baby knows today is a big day." I giggled as Sarah and Angel shared glances.

"Okay, well, let's get going. I stopped and grabbed you a tea." Sarah was shuffling me out the door after I gave Angel a good long kiss on his sweet lips.

After waiting around the township building for what felt like a million years, we finally signed off on all the papers. It was just about 9 o'clock and Sarah and I made our way to the school. I texted Angel to let him know that we were on our way.

Pulling up to the parking lot, I saw that Angel's bike was already there. Along with a handful of other cars. Sarah was so giddy getting out of the car; I couldn't help but laugh along with her.

"Stop. You're going to make me pee myself." I croaked at her.

"Oh my god, please don't pee yourself. I'll never let you live it down." She laughed. She took my hand and before she opened the door to the building she stopped me and looked serious.

"Al, I just want to say how proud I am of you." She spoke with loving tears in her eyes and my throat bobbed and tightened. "I love you like a sister and I wouldn't want to work with anyone else. You amaze me everyday and I know you'll be the best mother to this baby. You and Angel are one of a kind and made for each other. I'm just really happy that I am getting to be a part of all of this." The tears spilled over and we both hugged and giggled at our antics. After dabbing our tear streaked faces, we took a big breath and headed inside.

When I opened the door, Roman was standing in front of me and the building was too quiet.

"Roman, what are you doing here?" I said with a big smile. He stepped forward and then I heard boots in the far corner. When I turned my head I recognized Taylor and some of the guys from Los Demonios.

"We're here for you, baby girl." I laughed as he took my hand and laced his fingers with mine. Sarah on the other side of me, they led me out to what would be an open gymnasium. Angel stood in the middle of the floor; looking absolutely hot. He was wearing dark jeans with boots, a dark charcoal button down shirt with his sleeves rolled up exposing his tattoos and his hair was the perfect combination of sexy and messy.

As Roman and Sarah walked me out towards Angel, the volunteers, teachers, township committee person, Roger and a few colleagues stood all around the outside of the room.

"I thought that we told everyone ten o'clock." I asked Sarah under my breath, I was completely confused.

"Mhhmmm, we did. But Angel asked us to be here at 9." She said flatly as they let go of my hands and I stood in front of Angel.

"Baby?" I asked, my eyes finding his. His face was soft and relaxed. His eyes were bright with a gleam in them that made me smile from ear to ear. Just as I was about to ask what was going on, he knelt down on one knee.

"Holy shit." I blurted out and made Angel giggle at my reaction.

He took a small black box out from his pocket as the whole room started to spin. "Alexa. You came into my life and set my world on a tailspin I never could have predicted. From the second I met you; I've realized that I was lacking something that growing up, I never got a chance to witness for myself. You loved me without judgment, without hesitation and I fell so insanely in love with you; I knew I needed you in my life forever. I will die a happy man if you let me love you and our baby for the rest of my life. Will you marry me?"

As soon as those four words slipped out of his beautiful mouth, the world stopped spinning. Everything came into focus and all I could see was this amazing man kneeling in front of me and I never wanted to be without him.

"Yes." I cried. "Yes, yes Angel. I will marry you." Cheers and applause erupted all around us and Angel stood up and pulled me into his arms. We kissed so deep and fiercely, happy tears ran down my face as we laughed.

When we finally came up for air, I looked all around us and saw Angel's brothers from the MC standing all around us; clapping a congratulatory hand on Angel's back and Sarah, tucked up under Roman's arms. To say that this was the best moment in life would be miniscule in comparison to how Angel made me feel and the love that we were going to bring to our baby.

The End

Epilogue

Alexa

"So when do the adoption papers come through?" Sarah sat down next to me as we watched Harley dig his trucks into the heaping piles of sand.

"Should be any day now." I answered as I sat back in the lounge chair, rubbing soothing circles over my big baby bump. Sarah cradled a sleeping Matteo in her arms as she put up her now swollen feet.

"Ugh... how much bigger are my feet gonna get!" She moaned quietly.

"Haha. Don't worry. You've got two more weeks til that baby comes and then you'll be just as crazy tired as I am." I teased. Sarah was due anyway now. She looked stunning with her long blonde hair, her sweet belly and her glowing skin.

Angel and I were overjoyed when Harley came into this world. Of course it wouldn't be as sweet and memorable if I didn't go into labor and delivered on Father's Day. Harley arrived almost 9 pounds with beautiful brown eyes and a full head of dark hair. Angel would never admit it, but he cried like a baby the first time he held his baby boy in his arms. The first few months were rough, new parents and business owners and all. But we make it work and I've never been so happy.

When Sarah told us about Matteo, Angel and I didn't even bat an eye before we were applying for emergency foster. We've had Matteo since he was three months old and he's a dream. He was left at one of the partnering shelters with no milk, a dirty diaper and no trace of his mother. Last week we got word that we've been approved to adopt him when I found out I was pregnant again. A little girl. Angel cannot wait to spoil his little girl.

Angel's motorcycle shop is booming, he's got three mechanics and a full garage. He takes care of all Los Demonios's bikes minus the illegal stuff. And the school is doing amazingly. We're fully staffed and have even received several awards. Sarah and I are closer than ever; she even bought a house across the street from us! We see Roman almost every day. He's the best and goofiest Uncle you could ask for.

All in all the last few years have been a whirlwind but we wouldn't have it any other way.

About The Author

Kristen L. Proc

New and rising author, Kristen L. Proc lives in rural Virginia with her amazingly supportive husband and kids. She writes contemporary romance with angsty, steamy love scenes with relatable family dynamics.

Books In This Series

The Harder They Fall

Angel's Downfall

Roman's Empire

Taylor's Takedown

Made in the USA
Columbia, SC
22 June 2021